The Burnt District

Gary Link

PublishAmerica
Baltimore

© 2003 by Gary Link.

All rights reserved. No part of this book may be reproduced in any form without written permission from the publishers, except by a reviewer who may quote brief passages in a review to be printed in a newspaper or magazine.

First printing

ISBN: 1-59286-510-0
PUBLISHED BY
PUBLISHAMERICA BOOK PUBLISHERS
www.publishamerica.com
Baltimore

Printed in the United States of America

For Terri.

Acknowledgements

Readers who enjoy this tale owe a great debt to my wife, Terri, who from the first paragraph admonished me to resist teaching history and simply "tell a story." There is an old maxim that two things that the public should never see being made are sausage and politics. To that list I believe my wife would add *writing*. Her proof reading of my tortured drafts showed the true measure of her love for me. Her on target corrections and suggestions helped make this book a better read than it would otherwise have been.

Thanks to Michael Murphy for introducing me to the Great Fire of 1845 with his presentation many years ago to the Lawrenceville Historical Society. Thanks also to Tom Josephi for lending me his collection of period newspapers. Thomas Glanville, former Executive Director of the Pennsylvania Canal Society, cleared up a question I had about the gate mechanism for canal locks. Grace Ravotti and Sue Johns at the Freeport Borough Building provided friendly help with the large historical map in their care and other information about the borough.

Writing is purported to be a lonely business, but this work brought people back together by prompting me to re-establish contact with some old friends. Military historian, and former partner in all things historical, Jeff Sherry provided some timely information on Mexican War-era volunteer uniforms. Deb Knox gave sustained encouragement, and was the first to suggest that this work merited publication.

Non-fiction works of course were essential for my attempt to provide as accurate a setting as time allotted. Three works that I relied on most heavily were Leland Baldwin's *Pittsburgh; The Story of a City*, Henry Mann's *Our Police; A History of the Pittsburgh Police Force*, and Stephan Lorant's *Pittsburgh; The Story of an American City*. I also consulted Howard Worley's *Pittsburgh's Vintage Firemen, 1790 — 1915,* and *City at the Point*, Samuel P. Hays, editor.

Local museums and related facilities also supplied information for the Great Fire, and life in Pittsburgh in 1845, primarily the Senator John Heinz Pittsburgh Regional History Center exhibits and Archives. A visit to the Soldiers and Sailors Memorial Hall's military uniforms displays enabled me to describe the volunteer units with some accuracy. The Community Library of Allegheny Valley, Tarentum Branch's Local History Department provided histories of communities in the Allegheny Valley and of Allegheny County. And finally, the wonderful web site *Historic Pittsburgh*, at http://digital.library.pitt.edu, enabled me to read many rare histories and biographies written in the nineteenth century without even leaving my home.

I wish to thank my parents, Charles and Rhonda Link, for though having nothing to do with this book, did have something to do with me. And I am even more proud of mother-in-law Marilyn Clark's courage and strength than she is of my writing.

And last but not least, warm and smiling thanks to the believers: Tyler, Megan, Connor, and Emily.

Just one more. I'd like to thank PublishAmerica for making publishing what it should be: accessible to all.

1

April 10, 1845

Pealing bells wrenched John Parker from sleep. His mind struggled to gather awareness around it. Blinking open his eyes, he saw that it was daylight and realized he had been sleeping in the Watchhouse. Bells? It was not Sunday, he remembered. It was not a feast day for any of the churches that he could recall, and there were no large weddings that he knew of. That meant that the bells signaled "Fire!"

Parker heard people yelling outside. Smoke stung his nose, making him think that it must be *his* building that was on fire. Already fully dressed including overcoat and boots, Parker ran from the office into the reception area. Empty. He raced down a flight of stairs and burst through a large wooden door onto the street below. He stopped behind a crowd of people. Standing frozen and staring, John Parker saw that it was not his building that was on fire — it was the rest of the city of Pittsburgh.

From just beyond the buildings immediately in front of him rose a wall of black smoke rolling and curling up into the sky. The wall spread both right and left as far as he could see. Above the clang of bells and shouts of people a monstrous roar thundered with occasional bursts and explosions. He turned and sprinted back into the Watchhouse up the wooden stairs. Once on his floor again he climbed a small set of steps to the attic, opened a small window, and pulled himself out onto the roof. He clambered to the rooftop and, straddling the apex, surveyed the scene.

From his building halfway up Grant's Hill, John Parker looked down onto the city of Pittsburgh. Far to his left the Monongahela River flowed alongside the town to the northwest. To his far right the Allegheny River, flowing in from the north, curved westward to meet the Monongahela. At their convergence they formed the Ohio River that moved northwestward. The land between the Monongahela and the Allegheny rivers that contained the City of Pittsburgh sloped gently downward and narrowed to a tip that Pittsburghers called "the Point." Facing northwest directly toward the Point, Parker saw what at first glance looked like the end of the world.

Entire blocks of the city were on fire. The area from which the smoke poured was bounded on Parker's right by Diamond Street, which roughly bisected the city. The fire swept to the left across town to the banks of the Monongahela River. Driving winds threatened to knock him off of his perch. The wind drove the fire onward, blowing flames to adjacent buildings and sending embers across streets to land on wooden rooftops. The gale carried burning chunks of boards aloft that landed on nearby blocks and started still more roofs afire. Parker could not see where the blaze had originated, but its general movement at that time spread from city center to the southwest along the Monongahela River.

In the block in front of him Parker could see the men of the Vigilant Volunteer Fire Company fighting to halt the fire at Smithfield Street. He climbed down off of the roof to go help them. John Parker knew the men of the Vigilant. And they knew him, as most of Pittsburgh's five fire companies did. As a city constable, Parker had broken up many a fight between two or more companies.

Parker bolted out of his building again and ran down Fourth Street toward the firefighters. He dashed across Grant Street, dodging teams of horses pulling wagons and drays filled with furniture and other possessions. He reached the Vigilant Company at Smithfield Street where many civilians helped fight the flames. They concentrated not on the engulfed buildings across the street, but rather on the intact ones on the near side to stop the fire from crossing. Firefighters with hooks pulled burning pieces of roof off of buildings while others used axes to chop off burning corners and downspouts. Others smothered small fires with wet blankets. A line of men and women formed a bucket brigade bringing water from a well inside a nearby house.

Nearby, Parker saw a fire engine sitting idle. Reflections of flames flickered off of its brass fittings and nameplate. Long pump handles curved wave-like from its center toward both the front and the back. Between the handles a central cylinder rose with a short section of hose attached. The entire apparatus sat atop the engine's water tank housing. Several ropes hung from its front. For reasons Parker did not quite understand, the firefighters themselves shouldered these ropes and towed their engines at breakneck speed to the fire. Some unwritten firefighters' honor code allowed horses to pull their engines only for parades.

Parker recognized one firefighter, Jim Cowan, hacking at a wooden downspout with an ax. A large ember had blown down inside, and the downspout blistered almost to the point of ignition. Parker grabbed a pry bar off of the engine and helped with the downspout.

"What's wrong with the fire engine?" he asked the firefighter.

"There's nothing wrong with our engine," Cowan replied. Both men shouted to be heard over noises of the fire and the battle to stop it. "The damned reservoirs are empty!" He cocked his head toward Grant's Hill where Parker had just come from. An old reservoir remained on Grant's Hill; a newer one sat on Quarry Hill, on the eastern edge of the city. "This dry weather we've been having dwindled our water supply."

"How do you think this devil got this far?" Cowan continued. "Where have you been, anyway, Constable?" It was not so much a question as to Parker's whereabouts as it was a statement that everyone else fighting the fire here was already well aware of the water situation.

"Sleeping," Parker said flatly.

"Sleeping?" cried Cowan. "My God, man, do you sleep with the dead?"

Parker kept his gaze on his work and did not reply. Jim Cowan stared at him for another second as he worked his ax, and then started relating what he knew so far.

"It started behind Bill Diehl's icehouse at Second and Ferry sometime around noon. A washerwoman left her fire untended. The icehouse went up first. We were the first company on the scene. We hooked up our hoses to the plug on Front and Market and started hitting the houses next to the icehouse with a full stream of water. But after a few minutes, our stream of water dwindled into a dribble of mud. We opened the plug: the feed pipe was dry.

"The wind's been in cahoots with this fire the whole time, feeding it and blowing fire and embers everywhere. It's as if the devil himself were driving it before him. Once the water ran out, the fire ran mad and started taking entire blocks. It's been crossing streets like there was no gap at all between the buildings.

"We had a few victories early. By the time the Third Presbyterian Church caught, the Eagle and the Niagara companies arrived and the congregation helped out, too. Some of Eagle Company's men chopped off a piece of the corner that was burning, then the wind changed directions and left the church be. Our boys and the Neptune Company got up enough water to save the Post Office and the Gazette's building. But that was early. Since then we've been fighting and retreating. Always retreating.

"At one point we got some explosives and blew up a few houses to try to make a fire break, but it just wasn't enough. Now here we are. We should be able to save these houses since the wind is blowing away from us. But it's just going to get the houses in the other direction."

Cowan heaved another blow with his ax and the smoldering section of downspout broke free. "And every piece of wood in the city is as dry as tinder because it hasn't rained for weeks."

Parker looked over at the bucket brigade working on a corner house. The men and women in line worked at a frantic pace with only a few buckets, but their efforts were almost pitiful in the face of the conflagration that raged in front of them. A tall, dark-haired woman looked over at Parker.

"You'd be more help swingin' a bucket than standin' and gawkin', Constable!" she called.

"That'd be Marina," Cowan said, mustering a grin, "You'd better join her or likely as not you'll get a bucket of water tossed at you."

Parker knew Marina Betts, a leader in nearly every bucket brigade called near her neighborhood who threw merciless barbs at any who dared stand aloof while fellow citizens battled a blaze. He ran over and joined the line next to her, where there was a bit of a gap. He tried to match the rhythm of the line, swinging full buckets in one direction and empty ones in the other. The men at the end moved to dump water wherever it was most needed at the time: to put out a sprouting flame or soak a wall adjacent to a structure that was already engulfed. They worked the same general area for about one halfhour. The entire time, Marina Betts encouraged the workers and exhorted spectators to help.

"This is the only way we fought these devils years ago, before the reservoirs," she told Parker. "The city made every household keep two leather buckets in their homes for firefighting. We'd make two lines: the men passed the full buckets up and the women and kids passed the empty ones back. Nowadays not everyone keeps buckets and most don't have wells in their houses like this one does. They think they can rely on the fire companies and the reservoirs to do everything."

Parker nodded. He was concentrating on grabbing and passing, grabbing and passing.

He barely looked up from his task. Marina, however, watched everything around her.

"There might be business of yours yonder, Constable," she said as she gave a quick nod over her shoulder.

Parker turned from the brigade and looked down Smithfield Street toward the Monongahela River. Flames and embers blew furiously southwestward. Soon the fire would cross the street.

The incident to which Marina pointed, though, was much closer. A teamster stopped his wagon in front of a burning building across the street, climbed down, and tried to pick up a wooden crate that lay in the street. Looting was a common accompaniment to fires, but Parker could not believe a teamster would engage himself so. Something else must be afoot.

"With your permission, ma'am," he said to Marina.

"Any excuse ..." she returned, shaking her head. Then she turned toward a small group of spectators nearby, "You men, there, you'd be more help swingin' a bucket than standin' and gawkin."

The teamster tried again to lift the large crate off of the ground as Parker arrived. "Quick work here, Constable," he said. The box was marked "GUNPOWDER." Parker quickly bent down and grabbed the other end of the crate. Already the heat from the house burning beside them seared his face. Sweat stung his eyes as he and the teamster heaved the crate onto the wagon. The horses jittered and reared their heads. The teamster hefted himself up to drive the wagon off and Parker jumped up onto the wagon beside him. The teamster flicked the reins and yelled to his team, which started off with a jerk. Closer now to the Monongahela than to the fire's front at the city center, the teamster hauled his dangerous freight down Smithfield Street toward the river.

As they passed houses and other buildings Parker saw burning furniture along the streets. In smaller fires, it was a natural reaction for people to pull valuable items out of their houses to save them. Fire companies assigned Fire Marshals to guard the goods, using long red poles to fend off looters. Today, however, the practice of moving out furniture proved useless, as the fire consumed the piles along with everything else in its path.

Flames engulfed all of the buildings on the right-hand side of the Smithfield Street. Waves of heat blew at the riders. The thick smoke blowing overhead formed a dark canopy that blotted out the afternoon sun, making the street more like a tunnel. Flames in this canopy's underbelly reached ever across, licking the buildings on the other side. Many embers made it across, and Parker could see fires start on the rooftops of the buildings on the left. Suddenly a loud pop and crash sounded on their right as a building collapsed. Smoke belched out and embers showered the wagon. Parker bent over and covered up, as did the teamster while still controlling his horses. Parker sat up again and looked to see if any embers had landed on the horses. Seeing none, he then checked his own clothes.

"Constable!" cried the teamster. He gripped the reins with one hand and reached behind them with the other. Parker turned around and saw glowing embers in the wagon and on top of the crate of gunpowder. Parker jumped into the wagon and almost lay on the crate as he used his sleeves to smother small embers on the top and sides of the wooden box. Then he looked the crate over quickly for any tiny glowing red. None? Was it out? A small fire started in some debris in a rear corner of the wagon. Parker crawled to the back of the bouncing wagon and stomped the flames out with his boots. He turned around toward the front. The gunpowder crate was on fire.

The wagon crossed Water Street and headed straight for the Monongahela

Bridge. But instead of entering the covered span the teamster veered his team to the right down onto the Monongahela Wharf. The wagon rocked from side to side as Parker struggled to reach the gunpowder. He half dove and was half thrown onto the crate. He furiously slapped at the flames with his hands and the flaps of his overcoat. Every time he lifted his hand off of a smothered flame, it sprouted anew. All the while he struggled to keep the wagon's rocking from tossing him out completely.

The team reached the river and screamed to a halt at the shoreline, forcing Parker to hold on to the sides to keep from being thrown out of the wagon. Finally with all his strength he heaved the smoldering crate into the river. It thunked in the mud just inside the water's edge. The river lapped up and silenced the hiss of the last burning embers.

Relieved of their burden, both men hopped off of the wagon and stood staring at the crate. The teamster turned to Parker. "Now, Constable, why on God's earth do you think that a box of gunpowder was just sitting out on the street?" he asked.

"One of the firefighters told me that they blew up some houses to try to make a firebreak," Parker replied, "I guess in the hurry and confusion, one box of gunpowder was forgotten."

"One box was enough," the teamster quipped.

John Parker nodded in agreement. He looked around them. The packed-dirt beach of the Monongahela Wharf sat between Water Street and the river and ran roughly from the Monongahela Bridge to the Point. A wide section of it closer to the Point was paved with large cobblestones. On any normal day, stacks of freight dotted the wharf as drays and people moved about loading, unloading, and transporting goods. But today stacks of goods almost filled the wharf, piled as high as humans could reach as the factory and warehouse owners moved their stock there to save it from the advancing flames. Everywhere stood mountains of furniture, lumber, dry goods, bales of cotton, bolts of fabric, and crates of all sizes that did not reveal their contents.

Then, about thirty yards downstream toward the Point, Parker saw Jonas Burbridge, owner of a dry goods commission house on Front Street, holding a long, red Fire Marshal's pole out in front of him. Jonas menaced a looter who was trying to grab some merchandise to carry off. Although many people bustled around the wharf at that moment, the stacks of goods isolated many areas, and few people standing anywhere other than where Parker stood could see Mr. Burbridge's plight. Parker turned to the teamster.

"Constable, I've got to go now if I'm going to get out of here," the teamster said. "I'll not make it through Smithfield Street now. Maybe I can get up to Grant and get through town."

"It looks like I have more work here," Parker said. "Thanks again, for what you did."

"You have a care, now, Constable," the teamster said. He turned and jumped onto his wagon. He flicked his reins and the team wheeled around then galloped up off of the wharf.

Parker turned and ran toward Jonas Burbridge. Mr. Burbridge swiped at the looter, who ducked and tried to grab the pole. As Parker got close he yelled so the looter would see him approaching. He wanted to scare the man off, not arrest him. There was too much going on now to have the burden of trying to haul a looter up to the Watchhouse.

Suddenly something crashed down on Parker's back. The force of the blow and blinding pain sent him straight down into the dirt. Sparks flashed inside Parker's eyelids. He lay prostrate on the ground, the left side of his face pressed into the dirt. The crushing pain rendered him immobile. Two mammoth boots walked to his shoulder then squared themselves to his body. They stayed in place but the heels lifted, and Parker's body braced for another blow. But instead he heard a loud crack, then a yell of pain and anger. A heavy, dark object thudded in the dirt beside him. Parker saw the huge boots turn around toward a smaller pair of shoes behind them. The smaller shoes lifted completely up off of the ground out of Parker's sight, while a red Fire Marshal's pole dropped onto the ground. Then Jonas Burbridge landed with a crash at the foot of a pile of crates a few feet away.

The large boots walked away toward the Point. Parker rolled his eyes up and moved his head to see the boots' owner come into view as he walked away. He was larger than any man John Parker had ever seen. He wore blue overalls with a linen work shirt, the sleeves rolled up to his elbows. Under a tan saucer cap his short-cropped reddish hair was flecked with gray. It looked as if it would've been flaming red when the man was younger. The large man barked something at the first looter, and then helped heft a large sack onto the smaller man's shoulder. The first looter staggered a bit under the sack, then, bent under its weight, walked downstream. The large man picked up two similar sacks and followed. He carried one sack under each arm with no more effort than if they were two pillows. The two continued downstream along the river's edge, then veered right and disappeared around the stacks of goods.

John Parker watched the pair of looters as long as he could, then his eyes closed and his world went black.

"Constable! John! Are you all right?" Parker awoke to someone shaking him. Jonas Burbridge knelt beside him, peering into his face.

"Are you all right, John?" Jonas asked again.

Parker tried to get up. When he moved, the blinding pain returned to his back. He groaned and almost fell, then managed to get up on one knee. He looked at the object stuck in the dirt beside where his head had just been. It was a wooden box of nails about the size of one of the footprints that trailed away.

"How long was I out?" he asked.

"I'd have to know how long *I* was out to be able to answer that," Jonas replied. "It's been several minutes, at least. The wharf seems more deserted, and I think a lot of the merchandise stacked here is catching fire."

Parker looked around as much as his aching neck and shoulders would let him. It did seem that the smoke pouring from above the stacks that surrounded them was closer than before.

"The Monongahela House is going!" Jonas cried as he pointed upstream. Parker turned around slowly, still on one knee, to look where Jonas pointed. One hundred yards upstream, Pittsburgh's finest hotel sat on the corner of Water and Smithfield streets near the entrance to the Monongahela Bridge. The flames consumed an entire side of the building. Then the whole structure collapsed. Flames and embers erupted from the crash and blew onto the Monongahela Bridge, setting it on fire.

Both men watched mesmerized as the flames raced along the covered bridge. *Dry as tinder*, firefighter Cowan had said. Parker thought it looked more like the bridge had been soaked in lamp oil by the way the fire ate it up. Within ten minutes the bridge was afire along its entire length. The sight was as spectacular as it was horrifying. The fire ate away the wooden covering, exposing the timbers that made up its combination trusses and arches. After a few more minutes the first section of flaming timbers closest to shore broke and crashed into the water, which extinguished it with an audible hiss. Section by section, starting from the left, the burning bridge fell into the river.

Parker looked on silently. He had watched men build that bridge when he was a boy. It was many years ago, after a spring flood had washed away half of the Monongahela Bridge. Now, before his eyes, the entire bridge was destroyed. The last sections on the far side of the river fell into the water, revealing crowds of people standing on the opposite shore watching the spectacle of Pittsburgh's fire. More people walked up from the direction of Birmingham, just a short distance upstream on the other side of the Monongahela River.

Steamboats pulled away from shore to escape the fire ravaging the piles of goods on the Monongahela Wharf. Crews lined the ships' decks, watching the blaze. Seeing the steamboats move away demonstrated to the two men the immediacy of their own situation.

"We'd better get out of here," Jonas said.

Parker looked around, his back shooting in pain as he turned. The tops of the piles of goods immediately surrounding them had caught fire. A thick wall of smoke arose from beyond them on all sides. The heat and smoke choked them and burned their eyes as they looked for a way to escape. They might be able to step into the water and pick their way along downstream to the Point, Parker guessed, but could not see for sure. The path along the water's edge upstream toward the Monongahela Bridge was blocked by even more ruin. Parker looked out over the river. The crew of one of the steamboats waved to him in a circling manner, signaling him to come out to the ship.

"Jonas," Parker tapped Burbridge's shoulder and pointed to the boat.

"I'm not a good swimmer," Jonas worried aloud.

"I don't think we'll have to swim that much," Parker replied. "There hasn't been any rain for weeks. The river's pretty low."

"Okay," Jonas conceded, "but if I start to sink, I'm grabbing onto you!"

The two men stepped into the water and waded out toward the steamboat. For several yards, the water came only up to their knees. A little farther out, they were in over their waists. The crew of the steamboat watched them advance and lowered a small skiff into the river. About twenty yards from the steamboat, Parker and Jonas reached a shelf with a drop-off to a depth they did not know.

"Are you ready?" Parker asked. Jonas looked over at Parker and nodded quickly, with no confidence but with a compelling urge to get going. Both men pushed off into the deeper water and shuddered from the cold. They may have been having August-like weather in April, Parker thought, but this was still the freezing river water of early spring. Parker's hands met just under his chin, sliced the water in front of him, then pushed backwards in wide arcs. As he did this he kicked his feet the same way a frog's legs move in the water. With each stroke a stabbing pain wrecked his entire upper back. If he'd had the presence of mind, he thought, he would have taken off his overcoat and boots before starting into the water. He was a good swimmer, but their bulk made it difficult. His clothes, coupled with the pain in his back, made it a struggle for Parker to reach the steamboat. He looked over at Jonas, whose stroke was short and choppy as he doggie paddled. Jonas gasped and grunted as he moved, but appeared to be able to make it.

They reached the skiff at the same time. The moment Jonas stopped paddling to reach up to take hold of the boat, he immediately sank completely under the water. Parker grabbed his hand just as it slipped under the surface, but Jonas' weight pulled him down under also. Parker grasped Jonas' wrist and coat to pull him upward. Jonas, in full panic, seized Parker's hair and pushed him downward in an effort to reach the surface. Both men sank as they struggled. Parker tried to push Jonas upward, but Jonas' flailing only sent them farther down. Jonas kicked his feet until he was almost standing on Parker. Parker — tired from the swim, freezing, and his lungs bursting for air — felt fatigue quickly move into his arms. He felt he was about to lose the strength to fight off Jonas or even swim to the surface.

Suddenly Parker's feet touched solid ground. It was so unexpected that he was almost sitting before he pushed with his legs to stop their descent. Jonas felt the resistance from below and relaxed his grip on Parker. Parker took hold of Jonas' feet and thrust him upward. Jonas pushed off as Parker's arms extended. Parker then pushed off to propel himself upward. He could barely raise his arms to stroke downward to hasten his ascent. He saw the surface coming, but thought his lungs would explode even before he got there.

Parker let out a monstrous gasp for air as his head burst out of the water. But his arms simply would not move to keep him afloat, and he started to slip back under. Suddenly, two hands grabbed his coat and hauled him aboard the skiff.

"There you go, now," a voice said.

Minutes later Parker and Jonas lay in the bottom of the skiff gasping for breath. Two men stood over them.

"We saw you two go under," the voice said again. "The captain ordered us down to get you, but we really didn't think we'd see you come up again."

Parker tried to say "Thank you," but instead started coughing uncontrollably. The crew on deck pulled the ropes that suspended the skiff from the winch, lifting the small boat to the deck. The two crewmembers climbed out of the skiff, and then helped Parker and Jonas out. The captain met them there.

"I'm Silas Sayre, Captain of the *Eliza*. Welcome aboard, boys," he said.

"Captain, we are much obliged to you and your crew," Parker controlled his panting sufficiently to talk. "You seem to have saved us twice in the space of a few minutes."

"Don't mention it, boys," Captain Sayre said. "But I see now that you're going to shiver yourselves to death."

"Mr. Haus!" the captain called to one of his crew, who came over immediately. "Take this gentleman's coat and hang it in the boiler room. We'll see if we can dry it out a bit. Then bring back two blankets."

Mr. Haus took Parker's overcoat. Jonas did not have one on. Parker's constable badge glinted dully in the late afternoon sun as he handed the coat over.

"From the constable corps, I see, Mr ...?" the captain asked.

"John Parker, sir," Parker said, extending his hand. "Yes, I'm a constable for the City of Pittsburgh."

"I know your High Constable, Abraham Butler, very well, Mr. Parker," Captain Sayre explained. "He and I ran a line of keelboats on these rivers many years ago. He left the water for life on dry land. I never could."

Mr. Haus returned with two blankets. Parker and Jonas wrapped them around themselves. Parker's body let out one last shudder before he started to warm up.

"The river's got to be frightfully cold, I see," Captain Sayre said. "I must confess I did not expect you two to come up again once you went under together in a tangle."

Jonas put his head down while Parker explained, "Well, we hit bottom, sir, and were able to push ourselves up again."

"Bottom, you say?" asked Captain Sayre. "Ah yes, that was probably the remains of the sandbar. The thing used to make an island in the summertime when the river was low, the length of several city blocks. Pittsburghers even planted crops on it. Over the years floods and freshets washed the top of it away. Still, the Monongahela is quite low for this time of year. You wouldn't have pulled that stunt off in a proper spring river."

"Yes, sir," Parker agreed. They all turned toward the city. Looking at the wharf, Parker saw that they probably could have walked in the water along the shoreline toward the Point, after all. The Point and the first several blocks upstream from it remained untouched by the fire as the wind continued to blow steadily southward up the Monongahela River. People massed on that end of the wharf and in the streets near the Point. Moving to the right, flames engulfed the bulk of piled goods and merchandise on the wharf for the rest of its length to the Monongahela Bridge.

From his vantage point on the steamboat Parker saw that the blocks on the end of Water Street closest to the Point were still intact, but from there on the fire raged the entire length of the city along the Monongahela River. City blocks farther away from the river burned starting farther to the left, including the block on Ferry Street. Just how much farther into the city the fired raged, Parker couldn't see through the smoke, but he knew firsthand that it burned for several blocks beyond what he could see. Many thick, spiraling columns of smoke rose from each block, then all of the columns joined above to form a billowing roof that rolled southward to the right and obscured the city from view. The steeple of the Third Presbyterian Church rose defiantly through the smoke, but all else around it burned.

The Monongahela Bridge no longer stood to obstruct their view farther to the right. Parker saw that the fire crossed Grant and even Ross Street and advanced steadily upstream along the river. Beyond these two blocks glimpses of Grant's Hill occasionally came into view through the smoke. Its sparsely housed slope stopped the fire's progress in that direction. To its right Boyd's Hill arose much higher. Its dramatic cliffs dropped next to the Monongahela, leaving only a ribbon of land between hill and river.

Prevented by the hills from moving southeast into the hinterland, the fire continued consuming the blocks upstream along the Monongahela River. From where he stood on board the *Eliza*, Parker saw that the fire had even crossed the canal into Kensington. This community on the narrow flats between the river and the cliffs of Boyd's Hill contained the factories of several different industries and the homes of the people who worked in them.

"It looks like it's going after the boatyards," said Captain Sayre. "The very steamboat that you're standing on was built right there in Kensington."

Jonas turned to Parker, his face pale with dread. "The Gas Works!" he said.

Parker looked over again, straining to peer through the chaos to see the area of Kensington. Among its glass works and iron foundries sat Pittsburgh's Gas Works, which manufactured gas for the lamps that lit the city's residences, businesses, and streetlights. It was from this area that the explosions now sounded that heralded the front-line advance of the fire. Suddenly a colossal ball of flame swelled and blew into the sky above Kensington. One second later the pound of the explosion reached the ears of the men on the *Eliza*.

Parker shuddered. His city burned in front of him. Everywhere in the streets on the fringes of the conflagration people scurried in all directions. Teams pulling carts and wagons sped along all streets outside the engulfed area. He heard the screams of horses and the shouts of men and women from across the river. "Captain Sayre, sir," he said at last, "could I trouble you to take us over to the Point?"

"Do you think you are going to go put out that monster?" asked Captain Sayre.

"I don't know about the fire," Parker replied, "but I am a constable for the city, Captain, and at the moment, much needed."

"I won't argue that," said Captain Sayre. "It'll take some time, though. I'll have to turn her all the way around, then wend my way through all of these boats."

Then turning to his crew, "Mr. Haus, go into the pilothouse and tell Mr.

THE BURNT DISTRICT

Tindle to turn us hard astern toward the Point. I'll be along in one moment."

"Thank you, sir," said Parker.

"For someone who desires to go do his duty, Mr. Parker, you are welcome," replied Captain Sayre. He walked over to the crew gathered at the railing. He spoke to a few of them, who then moved to their posts. Then Captain Sayre went into the pilothouse as the ship started moving. Parker and Jonas were alone on deck.

"John," Jonas said quietly, "I'm sorry about what happened ... in the water."

"It's all right, Jonas," Parker replied. "It can scare you to death, being under the water. Can't breathe. Can't get out. It hits you very quickly that you *really can* die."

"You didn't seem so scared," said Jonas.

"I've never been afraid of water," Parker said. "I learned to swim when I was a child and it's always come pretty easily to me." Then he looked at Jonas with a sidelong grin, "That is, except when some madman is pulling my hair and kicking me in the ribs."

Jonas' eyes started to widen, but then he laughed and said, "Thanks a lot, John." He paused, "But really, thank you."

Parker nodded a "You're welcome" at him. Both men walked to the rear of the deck as the ship turned toward the Point. Parker stared at the piers of the now-destroyed Monongahela Bridge. They rose up from the river, dark stumps now isolated from each other. Between them the charred timbers that had formed the bridge's trusses protruded through the surface of the water. *Those trusses* were *the bridge*, Sammy would've said.

Thirteen years ago Sammy Reppert and Johnnie Parker sat on the banks of the Monongahela River almost every spring day and watched the workers construct new spans for the Monongahela Bridge. A flood that February had washed the two sections on the Pittsburgh side away. Parker enjoyed watching the sawyers cut the wood and the carpenters piece the timbers together, but it was Sammy who really loved learning how the bridge worked. It was a grand sight for two twelve-year-old boys. Workers lifted huge beams into place, and then connected them together to form the trusses and arches that reached from one pier to the next. Sammy loved the patterns the trusses made, and asked questions whenever a worker would answer about just how they held that bridge up. He was disappointed when workers affixed the wooden housing over top of the trusses that concealed them from his view.

That was the spring when Sammy and Johnnie became best friends. It was the spring when they learned how bridges were built. It was the spring when they found Ruthie Bowden dead on the banks of the Monongahela River. Sammy had walked upstream a bit to relieve himself. He went up into an area of scrub bushes and grass, near a rocky part of the shoreline. He ran back screaming at Johnnie and at the workers — screaming that there was a dead girl. They all ran to where he led.

Ruthie Bowden lay in the brush. She was soaking wet. A few in the crowd said she must've drowned. Her wide-open eyes stared at nothing and her mouth remained open in what looked to Parker like a permanent scream. Parker remembered thinking that she looked more like she'd been scared to death than drowned. Her head turned in a strange angle. Someone in the crowd mentioned something about another girl and then something that sounded like a man's name. Parker didn't understand the man because of his thick accent. The workers carried Ruthie's body to a wagon to take her up into town.

Parker remembered how incredibly lonely Ruthie looked lying in the grass. Even when the men crowded close to her, she seemed alone and removed. Even as they gently lifted her while the foreman said, "Easy now, boys, this is somebody's little girl," Parker felt her separation from them all, never again allowed to join them.

The crews went back to work, but Sammy and Johnnie didn't go back to watch them that day. They did go back the next day, but didn't mention Ruthie Bowden. They rarely spoke about her that spring while watching the crews put the bridge together. Occasionally one might mention that they'd seen her parents or they'd heard somebody report some piece of news or gossip related to her death.

That was thirteen years ago, when he was a boy — far on the other side of the dividing line that marked the end of John Parker's life and the beginning of his existence.

In his eighteenth year he met Angelina Dougherty. He courted her for a year while he established himself as an excellent worker at Bakewell's Glass Works. They married in the spring of 1839. John Parker adored his wife. In those days, he did not work all night long as he did now. Although he aspired to be a shop foreman, he was out the door when his shift was over, anxious to be home with his beautiful bride. When she told him that autumn that they were going to have a baby, Parker thought he could not possibly be happier. This was the life that people were supposed to live. Six months later Angelina Parker died from cholera.

In one stroke John Parker's wife and unborn baby were taken from him forever. He never understood how it could be allowed that his life be so completely shattered. Withdrawing into himself, Parker became like the piers of the Monongahela Bridge — dark and isolated. The trusses that had held him up and connected him to his world lay in ruins around him. He made no attempt to reconstruct them.

"John," Jonas could see that he was calling Parker back from some distant place. The *Eliza* allowed only the slightest lurch as she stopped near the shore.

Jonas started again, "John, we're here."

2

John Parker and Jonas Burbridge stood at the top of the gangway with Captain Sayre. Mr. Haus brought Parker's coat out and handed it to him. If felt warm but still damp.

"Captain Sayre," Parker said, "we are very much obliged to you, sir."

"You're welcome, gentlemen," replied Captain Sayre. "Constable Parker, you tell Abraham Butler that if he ever gets his mind back in the right place and decides to return to the river, I've got a place for him on my boat."

"Yes, sir. I'll tell him," said Parker. He and Jonas turned and walked down the gangway.

Captain Sayre had taken the *Eliza* around the Point to shore about one hundred yards up the Allegheny River. The Point was behind the fire, which raged away from it up the Monongahela River. Parker and Jonas disembarked and walked for a short distance along Duquesne Way, which paralleled the Allegheny River. Many of the warehouses and dry goods distributors piled their goods here, too. The strong winds still blew steadily southward, away from this area. Warehouse owners and workers stood vigilant, but it appeared that they had been spared this fire.

Parker and Jonas turned right onto Hay Street. While most of the city's blocks oriented on the Monongahela River, the first two blocks along the Allegheny River ran parallel to the latter stream. The two completely differently oriented sections of the city met along Liberty Street.

But no matter what the direction of the street, most of the traffic on it moved away from the fire. Horse-drawn carts, wagons, and drays clogged the streets as people carted their possessions away from the burning section of the city. Pedestrians added to the congestion, many carrying what few possessions they could. A few individuals moved toward the fire, coming in from other parts of the city to view it. People moved with urgency, but not panic. Even so, as he moved through the streets, Parker marveled that there were no traffic accidents.

When they reached Liberty Street, Jonas stopped. "John, my business is gone. I should go home and let my family know that I'm all right," he said.

"Take care, Jonas," said Parker.

"You too," Jonas said, and then disappeared into the human flow moving away from the city center.

Parker crossed congested Liberty Street to Fourth Street. He made his way up Fourth to Wood Street, where several fire companies played their hoses on the burning buildings. Long hoses connected two fire engines to each other as they worked in tandem to maintain the force of their stream. Barring a major shift in the winds, there was no longer much danger of the fire spreading in this direction, but there were still burning buildings to extinguish. Parker hurried to the nearest crew of firefighters. They wore the green of the Eagle Volunteer Fire Company.

"Where'd you get the water?" Parker asked.

"We got close enough to one of the old cisterns from the days before the reservoirs," replied one firefighter.

"Where can I help?" Parker asked.

"Join one of the pumping crews," the firefighter said, pointing to the engine closest to the fire.

Parker ran over to the green fire engine. One group of men pumped furiously on the twin handles that seesawed out from the engine's center. Another group sat resting nearby. One of their number stood up as Parker approached.

"Where do you want me?" Parker asked him.

"Join our crew," the firefighter replied. "We're pumping in twenty-minute shifts. My boys are starting our next turn now."

He turned to his men, "Up now, boys. Let's have at her!"

The men, though just finishing a respite, were clearly exhausted from fighting this fire the entire day. But once at the engine, they quickly switched places with the crew manning the pump handles. Parker grasped the wooden handle. It felt warm from this fight and smooth from many fights past. He matched the rhythm of the crew and pumped as hard and fast as he could. As he started, the pain in his back flared almost beyond endurance, but either because of exhaustion or his concentration on staying with the crew, it soon passed from his notice. The crews exchanged countless turns at the fire engine. With each new shift at the pump, fatigue seemed to settle into Parker's arms and back a little earlier than the previous shift. Women brought small buckets to the resting men and ladled out water for them to drink. During their breaks the men were usually too exhausted to speak. One young firefighter did strike a conversation with Parker as they sat down to rest after a shift.

"You're Constable Parker, aren't you?" the young firefighter asked.

"That's right," Parker replied. "You look familiar."

"Andrew Brody," said the young man. "Our boys got into a fracas with the Niagara Company a few months back while taking the engine back to the house from a fire on Irwin Street. You came in and broke us up. I remember 'cause it was nighttime and we were surprised to see a constable out."

"That was me," Parker laughed. "At least that time you boys waited until *after* the fire to mix it up."

"We *do* get into it," Andrew Brody agreed.

Then they were up working the engine again. When Parker had first joined the firefighters it was late afternoon, but nighttime had long since come. With the Gas Works destroyed, the city stayed completely dark except for the fire that they fought. Women brought lanterns while small boys held torches to enable the firefighters working around the engines to see. They worked into the night until they'd extinguished all of the fires and threats of fires that they could reach. The gale-force winds that had driven the flames earlier in the day had by now ceased. A slight breeze pushed coolly back into the burned area. In the darkness of the burned section of town, embers glowed and small fires licked up from the ruins in foundations, but they were no longer any threat. There was nothing left for them to catch onto. The fire had eaten up all of the fuel in the area.

Finally, the captains of the fire companies came around giving the orders to cease, pack up, and go home.

"That'll do, boys. The fire's burnin' out over in Kensington, only because it's run out of city over there to burn. We've done the best we could with what we had. God knows you've all worked harder and longer than anyone has any right to expect of ya. No one will be able to thank ya properly for the work you've done today. Roll 'em up and let's head back to the house."

With that the Great Fire was over. There were no *huzzahs* of triumph at this order. The firefighters' arms dropped to their sides, finally relieved of their burden. Some slumped against the engine, some sat on the ground with their tall conical fire helmets beside them. Slowly, they started to uncouple hoses and roll them up. The firefighters moved as if they were drunk with exhaustion. Civilian helpers, both men and women, stood tired and disoriented. They seemed to not quite know what to do next. Some allowed the emotions to burst forth that they'd been keeping in check as they'd worked for hours assisting the firefighters. One woman sat on the ground with her face in her hands and wept. A great darkness surrounded them.

Parker helped the hose company wind its fire hoses onto two large wheels that sat atop their carriage. The firefighters secured their own hoses and equipment, then shouldered the towropes and pulled their engines to their engine houses. The Vigilant Company suffered the loss of much hose, destroyed during the fight. But even worse, the fire claimed their engine house itself. After some discussion they decided to take their engine to the

Diamond Market to find temporary housing for it.

As the engines and hose carriage rolled out, Parker turned away from the scene and trudged up the street toward the Watchhouse. He walked along Fourth Street, where the blocks on both sides were destroyed between Wood and Smithfield streets. Once across Smithfield Street, Fourth Street became the borderline of the devastation. The block on his right toward the Monongahela River was burned. The block on his left, where the slope of Grant's Hill started, stood intact.

He turned left onto Grant Street. Up ahead in the darkness, the courthouse stood on high ground on the other side of the street. People crowded in front of it and up both sets of front stairs that led to its columned portico. Here and there government officials and courthouse staff moved among the throng, carrying lanterns. The officials had opened the courthouse doors to fire victims to give them a place to stay for the night.

Parker continued past the courthouse, which occupied the entire block on Grant Street between Diamond Alley and Fifth Street. He crossed Grant to go into the Watchhouse, which was situated on the small block just past the courthouse. As he approached the Watchhouse door, a few watchmen emerged from inside and passed him on the street. They nodded to acknowledge Parker and he nodded back. He went inside and up the stairs.

Pittsburgh's police force consisted of two different and separate departments. Sixteen watchmen walked specific beats in the city starting late in the evening through the early morning hours. During the daytime five constables patrolled the city, rotating attendance at court sessions, City Council meetings, and the Diamond Market on market days. The watchmen reported to duty on the ground floor of the Watchhouse, while the constables' offices occupied the second floor.

Parker reached the top of the stairs as the other four constables came out of the High Constable's office. They gave short greetings as they passed each other. Everyone moved in the same depleted mode. Oil lamps flickered in the building while the gas fixtures remained dark. Parker entered High Constable Abraham Butler's office.

"Constable Parker," the High Constable said, raising an eyebrow. "Come in and close the door."

Parker closed the door and stood in front of his boss.

"Constable Parker," High Constable Abraham Butler said. "No one seems to have seen you anywhere around during the late morning hours today, nor when the fire started. Might you tell me where you were?"

"I was here, sir," replied Parker, "in the Watchhouse."

"Not out on your rounds? What were you doing here?"

THE BURNT DISTRICT

"I came in to write down some notes from my rounds this morning. Then, I," Parker stopped and looked down, "as I sat writing, I — I fell asleep in the chair, sir."

"Constable Parker," the High Constable spoke louder now, "You are a Constable of the City. If you want to walk the city streets all night on your own time, I cannot stop you. But during the daytime you are *on duty*, answerable to me, and with an obligation to people that you protect. Do you understand me, Constable Parker?"

"Yes, sir," Parker answered.

High Constable Abraham Butler studied Parker for a moment. "Sit down, John," he said finally.

Parker sat in the small wooden chair that faced the High Constable's desk.

"John," High Constable Butler spoke quietly and calmly now, "I don't ask questions, and I guess I don't have to. I've been friends with your father for many years and we both watched you go down hill after — after Angelina died. You lost your job and seemed to lose all interest in life itself. I recommended you for appointment only because I've known you since you were a boy and I knew that you were a good man. A lesser man might've turned to the bottle on the way down. You did not, and I thought that said something about you.

"You've become a good constable, maybe the best I've had. And no one seems to mind your walking a beat at night after your regular hours. But John, it catches up with you, as it did yesterday. And I'll tell you, if anyone else had been sleeping on duty, I'd kick them off the corps on the spot."

"Yes, sir," Parker acknowledged.

"John," the High Constable continued, "I thank the Lord that I've never had to go through what you went through. But that was several years ago. At some point you need to, well, to come back to life on the inside. Do you know what I'm saying, John?"

"I think so, sir," Parker answered.

"Why do you think it's taking you so long, John?" the Butler asked. "Are you blaming yourself? Are you thinking that there's something you could've done?"

"I don't know, sir," Parker said while looking at the floor. "Sometimes I do."

Butler spoke in a reasoning voice, "John, how could you have helped her when the doctors themselves couldn't? What could you have done?"

"I don't know," said Parker looking up. "Something. *Anything.*"

And there it was. High Constable Butler reached the heart of the matter. He decided not to push anymore for the moment. He was a large man with a fleshy face whose expression registered genuine concern. A small mop of black, curly hair topped his high forehead. He folded his thick hands on the desk in front of him. "Well, John," he said, "I cannot stop you from doing that to yourself. It's something you'll have to come to on your own."

"But now," the High Constable changed the subject and lightened the tone of his voice, "Here's a fine thing. After lecturing you on staying out all night, by God I've got to ask you to stay out all night *tonight*. The Watch will need extra officers patrolling tonight. Lots of people will need help. People are homeless. They're lost. We have only one confirmed death from the fire so far that I know of, but several people are still missing. And, of course, there'll be looters about."

"Believe me, I know," said Parker. As he stood up, the stabbing pain flared in his upper back. He groaned out loud.

"What happened to you?" the High Constable asked.

"A looter hit me in the back with a box of nails," Parker replied.

"I take it that you didn't catch him, then," said the High Constable.

"Knocked me out cold," Parker said.

"Did you get a look at him?"

"No. I really don't remember much after he hit me — just a colossal pair of boots. Then I woke up to Jonas Burbridge's face in mine," Parker said.

"Now there's a sight," the High Constable laughed. Then he looked at Parker's wet clothes. "Did you step in the path of a fire hose?"

"No. I took a swim in the Mon," Parker said as he turned toward the door. "By the way, Silas Sayre says 'Hello.'"

"Hah!" Butler shouted. "That old gouger! He'll be on a boat on the day he dies."

Parker reached the door, then turned around. "Thank you, sir," he said.

"Be on your way now, Constable Parker," High Constable Abraham Butler said. "Grab a lantern on your way out. You know the Gas Works are gone. The city is completely dark.

"Oh yes," Butler remembered, "and tell anyone you see wandering around in the burned area to stay away from walls and chimneys that are still standing. They're weak and liable to fall over if you even touch them. The Select and Common Councils will have to hire men just to go around and knock them all down. They're a danger as long as they stand."

Parker walked out of the High Constable's office and over to a table where several lamp-oil lanterns sat. He selected a small wooden match from a pile and Parker lit one of the lanterns. He carried the lantern down the wooden stairs and stepped outside. To his right the streets were dark, but small lights glowed from oil lamps inside peoples' windows. Looking left, one block down the street, a more complete darkness hid the desolation that used to be the first and second wards of the city. He stepped onto the street and turned left.

As Parker passed the courthouse a woman ran over from the crowd in front of it and grabbed his arm. It was Addie Milligan, who until this afternoon had lived on Second Street in Parker's beat.

"Constable," she said urgently, "my daughter, Grace — we can't find her. My husband is out looking for her now. Will you help him? Will you please help him find our girl?"

"Of course I will, Mrs. Milligan," Parker replied. "I'm going out on rounds right now. I'll see if I can find her and your husband."

"She's our baby," Mrs. Milligan cried, "our only one."

"I'll certainly do what I can, Mrs. Milligan," Parker said.

Parker walked down Grant Street toward the Monongahela River. At the intersection with Fourth Street he entered the burned section of the city. His lantern did not throw light much farther than his immediate area. He walked up to a tall, thick shape in the darkness. He held the lantern up to it. It was a chimney, its bricks blackened by the fire and soot. He moved the lantern beside the chimney and looked past it into an open basement. Ashes and charred wooden beams filled the small area of light. Pulling the lantern back, he saw some of the timbers still glow red.

He stepped back and continued down Grant Street. He crossed Third Street, then turned right onto Second. As he walked, he felt his feet sink into a soft powder, as if the city had just gotten a mild snowfall. Letting his lantern arm hang and looking down, he saw that a layer of ashes about an inch thick covered everything. He felt disoriented, a condition only partly caused by the absence of streetlights. Even in the slightest of moonlight, he would be able to see the *buildings* on each side of the street. He would feel their presence without thinking about it. But tonight they were simply *not there*. He felt as though he walked through some strange, lonesome wood. Instead of trees it had thick, dark shapes scattered about. The streets, instead of passages between buildings, became trails to keep to, to keep from getting lost. In some places the piles of rubble in the streets made even this difficult.

Up ahead a small light appeared in the middle of the street. It grew larger until Parker saw a dark figure attached to it. As the figure approached, he saw a man walking toward him holding a torch. From the torch's light Parker realized that the haze around his lantern was not the result of its dirty glass. The haze surrounded them. As the man came nearer, Parker saw that he did not have a long watchman's coat on. He was a civilian.

"Mr. Milligan?" Parker asked.

"No. Thad Bell," a young man replied as his face came into view. "I'm looking for my father, Benjamin Bell. He hasn't been seen since the fire started. Have you seen an elderly man tonight, sir?"

"No, I'm afraid that I haven't," Parker said. "Have you checked the courthouse? Lots of folks are spending the night there."

"Yes, sir," Bell replied. "I looked for him at the courthouse. The English Lutheran Church on Seventh Street is also taking in fire victims. I checked there, and a few other churches."

"Well, there's still some confusion about," Parker reasoned. "It's hard to find your way around in the darkness. Maybe the daylight will bring some calm and better luck. He may find his way home then. In the meantime, I'll keep an eye out for him tonight."

Then he added dutifully, "Stay away from the standing walls and chimneys — they're weak, and liable to fall on you if you touch them."

"Yes, sir. Thank you, sir," Thad Bell said, then continued down the street.

Parker walked down Second Street. With the buildings gone, he could see across on other streets several small lights moving about just like Thad Bell's. Every once in a while someone called out a name in the darkness two or three times in a row. Then, nearby, Parker heard a very familiar call.

"One o'clock — the sky is clear but it's hazy down here," the voice called loudly and slowly.

Parker had to think for a minute to determine whose circuit he was on.

"One o'clock — the sky is clear but it's hazy down here," the watchman called again. Parker realized that it was Everett Hay's beat. In the distance he heard several other watchmen calling the hour and weather. Hay stood just around the corner on Smithfield Street. He faced the other direction as Parker approached. He wore a long, watchman's overcoat and a weathered, wide-brimmed leather hat. He held a lantern in one hand and his club in another. The watchmen carried clubs long enough to double as walking sticks. Parker, like the other constables, carried a shorter nightstick of turned oak, with a hole at the end for the rawhide strap that went around his wrist when he used it. But Parker seldom used or even displayed his club, carrying it on his belt under his overcoat. In fact, many people who routinely saw him on his rounds would be surprised to know that he carried one at all.

Everett Hay saw Parker's lamp lighting the ground beneath him and turned around.

"Hello, Everett," Parker said.

"Hello, Parker," Hay said, "What a mess, eh?"

"I've never seen or felt anything like it," Parker replied. "It's having a hard time sinking in."

THE BURNT DISTRICT

"Tell me about it, Parker," Hay said. "We started our watch late because everyone was fighting the fire. It took some figuring just for me to find my beat. It's not even the same place, anymore. It's not even *a* place. It's just — ruin."

"Any problems?" asked Parker.

"Nah," Hay said. "Not in my area. There's nothin' here to protect or loot. Anything moved outside got burned along with everything else. Now, Kevin's beat is a different story. He patrols Ferry Street over to Liberty, part burned area and part clear. People who moved their stuff over there are out all night guardin' it. That's where the looters'll be if they try anything."

"Do — did you live in the burned area?" Parker asked.

"Me? Nah. I live on O'Hara Street, way over on the other side of the canal," Hay answered. "How about you?"

"I board over on Sixth Street, near Cherry Alley," Parker said.

"We're two of the lucky ones, then," said Hay. "Well, I'd better get back on my rounds. The Lieutenant comes around every two hours to check on us. See ya around, Parker. And hey, don't touch any walls or chimneys — they're weak and liable to fall on top of you."

"Thanks," said Parker as they both walked away.

Parker stepped back onto Second Street and continued toward the Point. Odd-shaped silhouettes of partial brick walls showed black against the night sky. Some brick buildings had a front or back corner section still standing. Even brick buildings with all four walls still standing looked different. Looking up into their glassless windows Parker could see the stars up through their roofless tops. He realized that Hay was right: the haze surrounded them, but the sky above was clear. Through the doorways and bottom windows he saw small flames still flickering in some of their hollowed insides. From a nearby building he heard what sounded like a falling tree and then a crash. A burst of embers sprayed from its open basement.

Crossing Wood Street, Parker saw the steeple of the Third Presbyterian Church rising two blocks away. For the first time on this walk he found something familiar. The city's tallest landmark gave him an orientation point, enabling him to get his bearings. He crossed Market Street and approached Ferry Street, where Cowan told him the fire started. On his right stood the Third Presbyterian Church. He saw that two other buildings had been saved on that block. To his left the warehouse for the Globe Cotton Factory still stood; the factory itself was the fire's first casualty. The buildings in front of him lining the other side of Ferry Street were burned, but buildings behind those were untouched. Then Parker noticed a noise — faint but regular. He looked over at one of the unaffected blocks and saw lights through the windows of the *Gazette* building. The noise, he realized, came from their presses. *Tomorrow*, he said to himself, *people will be reading the news of the fire that hasn't even cooled yet.*

Parker crossed Ferry Street and walked into the unburned section of the First Ward. The edge of his light passed two figures sitting in the dark along the street. He walked over to a man and a boy sitting under a blanket. They leaned up against a moving trunk and a pile of furniture.

"Is everything all right here?" he asked them.

"Yes, sir," the man answered. "We'll be out here until daylight and I can find a place to store our things. Our house is gone. These items that we pulled out are all we've got left."

"Has anyone bothered you?"

"No, sir," the man said. His little boy had a small coughing fit as the father spoke, "My wife and daughter are spending the night over at the church. Our watchman's been by several times to check on us."

"I've got things covered in this area, Parker," said a rough voice from an approaching light. It was Kevin Fisk. Kevin was the longest-serving watchman in the city. Most of the other watchmen didn't mind Parker's nighttime rounds. Some appreciated the company. They felt the camaraderie of a fellow police officer. Kevin Fisk, however, took it as an intrusion into his area of responsibility and a tacit suggestion that he wasn't doing his job.

"Of course you do, Kevin," said Parker. "Earlier I saw a lot of goods from the warehouses piled on the Allegheny River side of the Point. I just wondered if they were proving too much of a temptation for looters."

"The warehouse people started to put their stuff back inside as nightfall came and they saw that they were safe from the fire. But it got too dark to finish everything. Their workers are taking shifts guarding the stuff. And I'm over there every couple a' minutes. I can spot people who have no business in my area," Fisk continued, glaring at Parker, "and I show them the way straight out."

"Um, right," Parker said. "Well, I'll be on my way, then. Good night, Fisk." He turned to the man and his son, "I'm very sorry about your loss. Good luck to you."

Parker turned around and walked back up Second Street. At least the weather was mild for the people staying outside all night, he thought. He spent the night walking the streets in the burned area. He heard coughing many times through the night. If the cough was nearby, Parker walked over to find the people to make sure they weren't injured or trapped. After making sure they were all right he always reminded them to stay clear of the walls and chimneys, and informed them that the courthouse and several churches had opened their doors to fire victims to stay overnight.

The desolation covered many city blocks. As he walked by each open foundation or partial wall, Parker tried to envision the building that had been there. He named to himself the business or the family who had lived in it. He realized that some of the city's poorest citizens living in the oldest sections of town lost their homes. Many of them lost both their homes and their jobs to the fire.

At dawn Parker found himself standing on the abutment of the Monongahela Bridge, staring out over the line of dark, squat piers in the water. He had no idea how long he'd been standing there. The stars disappeared as the sky turned an increasingly lighter blue. Sunlight touched the top of Coal Hill across the Monongahela River. The line of light slowly descended the several hundred feet of its steep face as the sun rose over the hills behind Parker. Soon the morning light showed the hill's entire spring-green and brown slope, then the dark green waters of the Monongahela River. Parker turned around to view the city now in daylight.

During the night Parker mostly *sensed* the city's desolation. He felt it all around him and glimpsed pieces of it at a time in his small lamplight. But in the morning light it came into full panoramic view. Black mounds of charred goods covered the Monongahela Wharf. Beyond the wharf and up into the city, a forest of chimneys and walls started from about halfway to the Point on his left and spread to the right as far as he could see into Kensington. Soot blackened everything standing, and a blanket of ashes colored the ground a soft gray. For the moment, nothing moved. The area seemed entombed in layers of grays and black. Parker remembered from his schooldays listening to his teacher tell about an ancient city in Italy completely destroyed by a volcano. The teacher told them that the entire city lay under a layer of the volcano's ashes for hundreds of years. Parker wondered if this was what that city had looked like.

In the daylight Parker started feeling his own ills. The excitement during the fire pushed notice of its effects in him to the back of his mind. This feeling carried him through the night as he walked the streets. But now he tasted smoke throughout his mouth and felt it down his throat. He spat a couple times, attempting to expel the acrid taste from his mouth, to no success. Smoke lined the inside of his nose right up into his head. A sharp headache started just above his eyes. The pain from the blow he received the day before returned and throbbed unceasingly in the top of his back.

Beside Parker the open maw of the Monongahela House's foundation lay filled with charred timbers and bricks. Huge piles of rubble lay outside it on all four sides. He looked beyond it to Kensington and decided to go over and see the Gas Works. As he walked around the rubble toward Water Street he saw a few people appear out on the streets. Here and there individuals and small groups of people appeared, surveying the destruction. Most moved slowly, as if in a daze.

Parker walked down Water Street, crossing Grant and Ross streets almost to the canal. At an alley to his left between Ross and Try streets, Parker saw two watchmen and one of the Lieutenants of the Watch, Nathaniel Rowe, standing at the edge of the foundation of a leveled building. One of the watchmen squatted next to the foundation and all three peered inside it with grim faces. Parker walked over to see what was the matter. As he reached them, Lieutenant Rowe looked up.

"I'm afraid we have a very sad find here, Parker," he said.

Parker looked down into the foundation and saw a young girl lying dead. She lay on a tangle of burnt timbers. Ashes coated part of her clothes. When he looked at her face, John Parker's head jerked back as if he'd been hit by a stunning punch. *It's Ruthie Bowden,* he thought. Her eyes stared skyward from her smudged face. Her mouth, set wide open, seemed to scream a silent scream. Her neck twisted at an odd angle. Memories and feelings of a twelve-year-old boy flooded Parker. He became confused for a moment, unable to separate two visions. He tried to collect himself. *But it couldn't be Ruthie Bowden — she died thirteen years ago on the banks of the Monongahela River!*

"She's not burned at all," said the standing watchman. "Looks like she fell in during the night. Look, part of this chimney's been knocked away. I'll bet she leaned on it and fell in."

The men looked at the chimney. A small section of exposed bricks were clean — untouched by fire or soot. A few bricks lay on and around the girl. One brick lay in her sprawling blonde hair near her forehead. A deep gash there laid a section of her skin open. Parker noticed very little dried blood in and around the wound.

"My God, this is horribly sad," said the squatting watchman. "I wonder who she is."

"Grace Milligan," John Parker said in a toneless voice.

3

Lieutenant of the Watch Nathaniel Rowe looked down again at the body of Grace Milligan lying in the charred rubble. The frown playing on his sharp face pulled down the ends of the thin mustache lining his upper lip. He kept his hair close-cropped and wore a round, solid cap with a flat top and tiny brim in the front. A small City of Pittsburgh insignia adorned the front of the cap. A similar insignia hung on the front of his long watchman's coat. He showed deep sadness over the dead girl in front him. "My God, the poor child," he said. "Imagine how she must have come to her end: alone and lost, then falling in the darkness. God save me but I hope she died instantly in the fall and did not suffer pain."

He made the sign of the cross as he spoke the last sentence, then turned to his men. "Let's not leave her out in the open like this for the public to gawk at. Mr. Kern," he said to the standing watchman, "please fetch a wagon and we'll take her to the coroner."

"It'll be a job just to find a wagon today, sir," replied Kern. "Every wagon, cart, and dray in the city was pressed into service yesterday carrying things out of path of the fire."

Lieutenant Rowe stared hard at Kern. Anger clearly welled up from below but he stopped it from erupting. "Find one," he ordered.

Kern saw that the discussion was over. He stood up without another word and walked out of the alley, and then around the corner down Front Street. Lieutenant Rowe turned to say something to Parker, and then stopped when he saw Parker's distraught face.

"Bless me, Parker. Are you all right?" he asked.

"I, um, ran into Mrs. Milligan last night outside of the courthouse," Parker said. "She asked me to look for her daughter."

"Oh, I see," Lieutenant Rowe said quietly. "There's more pain to come, isn't there? Well, there's a task that I'm not looking forward to."

"I'll tell them, if you don't mind," Parker said. "I promised Mrs. Milligan last night that I'd help them — her and her husband."

"Yes, of course," Lieutenant Rowe said.

Parker looked again at the body of Grace Milligan. Her pale face seemed transposable with his vision of Ruthie Bowden. His eyes moved again to the gash on her forehead. It was pale, like the rest of her. Something about that struck Parker as odd, but he could not quite formulate a thought on why.

"Well, I'm going to go find her parents," Parker said.

"Parker, maybe you'd better not send them here," Lieutenant Rowe suggested.

"Right," Parker agreed. "It might be some time before I find them. They may still be at the courthouse, or they might be out looking for their daughter. You'll probably get Grace to Eichbaum's by the time I find her parents. I'll just tell them she's there."

"We'll watch over her until Mr. Kern arrives with a wagon," said Lieutenant Rowe while reaching up to rub his forehead. "I must confess that I can't think of anything else to do at the moment. Bless me but my mind seems a bit hazy. I've got a crushing headache that's keeping me from concentrating."

"So do I," said Parker. He said good-bye and walked down the alley toward Front Street. As he left, he looked back to see Lieutenant Rowe turn toward the foundation and look down at Grace Milligan's dead body. The Lieutenant bowed his head, then made the sign of the cross and closed his eyes.

From Front Street John Parker turned onto Grant toward the courthouse. A few more people walked the streets viewing the destruction in general or standing at one particular structure. The people moved around stunned. A few who stood staring at a particular wall or into a foundation wept. But Parker did not observe any mass wailing or general despair. Many people appeared to be assessing the damage and deciding upon their choice of actions.

As Parker neared the courthouse, people who'd spent the night inside walked past him on their way to the area he'd just left. He searched for a while inside the courthouse and on its grounds, but did not find Mr. and Mrs. Milligan. A courthouse official said that he thought he'd seen them leave the grounds and walk across the street.

Parker returned to the devastated area and turned down Third Street. Even in the daylight the altered landscape proved so disorienting that it forced him to think about where he was going. The steeple of the Third Presbyterian Church provided a fixed point of reference to help him determine his location. He turned left onto Wood Street, and then approached Second Street near where the Milligans had lived.

A man stood beside one of the blackened pieces of wall, staring into the charred rubble that used to be his house. A woman knelt beside him facing out toward the street, sitting on the back of her feet and holding some kind of cloth. As Constable John Parker got close to them he saw that it was a small girl's jacket. Mrs. Milligan turned toward him. For an instant the look of hope started on her face, thinking he may be bringing news of Grace's whereabouts. But when she read the look on Parker's face as he approached, her expression turned to horror.

"No!" she cried, "No!" The repeated word extended into a cry of pain. Mr. Milligan turned around as he heard his wife's cries.

"Mr. and Mrs. Milligan, I'm very sorry," Parker said.

"Noooooooo!" wailed Mrs. Milligan as she doubled over, almost lying on the ground.

Mr. Milligan bent down and grabbed her around the waist, "Mother ..."

"Don't call me 'Mother,'" she shrieked, "I'm not a mother anymore. Oh, my baby ..." As she cried, she pawed at the ground in front of her with her eyes closed, like someone searching for their lost spectacles. Mr. Milligan continued to hold her around the waist while she struggled. After a while she stopped, then laid her face in his enfolding arms and sobbed.

Mr. Milligan held his wife. He wore soiled coveralls typical of iron foundry workers. He was a large man whose facial features at the moment were altered by weariness and grief. His eyes were red and watery, but he did not sob. He appeared to have realized long before Parker arrived what his daughter's fate must be.

"Constable, do you know ... what happened?" he asked.

"The watchmen found her in the basement of a burned-out building," as Parker started, Mrs. Milligan wailed anew. "They believe she got lost during the night and fell in the darkness. The Lieutenant of the Watch, Lieutenant Rowe, was with them when I arrived. He's a good man, and he watched over your daughter with care."

"Where is she?" Mr. Milligan asked. "Where is my daughter?"

"They took her to Coroner Eichbaum," Parker told him. Mrs. Milligan wailed again at the mention of the coroner's name.

Mr. Milligan nodded his head. Parker stood there. He wanted to say something to help or to relieve their pain. He wanted to tell them that he knew how they felt. He knew their loss. But now was not the time. Those remarks would be appropriate at a funeral, he felt, or maybe in the days afterward, but not now.

"I'm sorry," he simply said again. "Is there anything I can do?"

Mr. Milligan looked at him for a moment. "There is nothing you can do for us now."

Parker turned to leave.

"Thank you, Constable," Mr. Milligan said quietly.

Parker turned around, "Mr. Milligan, I'm sorry to ask you now, but, can you tell me where you last saw Grace?"

"I was at work when the fire started, of course," Mr. Milligan replied. "I work at the Dallas Iron Works over in Pipetown — Kensington, that is. We had to stay to try and save the building if we could. We tried to soak the sides with water from the river. Of course it did no good. The fire took the mill along with everything else."

"Grace, my baby, was at school over at St. Paul's. My wife was home when the fire started. She tried to pull a few things out of the house. What little she got out burned anyway. She started to make her way over toward the school, but stopped to help with bucket lines. She assumed Grace would be safe at the school. By the time she broke away from helping fight the fire, it was almost evening. When she finally reached school, they told her that Grace had gone.

"I finally found Addie at the courthouse sometime after dark. Then I went out looking for my Grace ..." Mr. Milligan stopped. His face contorted in a strain to hold off crying. He could not continue anymore.

"Thank you, sir," Parker said. "I'm very sorry." He turned and walked away. Parker headed in the general direction of the Watchhouse, to report Grace's death to the High Constable. The image of her lying in the burned-out foundation stuck in his mind. It alternated with the vision of Ruthie Bowden lying in the grass along the Monongahela River thirteen years ago. At times he could not distinguish between the two faces. The twin specters followed him through the streets.

Morning was by now high, and Parker saw even more people about. Many now worked among the ruins, salvaging and scraping bricks from their destroyed walls and chimneys to use to rebuild their homes. Passing the McClurg foundry's foundation, Parker watched workers poke through the rubble looking for chunks of iron that might still be useable product.

Parker arrived back at the Watchhouse and walked up the wooden stairs to the constables' floor. He blew out his lamp and put it back on its table. He looked in the High Constable's office. No one was there. Then Parker heard footsteps coming up the stairs. High Constable Abraham Butler walked in carrying a newspaper.

"Hello, John," he said while walking into his office. "Come in."

Parker followed him into the office. High Constable Butler laid the newspaper on his desk. It was *The Daily Morning Post*.

"Look at this," he said, reading from the paper, "'Twenty squares of the city in ruins. From one thousand to twelve hundred houses destroyed. Loss estimated at ten million dollars.' My God, John, most of the First Ward is gone, all of the Second Ward, and all of Kensington. That's one third of the

THE BURNT DISTRICT

city. Look here, they've already got a name for the destroyed area. They're calling it 'the Burnt District.'"

Butler read silently the newspaper's account of the fire. His head nodded affirmatively as he read certain parts. He and Parker already knew the details.

"Look here," he said, "they started writing this last night before the fire was even out — after they'd tried to save one of their editors' houses. By God, those newspapermen are a tenacious bunch."

"The *Post* says two people are believed to be dead, one man and one woman. Well, *we're* pretty sure about the man — several people reported seeing Samuel Kingston go back into his house for something. There are a couple of women reported missing. And rumors have people trapped in the Monongahela Bridge when it went up, but that's unconfirmed. It'll take *days* to find all of the missing persons and really get an idea of just who actually got killed."

"And, of course, there's Grace Milligan," Butler said, looking up from under his dark, bushy eyebrows at Parker. "I ran into Lieutenant Rowe before he went off of his watch. He told me all about finding her. Did you find her parents?"

"Yes, I did," Parker replied.

"How did it go?" Butler asked.

"Badly," Parker said.

Butler nodded in understanding. "Lieutenant Rowe said that you appeared particularly shaken by the discovery," he said. "Are you all right?"

"I'm fine," Parker said, "It's just that …" He looked at the floor.

"What?" asked High Constable Butler.

"Well, sir," Parker started, "it just makes no sense, I mean, where she was. Why was she way over at the end of Try Street, near the canal? She went to school at St. Paul's, right here across the street from us. Her home was on Second Street on the west side of Wood. She had no reason to be way over at Try Street, almost to the river."

"John," Butler said, "you know the confusion that reigned yesterday. Anybody could've ended up anywhere. At least a dozen people are unaccounted for right now, and I'll tell you that most of them are just lost. She wandered over there, lost, John, and *who knows* how? Besides, doesn't her father work over in Kensington?"

"Yes," said Parker, "'Pipetown.'"

"Yes, yes. I know," said Butler, giving an impatient wave of his hand. "The point is that she could've been trying to make her way over to her father."

"I guess so," said Parker, unconvinced.

The High Constable changed the subject. "The Select and Common Councils are meeting this afternoon. I've got to attend. There'll be a lot to do. The Police Committee will meet. The mayor himself will need a place to work — he lost his office and his house."

The High Constable looked at Parker. "You don't have to go, John," he said. "I'm going to be there. Perry will be there, too. So we'll be covered. And besides, to tell you the truth, you look horrible. You should go home and go to bed."

"Sir, I …" Parker started to protest.

"I'm not joking, John," Butler said. "You look like death. Take the rest of the day off. Go home. Get cleaned up. Get some sleep."

Parker looked down at his clothes. They *were* a mess. And if his face *looked* anything like his head *felt*, he would look bad indeed.

"Yes, sir," he said. "Thank you, sir."

"I'll see you tomorrow, John," Butler said. "I'll fill you in on what happens at the meeting today."

Parker turned and walked out of the High Constable's office. He trod down the wooden steps and out onto the street. He turned right on Grant Street away from the Burnt District, past St. Paul's Cathedral situated between Fifth Street and Virgin Alley. Pittsburgh was divided into two completely different cities now. Behind him the Burnt District sat in absolute desolation. Beside it, however, stood the rest of the city untouched by the fire. The buildings that Parker walked among now knew no rumor of the destruction over by the Monongahela River.

Many of the people in the streets appeared to run their daily schedules. It was the time of the morning when most people who had paused from their early-morning work for breakfast now returned to their duties. Women returned from the Diamond Market, which the fire had skirted, talking about the calamity. All conversation that Parker passed concerned the fire. From five years as a constable, Parker knew the pattern and rhythm of the street traffic at this time of the morning. He noticed that more of the wagon and dray traffic than usual headed toward the First and Second wards. Most pedestrians also walked in that direction.

Parker turned left onto Sixth Street. Just before Cherry Alley on the right stood a beautiful two-story wood frame house. A railed and roofed porch occupied the entire length of the house's front. Ephraim Wright built the house many years ago for his beautiful young bride, Jenny. At that time the lot on which it sat was out in the "country" surrounding a much smaller triangle of Pittsburgh, which was then still a borough. The couple built a large house, planning for many children who would fill its rooms and play on its grounds. Mr. Wright was a surveyor who made a comfortable living through which they could fulfill their dream. After a son was born, however, Ephraim Wright was killed in an accident while surveying just north of Kittanning. Jenny Wright raised the boy alone, keeping a few boarders for income. Her son grew up and left for St. Louis, to work as a surveyor as his father had done.

Parker walked up the porch steps to the front door. Jenny Wright had enough rooms for three boarders, but currently only housed two: Parker and James Higby, who owned a chemist shop on Union Street near the Diamond Market. From the beginning she started a practice of choosing her boarders carefully to protect her young son from any harmful influences. And even now, after he was grown and gone, she never seemed in a hurry to fill a vacant room to increase her income.

Parker walked in and went straight back toward the kitchen, where he could see Jenny Wright removing plates from a small table. Her gray hair was pulled up and fastened under a small white cap that she wore when working in the kitchen. An apron covered the front of her dress, a dark plaid of brown, copper, and black. By Parker's calculation she was nearly sixty years old, but she looked and acted much younger than that. It did not appear to him that age had taken any spring from her step or put a bend in her back. In her personal life she followed the moral standards taught in the First Presbyterian Church that she attended every Sunday. Though proper in her behavior and respectful toward others, Parker had noted on more than one occasion that she had no use for fake civility toward fools or scoundrels. Her humor and her wit often sent a man in either category packing with his pride in tow.

At the moment Jenny worked with her head down. Parker saw a look of concentration, maybe even tension, on her face. Her movements seemed shorter and choppier than her normal smooth, graceful manner. She looked up as he stepped into the kitchen.

"*There* you are," she said, and instantly relaxed as she saw Parker. "I was wondering if you were going to show up today. James has just gone back to work. I saved you some breakfast." She slid a covered plate across the table toward him.

"Good morning, ma'am. Thank you," Parker said looking at the plate. He had not thought about food at all in the last twenty-two hours, and just realized that he was desperately hungry. "I should get cleaned up first. I'm an awful mess."

She looked at him. "Yes you are. You were in the middle of things yesterday, weren't you? You always are. And out all night." Then she paused, "What's it like over there, John?"

"It's the worst thing I've ever seen," Parker replied, as all the weariness of the past day seemed to descend upon him at once.

"Yes, I suppose it is," Jenny said studying him, as if coming from Parker that statement carried some weight. "Well, there's a bucket of hot water beside the stove. Take it and get yourself cleaned up. Your plate will be here when you're ready."

"Thank you, ma'am," Parker said. He walked over to the black pot-bellied stove. Two buckets sat on the floor beside it and a pot of water boiled on top. He picked up one of the buckets by its handle and walked upstairs.

In the hallway Parker stopped at a narrow closet and pulled out a washcloth and a towel. He walked into his room and shut his door. He set the bucket down in front of the green painted washstand that stood against the wall beside the door. A basin and pitcher sat on the washstand and a large, round mirror hung on the wall above them. On the next wall the midday sun washed through the thin curtains of the room's lone window, which faced Sixth Street. Below the window to the right sat his squat and near-empty bureau. On the right side of the bureau Parker kept a small bookshelf with a few books that he'd read many times each. The bookshelf sat next to the head of his bed. Near the foot of his bed stood a small, round table with one chair. To the right of the table, a wardrobe backed against the wall facing the bureau. On the other side of the wardrobe a tall coat stand posted guard beside his door.

Parker looked at himself in the mirror. He really *was* a mess. His dark brown hair plastered his forehead. An ugly two-day growth sprouted on his normally clean-shaven chin. Soot and ashes smeared his face and his overcoat. He took his coat off and hung it on the coat stand. He slid his nightstick out of his belt and hung it by its rawhide strap on the stand. He took off his boots and then his dark jacket and trousers, which were still damp from his swim in the Monongahela River. Then he peeled off his wet underclothes, leaving his dirty garments in a pile.

Parker poured the hot water from the bucket into the washbasin. He soaked the washcloth and wiped off his face, chest, and arms. He looked at himself in the mirror as he washed. He was twenty-five years old. People always mistook him for at least ten years older. He felt at least ten years older. His five-foot, eleven-inch frame ached from top to bottom. At the moment one area in particular hurt very much. He turned his shoulder to see in the mirror his upper back where the looter hit him with a wooden box full of nails. A large black and blue mark ranged between his shoulder blades almost up to the top of his back. A yellowish border surrounded the bruise.

Shooting pain erupted when he moved his shoulder to see it.

He splashed the hot water in his face then put his head nearly into the basin to wet his hair. He combed his hair back, then lathered up his shaving brush in a cup that held a chunk of soap. As he leaned forward toward the mirror to shave, he saw that his hazel eyes were completely bloodshot. *No wonder Butler told me to go home*, he thought.

Parker finished shaving then pulled from his bureau and wardrobe clothes of the same solid style and color that he'd just taken off. He slid his nightstick through his belt, put his coat over his shoulder, and then carried the basin and empty bucket downstairs. The basin he emptied outside behind the house. He took the bucket to the well to refill it before returning it to Jenny. Ephraim Wright built his house with a well in the back yard long before the first reservoir was installed in the city, and so Jenny always had her own supply of water.

As Parker returned to the kitchen and set the bucket down beside the stove, Jenny sat at the table reading the newspaper accounts of the fire. He saw that she had both the *Daily Morning Post* and the *Gazette and Advertiser*.

"Thank you, John," she said, as Parker sat down and uncovered his plate of food. "This fire was dreadful, John. It says here that hundreds upon hundreds of families are homeless. It's only by the grace of God that more people weren't killed. Do they know, yet, who this woman was?"

"No," Parker replied, "but we did find a little girl who was killed."

"Who was she?" Jenny asked.

"Grace Milligan," Parker answered.

"Oh my, that's Addie's little girl. She's their only child."

"How do you know them?" Parker asked.

"Well, it's actually Addie's mother, Nora Fischer, that I know," Jenny explained. "Nora's been active in church with me for many years. Her husband Tom couldn't abide by Addie marrying an Irish Catholic, and they've been, well, estranged from their daughter ever since. Nora says Tom hasn't spoken to Addie since." Then Jenny asked, "How do you know it was her … I mean, was she burned badly?"

"She wasn't burned at all," Parker said. "We found her lying in the basement of a burned-out building over on the alley off of Try Street. *It appears* that she was lost during the night and leaned against a weak chimney and fell in."

"It appears?" Jenny asked.

"Well, that's what it looks like, and that's what everybody thinks."

"But that's not what *you* think?" Jenny said.

"I don't know," Parker said. "Something just isn't right."

"What isn't right?" Jenny asked.

"I'm not sure," Parker said, then paused. "Ma'am, do you believe in ghosts?"

"No, John," she replied. "I don't."

"Neither do I," said Parker as he finished his breakfast.

"John Parker, are you going to tell me what in heaven's name you are talking about?" Jenny asked.

"As soon as I figure it out myself, I will," he replied as got up from the table. "Thank you very much for breakfast."

"You can almost call it lunch, by now," she said. "If some people wouldn't stay out all night, they might eat at a proper time. And then others could get a decent night's sleep instead of up worrying all night."

Parker smiled, "Good-bye, ma'am," then walked out the front door.

Before he put his overcoat back on, Parker shook it a few times to try to knock some of the ashes and soot off. He walked over to the morgue, near the courthouse. In a small office just off of the foyer, an elderly gentleman sat at a desk writing in a wide, cloth-bound register. He was a thin man, almost completely bald, with a width of thin gray hair just around his ears, traveling, presumably, around to the back of his head. He wore a dark business suit, and looked up over his spectacles as Parker approached.

"May I help you?" the man said as more of a greeting than a question.

"Mr. Eichbaum," Parker said, "I'm John Parker."

"Yes, of course, Constable Parker," Coroner Eichbaum said in a welcoming voice. "You and I have met before. I trust you are here about Miss Milligan. Lieutenant Rowe said that you would find her parents. And they mentioned you when they came in."

"Yes," Parker said, "I was just about to ask you if they'd made it over here yet."

"They left one-half hour ago," Mr. Eichbaum said. "It's very sad, of course."

"Yes," Parker agreed, "very sad." He paused, then asked, "Mr. Eichbaum, I was wondering, do you think that Grace Milligan's neck was broken?"

"Her neck was absolutely broken," stated Mr. Eichbaum.

"Did you think that was, I don't know ... unusual?" Parker asked.

Mr. Eichbaum put down his pen and leaned back in his chair a bit. "I would think it unusual if a little girl fell into a basement full of timbers and rubble in the total darkness and *didn't* break her neck," he said. "Why do you ask?"

"I'm not sure," Parker confessed. "Did the Watch tell you much about how they found her?"

"Lieutenant Rowe and I discussed her discovery in great detail," Mr. Eichbaum replied.

"I have a question, then, about the gash on her forehead," Parker continued. "You see, I know that if I got a gash on my head like the one that she had, blood would spurt out all over the place. But I didn't see that much blood around her cut, especially considering it was caused by a brick dropping from some distance."

"Of course I know the wound of which you speak," Mr. Eichbaum said. "Constable Parker, let me explain something to you. Inside of your chest your heart pumps blood through your body. It forces your blood through tiny vessels in every part of you — from the bottom of your feet to the top of your head. When you receive a cut deep enough, it is this force with which your heart is pumping your blood that causes it to 'spurt' out of the wound. Now, taking all that into consideration, if a body were to receive such a wound long after the heart had stopped beating, then blood would naturally *not* 'spurt' out, would it?"

Parker looked at Mr. Eichbaum for a moment. "Are you saying that she was dead before the brick hit her?" he asked.

"She was absolutely dead before the brick hit her," Mr. Eichbaum stated. "Constable Parker, were the bricks not lying on top and around Miss Milligan when you found her?"

"Yes," Parker answered.

"That is what Lieutenant Rowe said as well. Now, if Miss Milligan leaned on a chimney and pushed bricks in, then fell in herself, would *she* not have been on top of the bricks, rather than the *bricks* on top of her?"

"Yes," said Parker again, wishing at the moment that his mind had been functioning properly at the site where they found Grace Milligan.

"Then it is clear to me, Constable, that she fell in by herself and the fall killed her," Mr. Eichbaum continued. "Later on someone came by, bumped the chimney in the darkness, and knocked the bricks in. Or perhaps that part of the chimney was so weakened by the fire that it collapsed by itself."

"Yes," Parker said, "I wish I had thought of that. Thank you very much for your time, Mr. Eichbaum."

"You're quite welcome, Constable Parker," Mr. Eichbaum said, looking at Parker over his spectacles. He picked up his pen again and dipped it in his small ink bottle.

Parker said good-bye and walked out into the street. His mind began to spin, but this time not because of breathing smoke all night. He tried to absorb what Coroner Eichbaum just said. *Grace Milligan in first. Dead.*

Bricks in afterward. After standing in the street for a minute or two, he headed to St. Paul's School.

Parker arrived at the small schoolhouse, on the corner of Virgin Alley a few doors from St. Paul's Cathedral, and walked up a set of stairs into the building. Inside, a short hallway led straight through to a door that went back outside on the other side of the building. Two interior doors stood facing each other on opposite sides of the hall. Parker looked through the window of the door on the left. A man paced leisurely to and fro across the front of a roomful of young boys. The man spoke as he paced and the boys watched him, apparently listening attentively. Parker looked through the window of the opposite door. A woman sat at her desk in the front of the room as about one dozen young girls sat at their desks writing. The woman looked over at Parker and he held up his index finger to indicate that he requested a minute of her time.

The teacher walked over to the door. She wore dark, full-length skirt from under which her tiny boots peeked as she stepped forward. The collar of the blouse underneath her jacket stood straight up and covered most of her neck. She wore her light-brown hair pulled up in a bun in the back. She did not pull her hair up tightly into the bun, but rather it sagged as a whole in a more relaxed fashion.

"May I help you?" she asked as she opened the door just enough to speak to him.

Parker saw that she was a young woman. Two thin locks of hair had fallen from her bun and framed her smooth face. She looked a bit weary but forced a smile.

"Ma'am, I apologize for interrupting your class," Parker said. "I need to ask you some questions about Grace Milligan, if you don't mind."

The teacher's smile sagged immediately at the mention of Grace's name. "One moment, please," she said and closed the door. She gave her class some instructions while Parker went outside and walked down the steps. After a few seconds the teacher came outside and down the steps to Parker.

"I'm Constable John Parker, ma'am," Parker said, "and again I'm sorry to bother you."

"Alice Wickersham," she said flatly. "What would like to know, Constable?"

"Miss Wickersham, could you tell me when and where you last saw Grace?" Parker asked.

"All the girls were in my classroom when we were alerted to the fire," she started. "I kept them in the room all day, while I periodically came out to see if our building was in danger. I kept them here past regular dismissal time, some even into the evening. I thought they would be safer here than trying to go home through all the confusion, especially the girls who lived in the direction of the fire. I thought that this would be a safe place for their parents to come and get them when they were ready. Mr. Wharton sent his boys over to my room so that he could go assist in fighting the fire.

"The children who remained here into the evening were the ones who lived where the fire was. A few of them became very concerned that their parents might be injured or need them somehow. During one of the times that I came outside to view the situation, Grace snuck out the other door."

"Was it nighttime, then?" asked Parker.

"Yes," Miss Wickersham replied, "it was just after dark."

Miss Wickersham turned away from Parker and folded her arms in front of her. She brought one hand up to her mouth and began to cry. "I'm sorry," she sobbed. "I'm so sorry. I tried to keep her safe. I tried to keep them all safe from harm." She stood and wept. Parker walked over to her. He started to put his hand on her shoulder in a comforting gesture, but stopped and withdrew.

"Miss Wickersham," he said finally, "you did the right thing. You made the right decisions. You looked out for those children. But no matter what you do, you can't keep someone from slipping away who really needs to go. You can't blame yourself.

"Look, there's a whole section of this city in anguish today," Parker continued. "It's an area of pain so big that it has its own name. Don't get dragged into it. You don't deserve to be there. And besides, believe me, once you're in there it's very hard to ever get out again."

She looked up at Parker and nodded. "Thank you," she said. He could tell she understood and appreciated the first part of what he said, but he lost her a little at the end. He really didn't understand, himself, what he'd just said. The words just came out. "I need to get back inside with my girls, if you are finished with your questions," she said.

"Those are all the questions I have," Parker replied. "Thank you for your help." He stepped out onto Fifth Street and walked toward the Courthouse. Looking back at the schoolhouse, he saw Miss Wickersham standing outside the door, attempting to compose herself before going back inside.

At Grant Street Parker hesitated, unsure where to go next. Coroner Eichbaum's clear thinking and deductions stung Parker as an unspoken rebuke: *Why didn't you see that, Constable Parker?* Why indeed? What malaise clouded his head earlier this morning and gave him the splitting headache that broke his concentration? He needed to go back, he realized, to see what he had not seen before.

Parker turned down Grant Street toward the Monongahela River. By now it was past noon. The Burnt District, deserted at daybreak, now bustled with activity. People cleared the streets by loading rubble onto wagons. Others separated and stacked the reusable bricks nearby. Among the workers walked sightseers. They looked on in awe and concern, but not despair. Many he'd never seen before, probably in from the countryside or even nearby towns to see the results of the great fire.

He reached the alley off of Try Street. A small group of people stood at the foundation ahead. "That's where they found her," one of the group pointed. They gazed in, then noticed Parker approaching and moved on. Stepping up to the foundation, Parker inspected the ground in front of it. At daybreak the undisturbed carpet of ashes might have shown footprints to give clues to what actually happened here. But the day's traffic had long since ground them all into the sidewalk. He cursed himself silently for not looking the first time he was there.

Parker peered into the foundation. The fire's tremendous heat had reduced nearly everything within to ashes. Only the bricks and thickest timbers remained intact, but the timbers were charred completely black. He looked at the spot where Grace had lain. The area was disturbed as a result of the Watch climbing in to retrieve her body. He set his hand down on the clean section of chimney that the Watch believed Grace had leaned against when she fell. He put the slightest force on it, pushing away from himself. It did not move. He grasped the edge of the bricks and gave a solid shake. It didn't budge. Parker inspected the section. The bricks and mortar were definitely exposed *after* the fire, as soot covered the entire standing chimney except for that small area. Parker stepped back and kicked the section with the heel of his boot. The few bricks that he hit moved as their mortar cracked, but they remained in the wall.

Parker stared at the chimney, his mind trying to grasp what he'd just seen. *Bricks tumbled from a wall that was* not *weak, hitting a girl who was already dead.* Neither the Watch's nor Mr. Eichbaum's interpretations of these facts satisfied him. He stood back and cursed himself again for his failure to observe important details this morning. His anger at himself grew and he stepped away from the foundation, trying to take it all in. Seeing nothing else to help him, he left the scene exasperated at his own ineptness.

He felt a sudden need to do something more routine. High Constable Butler would not mind if he attended the Meeting of Councils after all, he decided, considering that he'd cleaned himself up. Stepping back from the problem might allow his mind to sort things out. He headed in the direction of Council Chambers. John Parker exited the Burnt District with the specters of Grace Milligan and Ruthie Bowden still shadowing him.

4

Parker slipped into the back of Council Chambers. He spied Constable Albert Perry standing in the back of the room. They nodded a silent greeting to each other as Parker walked over and stood next to him. He surveyed the assembly seated in front of him. In the front of the chamber the city's two legislative bodies, the Select Council and the Common Council, sat in joint session. Mayor William Howard sat in one of the rows of seats provided for the public to attend the meetings. Parker saw not only the mayor, but also many officials of the city government assembled in the audience. Among them were the Treasurer, the Wharf Master, the Street Commissioner, the Collector of Taxes and Water Rents, the Superintendent of Paving and Grading, the Superintendent of the Water Works, and, of course, the High Constable. The Chairman of the Joint Session read aloud at his seat.

"... and it is resolved, that it be requested and enjoined upon all our citizens who may own warehouses or other buildings, and also the churches, to throw them open for temporary shelter for those of our fellow citizens made houseless by the recent calamity — and that the citizens of our sister city, Allegheny, and of Birmingham, make the same arrangements and communicate to the mayor of Pittsburgh where such buildings are located."

"What did I miss?" Parker whispered to Perry.

"They met in committees earlier," Perry replied. "The Police Committee recommended hiring some extra help to patrol and to knock down weak walls. The Councils voted to authorize the mayor to hire some more people."

"Did they allocate him any money to pay them?" Parker asked.

"Not that I saw," Perry said. "I guess we won't see *that* extra help any time soon. The Common Council did give the mayor their Council Chambers to use as his office — his being burned down, and all. So they *have* given him *something*. He's to hold a town meeting tomorrow at two o'clock in the Diamond Market. They're going to talk about relief for the fire victims."

Next the Councils took up the matter of obtaining help from the state government in Harrisburg. Debate centered on the amount of assistance to request. They finally decided to describe the city's plight and let the legislators decide on the amount and type of relief to send. Someone pointed out that the current legislative session in Harrisburg would close shortly. The members drafted a letter to the governor, asking him to extend the session to give the state senators and representatives time to discuss the matter and allocate money. Councils appointed the Honorable Cornelius Darragh to travel to Harrisburg to lobby on the city's behalf.

By the time the debate ceased and the Councils adopted their last resolutions, it was early evening. Parker said good-bye to Constable Perry, leaving before High Constable Butler could see him. This wasn't difficult, as most of the officials stayed and conversed after the chairman's gavel closed the meeting.

Parker went home to the Wright House. He found Jenny and James Higby in the parlor sipping some after-dinner tea.

"Hello, John," Jenny greeted him. "I left some supper in the kitchen for you. Can you join us after you've eaten?"

"Thanks, Jenny," Parker replied. "Of course I'll join you. Hello, James."

"Hello, John," James Higby said. "We've got some news to catch up on."

"I'll be just a few minutes," Parker said as he left the parlor.

"Take your time, dear," Jenny called after him.

Parker took his coat up to his room and left his nightstick and jacket there also. He ate his supper in the kitchen, then joined Jenny and James Higby in the parlor. James just finished lighting the oil lamps. Jenny had never connected to the lines of Gas Works, and so that building's destruction meant no adjustment for her. "Thank you for supper, ma'am." Parker said to Jenny.

"Oh you're welcome, John," she replied. "James was just telling me about all the businesses that were lost yesterday."

James Higby sat back down in his chair and picked up his teacup and saucer. He was a small, slight man, always dressed in full business suit with spectacles on, no matter what time of the day or evening Parker saw him. He styled his hair back with some sort of cream that Parker assumed he got from the druggist shop that he owned and operated. "Oh, yes," he said sipping his tea, "my shop was filled all day with patrons telling about the losses their friends and acquaintances suffered. And it's curious, but nearly all of them complained of headaches."

He continued, "The fire destroyed some of the oldest portions of the city, you know. There were lots of businesses in those wards."

"And lots of homes, too," Jenny chimed in.

"Quite a lot," James agreed, "but businesses of every type suffered. Several iron foundries burned down. Even the McClurg Foundry on Wood Street is gone — it was the first in the city, of course. And the Dallas Iron Works in Kensington is gone.

"Bakewell's Glass Works, an establishment that John knows very well, burned to the ground. Several hotels burned down: the Monongahela House,

THE BURNT DISTRICT

of course, and the Merchant's Hotel on Wood Street, the Eagle, the American Hotel, and the Smithfield Hotel. There were others that I wasn't told of, but I'm sure they're gone, being located inside the Burnt District. Several coffee houses and taverns burned also."

"Those taverns can just stay burned, as far as I'm concerned," Jenny declared.

"Yes, I'm sure," James chuckled. "Oh, yes, and the Bank of Pittsburgh is gone. Now, they built that bank with a roof made of a special material, zinc, I believe. It was supposed to be fireproof, but people reported that that roof melted like nothing. Fortunately for its depositors, the bank's vault protected its books and their money."

"Some of your competition was eliminated, too, wasn't it, James?" Jenny said.

"Oh, quite," James replied. "Let's see now, there would have been about five or six druggists' shops burned. Oh my, when I think of my friends who had shops in the Burnt District: grocers, barbers, hardware merchants, blacksmiths, watchmakers, doctors, and exchange brokers. I could go on and on. There had to be at least ten or eleven cabinet and chair makers alone in that area. And of course there were all those commission merchants and wholesalers near the wharf."

"What do you think will happen to them, James?" Jenny asked. "Will they all go out of business?"

"Oh no, no," James assured her, "most of them will rebuild. Some have started already. Lot's of them are taking up business temporarily in available office and warehouse space around the city. Alan Turner, the tobacconist, has already spoken to me about renting the small office that I own next to my shop — just until his store is rebuilt."

"Now, they'll need money, of course," James continued. "Another devastating thing about this fire is that it burned most of the fire insurance company offices. Between them they've lost hundreds of thousands of dollars."

"Will their policyholders get their money, then?" Jenny asked.

"Well, the Mutual and the Fireman's declared that they will pay all their risks. Others are planning to pay just a few cents on the dollar," James replied. Then, turning to Parker, he asked, "What do you think we can expect in terms of relief from the government, John?"

"The city is sending Cornelius Darragh to Harrisburg to appeal for help," Parker replied.

"How much will they ask for?" James asked.

"It sounds like they're going to state our situation and leave determination of the exact amount and method of relief up to the Legislature," Parker said. "The mayor is conducting a town meeting at the Diamond tomorrow at two o'clock to talk about local relief — not just money but also food and temporary shelter for victims."

"Do you know if anyone else was killed, John?" Jenny asked.

"Except for Grace Milligan, the only names we have are of people reported missing," Parker replied. "People have reported relatives missing and witnesses said they saw neighbors go into buildings, presumably to save some personal item, then never saw them come out again. Until we find them, we won't know if they died in the fire or escaped while the witnesses were fleeing."

James and Jenny exchanged small anecdotes about neighbors' or acquaintances' activities during the fire. Parker listened for a while, but then his mind drifted. The flames in the lamps flickered dreamily. Suddenly Parker looked up with a start. James and Jenny both stared at him with small smiles on their faces.

"Is something wrong?" Parker asked.

"You were asleep, dear," Jenny replied.

"Sleeping sitting straight up," James declared with amusement.

"John, you're exhausted," Jenny said. "Why don't you go on up to bed?"

Parker rubbed his eyes, "You're right. I *am* tired." He stood up and sighed, "Good night."

Parker trudged in no hurry up the stairs and into his room. He didn't bother lighting a lamp, but rather simply took his clothes off and laid them across the chair at his small table. He stood staring at his bed in the darkness. He wished that he could skip the night and wake up in the morning and be brand new. After standing for several minutes he crawled heavily into bed. He lay on his side and stared at the dark bookcase and bureau for as long as he could. Then finally, his eyes closed and John Parker went to sleep.

5

John Parker stood in absolute darkness. He strained to see any hint of light or shape, or any movement at all. None. He reasoned that he must be inside some room or enclosed area, for darkness could never be so complete out of doors. He felt not the slightest breeze on his face; heard not the slightest sound. The total blackness disoriented him, and he could not decide which way to go, or whether or not to move at all. For all he could see, he might be standing in front of a wall or at the edge of a flight of stairs.

Suddenly a small oval of pale light appeared in front of him, about waist high. The light revealed his wife's face. She appeared to lay on her back, as on a bed or table, but Parker could see nothing more than her head, facing upward. He stared at Angelina for a few moments, wanting to reach over and touch her. Her eyes were closed and her skin showed none of its usual beautiful color. Then on the fringes of the slight illumination around her, he began to see outlines of dark hooded figures standing around Angelina. They murmured quietly among themselves. Parker could not make out any words — the murmuring seemed to come from many more people than could be standing there, and it sounded far more distant.

After a moment, Angelina's head started to move slowly away from Parker, as if the table were on wheels. He tried to follow but his feet would not move. Suddenly Angelina's eyes opened and she looked at him. "Help me, John!" she cried. "Don't let them take me! Don't let them take me, John, please! Help meeeeeee!"

Her pleas turned into a long, sustained scream. The scream increased in volume and intensity. The sound seared Parker's ears until suddenly he realized that he was the one who was screaming.

John Parker's head jolted backward and his eyes flipped open with a start. He looked around to see his dark bookcase and bureau beside him. He gripped the edge of his bed and realized that he was panting. He closed his eyes and turned his face into his pillow and wept, more from defeat than anything else. He wished that he could stop the nightmare. But no matter how many times the dream came, he never recognized it while it was happening. He was never able to stop the nightmare and say, "No! I've been here one thousand times before. This is not real."

Parker lay in bed for a while until he calmed down. The slightest hint of light showed through the thin curtains of his window. The sun would be coming up shortly. He got out of bed and started getting dressed.

Jenny Wright awoke at the sound of the screams from the next room. She, too, looked around for a moment in sleepy confusion at the ruckus, but then upon realization, relaxed with her head back on her pillow. The first time she'd heard the screaming from John Parker's room in the middle of the night five years ago, she thought that a thug might have broken in to exact some vengeance on the new constable. She threw on her housecoat and ran into his room to help. But all she saw was John Parker up on his knees, gripping the balustrades of the headboard, his eyes closed tightly. He screamed repeatedly until she ran over to him and called his name out. He woke up not knowing where he was. His wild eyes looked around until he realized that he'd been dreaming. After he calmed down he thanked her and told her that he was all right. But she could see that a deep grief set into him.

Jenny lay in her bed with her eyes open. He would go downstairs soon, she knew. She looked over at the table clock ticking on her nightstand. Almost five-thirty. Jenny got out of bed and put on her shoes and housecoat. She lit her lamp and took it down to the kitchen. She fueled and fired her stove, and then put on the pot of water that she'd filled last night before going to bed.

John Parker dressed without lighting his lamp. Just enough light came through his curtains to allow him to dress. He went downstairs and found Jenny in the kitchen making coffee. Long ago he gave up trying to tell her that she did not have to get up with him after these incidents. She would only smile and say that she was about to get up anyway. Conversation at these times usually didn't approach topics of any weight. Also, Jenny made sure that she never reminisced or even went back into the past farther than a few weeks. John enjoyed her stories during other times, but in these mornings she knew that she needed to bring him back to the present.

"James told an unbelievable story last night," she started. "He said that a man from a farm in Jacksonville way over in Westmoreland County brought into his shop yesterday a bank check from Pittsburgh with its edges burned. That would mean that those winds we had on Thursday carried that piece of paper twenty-two miles."

"I believe it," Parker said. "I watched the wind pick up planks and send them sailing over rooftops to the next block. The updraft from the flames probably lifted that check high in the air before carrying it away.

"So we had sightseers in from that far away, eh?" he continued. "I thought I saw some unfamiliar faces in the Burnt District yesterday afternoon."

"James said that people stopped in his shop from all over the countryside

— in town just to see the fire damage," Jenny said.

"I guess news travels fast," Parker observed.

The two made small talk until the sunlight showed through the kitchen window. Then Parker got up to go.

"Well, I'm going to get started," he said.

"Where are you going so early?" Jenny asked.

"I've got to go talk to an old friend of mine," he replied.

"John Parker, you're not old enough to have an 'old friend,'" she chastised.

"Okay, okay," he chuckled, then added solemnly. "Thanks, ma'am — for the coffee."

"Oh, don't mention it, John," she said. "I was about to get up anyway."

Parker walked out the kitchen door through Jenny's backyard onto Cherry Alley and headed toward Liberty Street. Activity in this part of the city, far away from the Burnt District, seemed normal. Storefront blinds raised with the sun. Farmers drove their produce-laden wagons to the Diamond Market while others delivered milk to their customers. Parker turned right onto Liberty Street and walked to the intersection where it met both Grant Street and the canal. The water in the canal basin at this crossing sat stagnant and devoid of boats. No canal boats moved on this side of the Allegheny River while the aqueduct was being rebuilt. Parker followed the canal's towpath to the river.

As he approached the aqueduct, Parker watched the construction workers arriving at the site. He reached the top of the bank that sloped down to the river. Some of the workers walked down this slope to a flat area where piles of timbers lay beside a small temporary sawmill. Others stayed at the top of the embankment and walked atop the aqueduct's flume, which appeared to be nearly complete.

The flume of the Allegheny Aqueduct looked like a long wooden box extending across six stone piers to the bank on the north side of the river in the City of Allegheny. Its tightly fastened timbers gave it a solid look. The box did not have a lid, however. Its open top formed a trough that was wider at its top than bottom. This trough would be filled with water for the canal boats to glide on — a river across a river. Extending along both sides of the top of the trough, flat planks supported by timber brackets formed walkways lining both sides of the aqueduct: the towpath on one side on which the mules would pull the canal boats, and the berm side on the other, on which pedestrians would walk.

On top of each of the aqueduct's six piers, stone towers interrupted the walkways on both sides of the trough. The tops of the towers raised just a few feet above the towpath and narrowed the walkway by a few feet at those points. From the top of each tower a thick cable plunged downward through a hole in the planks, curved through the wooden brackets jutting out from the underside of the flume, then rose up through again to the top of the next tower. This catenarian curve of the cable continued from tower to tower until it terminated at a small but thick masonry building near the top of the riverbank just in front of Parker.

By now all work crews engaged fully in their tasks. On top of the flume, workers fitted and secured timbers and planks into place. On the shore below, men sawed wood to the specified dimensions. Parker watched the bustle. One notably large man lifted a massive timber onto his shoulder and carried it to the sawyer. Something seemed familiar about the man's enormous size and strength, his coveralls, his tan saucer cap, and his graying red hair. Parker wondered if he should know who the man was. The top of Parker's back suddenly ached as he watched. Something started coming to mind.

"Can I help you?" said a voice from behind.

Parker turned around. A man with a bushy goatee and penetrating eyes looked at him.

"Can I help you, sir?" the man asked again. This time Parker noticed the man's German accent.

"I'm looking for the person in charge of building the aqueduct," Parker replied.

"I am in charge of building *this* aqueduct," the man declared.

Parker hesitated, "I'm sorry. I'm looking for the Superintendent of Construction."

"Ah, yes," the man said, now understanding who Parker wanted, "I shall tell him that the *polizei* are here."

The man walked onto the deck of the aqueduct's flume to a cluster of men conversing at its edge. He spoke to one of them, who then detached from the group and started toward Parker. The man looked the same age as Parker and smiled a familiar smile as he approached.

"Hello, John," Sam Reppert said. "What are you doing here?"

"Who was that?" Parker asked, nodding toward the man to whom he'd just spoken.

"Who's *that*?" Sam asked back incredulously. "John, that's John Roebling. He's the one who designed this aqueduct."

"Was I supposed to know that?" Parker asked.

"It's *only* the first suspension aqueduct built in the whole world, John," Sam said.

"Oh," Parker teased with a straight face, "Is that good?"

THE BURNT DISTRICT

Sam shook his head disgustedly. "Come with me, John." He walked down in front of the masonry building into which the cable disappeared and pointed to the cable itself.

"Do you see this cable? It's seven inches thick. Nineteen hundred metal wires laid together make it up. Each wire alone can hold eleven hundred pounds. The cable can hold over two thousand tons."

He pointed to the masonry building. "Do you see this anchorage? The cable connects to eyebars inside if it. It can hold down a weight twice as heavy as this cable will ever have to carry. Mr. Roebling designed them both. There are no cables or anchorages like this anywhere else in the world."

"So ... you're saying that this is the first in the world?" Parker deadpanned.

Sam Reppert was about to start a fit. "That's what I've been ..." He suddenly detected the small smile playing on Parker's lips. He scowled and narrowed his eyes at Parker in mock anger, then started to laugh. "Okay, John, you got me."

Parker laughed too, "So how have you been, Sam?"

"Good, John. And you?"

"Good. How are Beth and the kids?"

"Everyone's healthy. Beth asks me when you're coming over for dinner again. We haven't seen you for several months. Come to think of it, this is the first time that I've seen you at the construction site since we started."

"Yes, I know," Parker said while panning the entire aqueduct. "You folks have put this thing up pretty fast. When did you start? September?"

"Yes," Sam said, "we've worked all winter. Mr. Roebling is very adamant about meeting the deadline next month. He's been here working with us nearly every day."

"You've been in charge of constructing some of the major buildings in Pittsburgh in the last two years," Parker noted, "but it sounds to me that you don't mind playing second fiddle to Mr. Roebling on this one."

"The man's a genius," Sam said, "and he's a tireless worker. He plans everything, directs everything, and even solves problems that we run into." Sam looked at the aqueduct the entire time he spoke. His gaze fixed on an area on the flume where the crew worked. He pulled out a small, leather-bound notebook and began writing in it with a long, flat pencil.

Parker looked on as Sam wrote. He'd watched Sam's childhood fascination with the way things were built grow as Sam himself grew. As an adult, Sam made his profession constructing his own buildings, and built some of the finer structures in the city in recent years. He appeared to be more proud of this project than any of the others. Parker had never seen Sam as happy as he was at this particular task. He regretted what he was about to do.

"Sam, do you remember Ruthie Bowden?" he asked.

Sam stopped writing. He did not look up as he spoke. "You know I do, John," he said, irritated at the memory being brought forward. "I'll never forget it. Just like you won't. Why?"

"You remember, then, what she looked like — lying there. Just like I do." Parker continued, "You remember the look on her face. Everyone said that she must've drowned. But I never thought that she did. I remember thinking that she looked like she'd been scared to death. I remember her head: it was at a strange angle, sort of twisted or out of joint."

Sam's tone bordered on anger, "Yes, John. You're right. I remember. Now why are you doing this?"

"We found Grace Milligan lying dead in the ruins of one of the buildings in the Burnt District yesterday," Parker said.

"Yes, I know," Sam said, looking up finally.

Parker continued, "She was lying in an open basement. Everyone figured she must've fallen in during the night — maybe hit her head when she landed. She was lying among some charred beams."

"And …?" Sam asked.

Parker leaned forward a bit and craned his neck toward Sam, speaking in a more hushed but urgent tone, "She had the same expression on her face as Ruthie, Sam. Her eyes were wide open and her mouth looked set in a scream. When I looked at her, I saw Ruthie Bowden. Sam, her neck was twisted just like Ruthie's. Something nags at me when people say she just fell, the same way it's always nagged me when people say Ruthie drowned."

"If she fell in the dark into a tangle of beams, John, then she *could've* hit her head. She *could've* twisted her neck," Sam pointed out.

Parker looked down at the ground, then out over the river for a moment, then back at Sam, "What twisted Ruthie Bowden's neck, then, Sam?"

Sam started with an answer, but couldn't find one.

"When we found Ruthie on the riverbank she was soaking wet," Parker said. "That's why everyone just said that she drowned. But something always seemed, well, *not right* to me. I'd never seen a drowned person before, but I expected to see something different — the person to *look* different. But Ruthie didn't look any different — just wet. It was as if someone *covered* her with water. And yesterday, looking at Grace Milligan, I got the same feeling. She lay in a tangle of timbers, covered with ashes and bricks. I got the feeling that she had been covered with bricks the same way Ruthie had been covered with water."

"What are you saying, John?" Sam asked.

Parker paused for a moment, then stated, "I don't believe Grace Milligan fell, Sam. I don't believe she fell and I don't believe she hit her head and I don't believe Ruthie Bowden drowned."

"Are you saying they were murdered? And by the same person? John, they died thirteen years apart!" Sam said.

"*I* was here thirteen years ago," said Parker. "So were you. Lots of people are in Pittsburgh today that were here thirteen years ago."

"Okay, John. Suppose you're right. Suppose someone killed them. Then why aren't there more killings? If someone is going around killing people — murdering young girls — then why did they wait thirteen years to do it again? It doesn't make sense."

"I don't know, Sam," Parker replied. "I don't know why or what. And you're right. It doesn't make sense. Not yet."

"Sam, there's something about the day that we found Ruthie that I've been trying to remember that I need your help with," Parker started again. "Somebody said something when we were all standing there around her — he said a name, I think. I don't remember because I wasn't paying attention to anything but Ruthie lying there. But I remember somebody making a remark about another girl — and a man's name. I keep thinking he said the name 'Todd.'"

Sam closed his eyes, tilted his head, and thought for a moment, "Not 'Todd.' It was 'Toddstown.' That's the name they used to call Freeport, a ways up the Allegheny. The locals called it 'Toddstown' the same way we call Kensington 'Pipetown.' I remember he said something like 'She looks just like the girl they found up in Toddstown when we were digging the canal.' Only he was Irish or Scottish, I think, and it came out more like 'She leks like the wee lass they fend up'n Toddstn when we was diggin' the canawl.'

"I remember because no one else was saying anything at the moment. He was a little man, no bigger than I was at the time. It looked like the other men standing around knew him because a few beside him stared at him hard after he said that, then he just kind of shrunk away from the crowd."

Parker thought for a moment. "They dug the canal in twenty-eight, didn't they?" he asked.

"It opened here in twenty-eight," Sam said. "They would've been digging the ditch at Freeport about that time. They have two aqueducts up there that I helped do some repairs on a few years ago — one crossing a wide creek and a bigger one crossing the Allegheny River."

Suddenly a German-accented voice called from above, "Will you be joining us today, Mr. Reppert?" Parker and Sam looked up to see Mr. Roebling standing at the edge of the flume.

Sam waved to him and nodded affirmatively. He turned to Parker, "I've got to get going."

"I know," Parker said.

"John, this thing that you're thinking — I just don't know ..." Sam trailed off.

"I don't really know either," Parker said, "but I've got this urgent feeling that something's wrong. I can't shake it. I just have so many questions about the whole thing."

"What are you going to do, John?" Sam asked.

"Find answers, Sam," Parker said. "I've got to find answers."

"Where would you even start?" Sam asked.

Parker looked down at the work crews on the riverbank, then stared out at the Allegheny River swirling around the aqueduct's stone piers. Above, more workers assembled the aqueduct's flume. Just beyond, on the far shore, mules towed boats along the still-functioning Main Line of the Pennsylvania Canal. The man-made waterway followed the Allegheny River northward for thirty miles. Then, at a small frontier town, the canal made a sharp right turn to start its eastward journey across the state.

"At the beginning," Parker answered at last.

6

"You want to go *where*?" thundered High Constable Abraham Butler.

"It would only be for a day," Parker said. "I can take the canal and be back before duty tomorrow."

"And do you mind telling me why you want to take a whole day off of duty to go traveling around the countryside?" Butler asked.

"I wouldn't be off-duty," Parker pointed out. "I would be working."

"Doing what?"

Parker hesitated. He braced himself, then said quietly, "Sir, I don't think Grace Milligan's death was an accident — I can't say exactly why — but I don't. There might be something or somebody in Freeport that can help me piece together what happened."

Abraham Butler stared at Parker. There had been too much nonsense packed into those two sentences for him to absorb. He opened his mouth to speak, then stopped. He laid his hands on his desktop, closed his eyes, and leaned forward. He waited until his taut face relaxed, then opened his eyes and spoke slowly.

"Okay, John, let's see if I have this right. You think that Grace Milligan's death was 'not an accident,' but you can't say why?" he said.

"Well, there are a few reasons," Parker explained. "As I said before, there was no reason for her to be way over on Try Street."

"Except that her father worked over in that direction," Butler said matter-of-factly. "Go on."

"And," continued Parker, "her neck was broken."

Butler started, "By *falling* ..."

"By falling into a burned-out basement in the dark," Parker recited. "Yes, I know that's what everybody says."

"That's what Coroner Eichbaum says," Butler said. "I've talked to him already."

"Did Coroner Eichbaum tell you that she was dead *before* the bricks fell on her?"

"He told me that taking everything into account, he still feels that her death was an accident."

"Sir, I went back to the chimney where she fell in. Those bricks aren't loose. I tried that wall."

"Did it occur to you, John, that the *loose* bricks were the ones that fell in?"

Parker did not reply.

"Look, John," High Constable Butler said, "if the Coroner says it's an accident, how am I to justify an investigation? Especially when we need all of our manpower here for our current disaster?"

"You could just trust me," Parker said.

"I'm sorry, John," Butler replied. "Don't take it personally. I need you here. If you want to go do your investigating, you'll have to do it on your own time. Monday is your next day off. Go then.

"Now I'm going to make some announcements at Report," Butler said, "and everyone's here. C'mon now."

High Constable Abraham Butler rose from his desk and walked out of his office into the large reception area just outside his door. Several chairs sat in uneven rows in the middle of the room, facing the High Constable's office door. The other four constables waited there, sitting in the plain wooden chairs. They reported for duty at seven o'clock every morning. Usually they just reported in, and then went out to their rounds. Sometimes, as today, the High Constable held a short meeting that consisted mostly of his making announcements and giving instructions. Parker followed Butler out of the office and sat in a chair beside the others.

All five assistant constables wore city-issued overcoats — the closest the city came to issuing uniforms. Years of exposure to the weather discolored the coats' original butternut to a dull, dirty tan. Any constable leaving the force turned his overcoat back in to be worn by his replacement. Each constable wore a brass city seal pinned to his coat. Unlike the firemen who kept the brass on their parade uniforms and engines polished and shiny, the constables' brass was tarnished and dull. Theirs were work clothes, and none made any attempt to look sharp. Three of the men wore their own hats — weathered hats whose wide brims slouched from wear. Parker and Perry wore no hat.

Parker was the youngest, though longest-serving, assistant constable. At five years he had a full year's seniority over the next longest-serving, Albert Perry. The other three, Hugh Ihmsen, Charles Cameron, and Art Keller all joined the force within the last two years.

Although they maintained a professional camaraderie, they did not form a close-knit group on a personal basis. John and Albert worked well together. If Parker gave any thought to having friends, Perry might be one. The three newer constables stayed more tightly together. Their conversations at Report often recounted the previous evening's exploits in a local tavern — as patrons, not law enforcement officers.

"All right, men," High Constable Abraham Butler started, "we've got one-third of the city burned to the ground. The Burnt District covers about fifty-six acres. It runs along the Monongahela River from Ferry Street in the First Ward through the entire Second Ward and all of Pipetown. Between Ferry and Wood it goes inland to Third Street, although the block at Water Street was spared. Between Wood and Smithfield it reaches from the wharf all the way to Diamond Alley. Through the rest of the Second Ward it goes from the river up to Fourth Street.

"We estimate that the fire destroyed as many as twelve hundred buildings. Roughly seven hundred of those were residences. Right now we believe that around four thousand people are homeless.

"Several people are still reported as missing. Two are strongly feared to be dead. Witnesses say Mrs. Brooks from Third Street in the Second Ward wouldn't leave her house because she couldn't get her furniture out. Others saw Samuel Kingston from the First Ward enter a building and never come out. A few other people simply haven't been seen since the fire — Mrs. Maglone and Mrs. Wyatt from the Second Ward, John Johnston in Pipetown, and Mrs. Denning, who was living at Kevin Beale's place.

"John and Albert, those are your two wards. Obviously, you can't go knocking on doors searching for these folks. You'll just have to keep talking to people that you see out and about in your areas to find out if anyone's seen these people."

"Is Benjamin Bell on the 'missing' list?" Parker asked. "His son was looking for him Thursday night."

"He's not on my list," the High Constable replied, "and I haven't heard the name mentioned during any discussion regarding missing persons. The only person who's actually been confirmed as dead so far is Grace Milligan," Butler continued, and did not look at Parker as he said the name.

"We had some looting during and after the fire. For most of the missing property, at this point, we don't know if it was stolen or just lost in the confusion. The mayor set up a system whereby people who are missing property and people who have somehow 'acquired' property can submit a description of said property to his office. He will try to match up the lost to the found."

"How does someone 'somehow *acquire*' property, sir?" asked Albert Perry, half jokingly. The other constables chuckled.

"Hopefully honestly," quipped the High Constable. "Now, we know of a few cases already where horses who bolted in fright on Thursday wandered into strangers' property on Friday. Hopefully most of the 'acquisitions' will turn out to be that innocent.

"But I've got an even more serious situation to alert you to — someone tried to set the Reynolds & Wilmarth Boatyard afire yesterday. A worker found a small blaze in a woodpile. Apparently someone bound some wood chips together, stuffed the bundle in the woodpile, and lit it. The worker found the fire before it did any damage."

"Any idea if Thursday's fire was set, too?" Perry asked.

"No," the High Constable replied. "It was the washerwoman's fire behind the icehouse. Of that we're certain."

"Now, one last thing," Butler announced. "The mayor is holding a town meeting at the Diamond today at two o'clock. Parker and Perry, you two need to be there. You other three can go if you want, but I'm not requiring it. Now, any questions before you go?"

"Sir," said Albert Perry, "will they be hiring extra men to knock down the walls?"

"The Councils authorized the mayor to do that," Butler replied, "but I heard no mention of giving him the money to do it. We'll have to wait and see if that happens.

"Now keep your eyes peeled while on you rounds, men," Butler said. "As we saw yesterday at the boatyard, it's calamities like ours on Thursday that bring out the craziness in some people."

With that the meeting ended and the men rose to their feet. Parker walked out silently with Albert Perry, while the three others followed in a group.

"I heard they found old man Bell in a bawdyhouse over in Bayardstown," Cameron sneered to the other two. All three erupted in a round of laughter. Perry gave Parker a sidelong glance then rolled his eyes.

Out on the street the two groups separated en route to their beats. Parker and Perry walked down Grant Street toward the Burnt District. They passed the courthouse, from which emerged many still-homeless citizens. The massive building occupied a commanding position on Grant's Hill over the city. Walled stairs started on the opposite sides of its front and met in the center, leading onto its large portico. Thick columns lined the portico's front and supported its short, but substantial, roof. Beyond the porch roof a center dome topped the roof of the courthouse itself. Only four years old, its sandstone walls wore only a slight tinge of the soot from the factories that blackened older buildings in the city.

The two constables entered the Burnt District. They parted at Second Street with nodded "good-byes" as Perry walked toward the Point and his beat, the First Ward. Parker stood at the intersection of Grant and Second for a few minutes and watched the activity around him. In all directions workers continued clearing debris from streets and buildings. Two blocks away, close to the river, he saw the ruins of the Bakewell & Pears Glass Works. Memories of working inside the glass factory filled Parker. He remembered the bustle of the workers, heard the clatter of machines and clang of tools, and felt the heat of the furnaces. They were memories that, if allowed to progress, would lead to memories of tragedy. He abruptly cut them off and turned away from the glass factory.

Parker still wanted to see the ruins of the Gas Works, even though it was not in his beat. He started along Second Street toward Kensington.

The Second Ward and the city limits ended at Try Street. Kensington began on the other side. At this point the canal crossed Parker's path, following Suke's Run on its way from Grant's Hill to the Monongahela River. The small bridge that crossed the canal on Second Street lay in charred pieces. Looking toward the river, Parker saw that the locktender's house also burned down. In the opposite direction, the canal crossed Watson's Road, then disappeared into the darkness of the tunnel through Grant's Hill. From what Parker understood, city officials originally planned the length of the canal from the tunnel to the Monongahela River to meet a branch of the Chesapeake and Ohio Canal that was to come up to Pittsburgh along the Monongahela River from Virginia. But the "Cross Cut Canal" was never dug, however, and few locals had any use for the canal on this side of the basin at Penn and Liberty streets. Canal boats used the tunnel so rarely that it took on the nuisances of an abandoned building.

Parker stepped down the short embankment to the canal. When the prism-shaped ditch was properly filled, the water measured four feet deep. But with no need to maintain this unused terminus, canal officials long ago stopped any upkeep of the tunnel or the canal's last leg to the Monongahela River. The remnant of Suke's Run fed only a few inches of water into the ditch. Parker walked across and climbed up the embankment on the other side.

Kensington was a small industrial town built on the narrow slip of land between Boyd's Hill and the Monongahela River. It had neither the status nor the government of a borough. It never seemed to Parker to be anything more than an extension of Pittsburgh beyond the city limits. At the moment, however, it was mostly a wasteland.

Parker left Second Street and walked in the direction of the Monongahela River to the Gas Works. He passed two great charred circles on the ground, rimmed by rubble and as large as buildings. Walking past the circles and across Grenough Street, he found the several buildings that made up the Gas Works damaged but much more intact than he'd expected. Crews repaired sections of the buildings' exteriors. A group of men exited one of the buildings. As they passed, Parker spotted Adam Kimbal, one of the trustees that managed the Gas Works, whom Parker recognized from attending city council meetings.

"Hello, Mr. Kimbal," Parker called.

Kimbal stopped, "Oh, hello, Parker. What are you doing over here?"

"I was curious to see the damage to the Works," Parker replied. "From the ball of fire that I saw rise out of here, I thought things would be much worse."

"You saw our holding tanks go up," Kimbal said as he nodded toward the black circles on the ground. "The plant escaped by the luck of the wind, I suppose. It was so strong that it blew burning debris clean over some buildings to the tops of others far away. Few people in Kensington, it appears, were as lucky as we were."

"I see," Parker said.

"Well, I've got to be going, Parker," Kimbal said, motioning to the departing group of men. "We've got gas lines all over the Burnt District to find and repair."

The group continued toward the city. Parker turned from the Gas Works and surveyed the rest of Kensington. It was so small and narrow he could see all of it from where he stood. Almost the entire town was devastated. Kimbal was right: few people *were* as lucky as the Gas Works. Only a few houses stood untouched at the far end of the town. There was some distance between them and the rest of the buildings. Parker guessed that the fire must've burned itself out before it reached them.

He walked over to the Dallas Iron Mill next door. By the number of men cleaning up the ruins, it seemed few people lost employment at this mill. Workers knocked down any sections of walls still standing. In one area they stacked unbroken bricks and blocks for re-use. Other piles contained charred timber, broken brick, and other unusable rubble. Parker walked around and found a third set of piles, consisting of chunks of iron covered with soot and ashes. Parker stood in front of these piles. The large, misshapen hunks of iron looked not to be the "pigs" or blooms that the mill shaped into finished products, but rather, pieces that melted in the tremendous heat of the fire.

"Sheet iron, hoops, boiler iron, rods, nails — you name it, we make it," said a man's voice coming up beside Parker. "It's all there in big globs, now."

Parker turned around. "Henry Watts," the man said, "I'm a foreman here. Is there something I can do for you, Constable?"

"No," Parker replied, "I just wanted to see what things were like over here. It looks like you're preparing to start over again."

THE BURNT DISTRICT

"You bet," Mr. Watts said. "We're going to rebuild this place. We'll be up and running again in time. It will take some doing, though. That fire really gutted us out."

"It is a shame," Parker said, "especially considering the work your men did to try to save it."

"Save it?" Mr. Watts said. "Who tried to save it?"

"Your employees," Parker said, "they brought up water from the river and tried to soak the building so it wouldn't catch."

"Who told you that?" Mr. Watts asked incredulously.

"Kevin Milligan," Parker replied. "He does work here, doesn't he?"

"Kevin Milligan works here," Mr. Watts almost laughed, "and when the Gas Works' tanks blew, he ran out the door and far away just like everyone else. Nobody brought water up from the river. There wasn't no savin', just a lot of runnin'."

"I see," said Parker, now looking around at the mill workers busy at their tasks. "Is Kevin here today?"

"Didn't show up today. Why? You gonna arrest him for lying?" Mr. Watts laughed.

"No," Parker said, "I just wanted to talk to him."

"Well, I'll keep an eye out for him," Mr. Watts said. "If he shows up, I'll tell him you're looking for him. Excuse me but I've got to get back to work now."

"Thanks," Parker said. "So do I."

7

Throughout the morning Parker patrolled his beat just as High Constable Abraham Butler had ordered. But as Butler had also directed him to attend the two o'clock public meeting at the Diamond Market, Parker left the Second Ward in the afternoon to attend to that duty. He made a long detour, however, going first up to the courthouse where the Milligans might still be staying. He had some questions to ask Kevin Milligan, who, he had learned that morning, had *not* stayed at the Dallas Iron Works when the fire reached Kensington. At the courthouse he found neither the Milligans nor anyone who could tell him where they might be.

Just before two o'clock Parker arrived at the Diamond Market. The market square, about the size of a city block, opened at the intersection of Market Street and Diamond Alley. A long, curved Market House lined one end of the square and faced a straight row of market buildings on the other end. Today fire victims and public officials, rather than busy shoppers, comprised the crowd that filled the open area between the two buildings. Parker saw Mayor William Howard and some prominent citizens on a low, makeshift platform conversing before opening the meeting. Their platform sat in front of an old building on the west side of Diamond Alley that had served as the county courthouse for many years before being replaced by the new one on Grant Street.

Off in a corner of the square Parker saw a few of the men of the Vigilant Volunteer Fire Company standing in front of their engine, which was parked in an open space between two buildings. Walking over to them, he recognized Jim Cowan, the firefighter with whom he'd worked briefly on Thursday.

"Hello, Constable," Cowan greeted him, "getting proper sleep, these days?"

"Hello, Jim. I see you haven't found a home for your engine yet," Parker said.

"No," Cowan replied. "There's the devil to pay between us and the market people, but we've got no other place to put her for now."

"Are you going to rebuild the engine house where it was?" Parker asked.

"Don't know yet," Cowan said. "We haven't met yet to decide nothin'. We'll have to find a place to meet first."

"How did your men fare on Thursday," Parker asked. "Did anyone get hurt?"

"All of our men are okay," Cowan replied. "One of the Eagle's men caught a blast straight in his face and was carried from the fight. I haven't heard what became of him. The Neptune Fire Company lost their engine to the fire, and we all lost a great deal of hose."

As the firefighter continued, the officials gathered on the platform and called for everyone's attention. Mayor Howard opened the meeting.

"My friends and fellow citizens," the mayor said, "we are assembled here today to discuss relief measures that we will take to help victims of our calamity late on Thursday, the Great Fire. Our first order of business is to appeal to our state government in Harrisburg for assistance. I will now read to you a letter that we have drafted to send to Governor Shunk, to be carried to His Excellency immediately."

Mayor Howard then read aloud a short, one-page letter imploring Governor Shunk to use his executive authority to extend the current session of the state legislature to give that body extra time to discuss relief measures for the city.

The men on the dais with the mayor then conversed in committee to carry out the relief measures for the fire victims. First, the committee approved the mayor's letter to the state legislature. Next, the mayor held up a much longer letter to the Legislature and began to read:

"To the Honorable Senate and House of Representatives of the Commonwealth of Pennsylvania,

The people of Pittsburgh, in Town Meeting assembled, respectfully represent that in the midst of their prosperity and security they have been overwhelmed by a catastrophe that has no parallel in the annals of this country. The scourge of fire in its direct form has been upon them. The sun of Thursday, the 10th of April, which on the morning of that day, looked down upon their streets in one unbroken scene of industry, of animation and hope, threw its last parting rays at evening over a picture of widespread desolation and despair. A hurricane of flame swept over their deserted town, and so rapid — so irresistible — was its career that before nightfall, before its inhabitants had leisure to collect their faculties, or realize the imminence of their peril, one-third of their city, comprising a vast population and an incalculable amount of wealth, was in ruins. They are yet scarcely able to estimate the extent of the awful visitation, which they have experienced ..."

Just then Constable Albert Perry approached, joining Parker and the men of the Vigilant.

"... enough, however, is known to enable them to state that millions in property have perished in the conflagration. The houses of one thousand families have been desolated, and the inhabitants, in nearly every instance, stripped of their all, and left with scarcely a garment to cover their nakedness, and without a roof to shelter them from the winds of heaven ..."

Perry turned to Parker, "What're they doing?"

"Letters to Harrisburg," Parker replied.

"... if their calamity had been a partial one, the energies of our people would perhaps have ensured an effectual remedy. Its effects, however, were diffused so widely beyond the visible range of the immediate disaster itself, and must necessarily so deeply disturb the existing relations and resources of our whole people, that they cannot but feel a conviction of their own present comparative helplessness and inefficiency under the astounding effects of so awful and unexpected a visitation ..."

Perry asked, "What's he saying?"

"He's begging for money, I think," Parker replied. "I'm still wading through the verbiage."

"... under these circumstances, therefore, in view of the important in intimate relation which the people of Pittsburgh occupy with the parent Commonwealth, and of the deep and vital injury which it must sustain from the desolation of one of its fairest cities, as well as of the ample power of its legislature to interpose effectually in this great exigency for their relief, we have thought it fitting to invoke their aid on behalf of the suffering and destitute of our people ..."

"Yep," Perry said, "I think he just begged for money right there."

"... we accordingly leave entirely to their hands with a full assurance that a paternal government will not be found wanting to its children in the day of their extreme and unprecedented calamity.

Your faithful servants,

The Citizens of Pittsburgh."

"By God, that was a mouthful," Albert Perry declared.

"I don't know exactly what he said," Jim Cowan mused, "but I hope in there somewhere he asked them for some help."

The committees adopted the letter as read. Next, they passed a resolution appealing to the farmers and millers in the areas surrounding the city to send donations of food to the fire victims. Mayor Howard announced that he would receive the donations and store them in the old courthouse behind them. The mayor then appointed three people from each ward to carry out the measures for immediate relief of the fire victims. The committee appointed one person from each burned block to list the names of the victims in their block. Victims so listed would receive a certificate authorizing them to receive the relief.

The public meeting lasted for just under two hours as the committee members discussed and passed these resolutions, and then answered questions from the victims assembled. It ended after the committee adjourned and the victims were satisfied that they'd gotten all of the information that the city fathers could give at the time. As the crowd dispersed, the two constables said good-bye to the Vigilant Volunteer Fire Company and their homeless engine.

As they left the Diamond and entered the Burnt District, Parker turned to Perry, "Albert, I'm looking for a couple: the Milligans, from my ward — do you know them? They were staying at the courthouse, but they're no longer there."

"No, I don't know them," Perry replied. "Have you looked in the Third Presbyterian Church? Lots of people are staying there."

"Well, come to think of it," Parker said, "they're Catholic. I should try St. Paul's first."

"That doesn't matter much right now," Perry pointed out. "Nobody's asking the religion of fire victims that they're giving shelter to. You might as well try the Third Presbyterian, since you're so close to it right now."

"You're right," Parker said. "I'll stop there first."

Perry stopped, then looked at Parker, "Milligan — isn't that the name of the girl that died in the fire?"

"Yes. I'd just like to talk to Mr. Milligan," Parker replied.

"I know you were with the Watch when they found his daughter," Perry said, his slightly rising voice asking the question that his words did not.

Parker looked at him. "Something's just not right," he said. "I need to piece it together."

"Is that what you and Butler were arguing about this morning?" Perry asked.

"He wants me to drop it," Parker said. "He says we've got too much to do already."

"Well, we do," Perry said, "but in the midst of all the other things that are going on, we still have to do our job."

By then they were near the Third Presbyterian Church. "Thanks, Albert," Parker said.

"Good luck, John," Perry said. "If there's anything that I can do to help, let me know."

"I will," Parker said. Perry continued straight toward the wharf as Parker turned toward the Third Presbyterian Church. Its steeple towered above all else around it, as it had even before the fire. Its brick walls, which had forced the fire to go around them, stood soot-stained but solid. Only a hacked-off corner of the roof showed how perilously close it had come to joining the buildings around it in succumbing to the flames.

A few people loitered outside as a continuous stream of traffic went into and out of the front doors. Parker went inside and followed the line down a set of stairs into the basement. There, in a large room that was as long as the body of the church above it, people crowded on and around rows of makeshift beds. Women and small children made up most of the multitude. The room felt uncomfortably warm and there seemed to be little fresh air. Amid the talking of the adults, children cried from hunger or simply the continued distress of being displaced from their homes.

Parker walked through the aisles looking for the Milligans. At the far end of one aisle he spotted a woman that looked like Mrs. Milligan, dressed in clothes like those she wore the previous morning, when he had found the couple at their burned-down home. She sat on the end of one of the beds, facing away from the crowd. Unlike most of the other women in the room, she did not occupy herself with any task to help her situation or just pass the time. She just stared blankly at the next bed in the row. As Parker came up next to her, he saw that it was indeed the woman he sought.

"Mrs. Milligan?" he said. She made no response. "Mrs. Milligan?" he asked again. This time her head slowly turned toward him. Her eyes pointed at his face, but he didn't feel that she was really looking at him. If she recognized him, she did not show it.

"Mrs. Milligan, I'm John Parker. Constable Parker."

"What do you want?" she said in a flat voice.

"Ma'am, I need to talk to your husband. Can you tell me where he is?" he asked.

"My husband?" she said, and then turned her face straight ahead again. "He went to work."

"He went to work today, ma'am?" Parker asked.

"Yes," Mrs. Milligan said, "over at the mill in Kensington. He said they were cleaning up. He said if he helped clean up and rebuild the mill, then he could keep his job. He's been working a lot of extra shifts the past couple of months — working into the evening, working days that he'd never worked before. It's like I hardly see him anymore." She turned to Parker again, "It wasn't always like this. He took that job for me in the first place, you know — did it for me."

"Yes, ma'am," Parker said.

"He *did*. Before we were married, he worked labor and carpenter work in towns all over the countryside. He's been all over, you know.

"I made him stop, though, after we met and he started talkin' marriage. I said 'Kevin, if you want to marry me, you're going to have to settle down. You get yourself a steady job right here in town and stay here.' And he did. Then we got married and … and …" Mrs. Milligan cupped her hand to her mouth and started crying. "And our baby. Oh, my girl!" She collapsed into sobs.

Another woman came from around the bed and sat beside her and held her. "Oh, Addy," the second woman said as she tried to comfort Mrs. Milligan. It was Gladys Dilworth, who had lived next door to the Milligans. Mrs. Dilworth looked up at Parker with a hard stare to dismiss him.

"Thank you, Mrs. Milligan," Parker said. "I'm sorry to have troubled you."

He turned and walked back the aisle past the rows of beds, women, and children. Most of the women wore dark clothes, as many women who lived in Pittsburgh's constant smoke from its factories and mills, chose to wear. The room appeared darker as the light from the few windows seemed to dim. It became to Parker more crowded, closer with the dark figures. The wails of babies became more prominent in his ears as the conversation of the adults receded to a dull, distant murmuring. He quickened his steps and slipped between groups of people crowding the aisles. Trotting up the stairs and out of the church, he stepped into the sunlight and caught his breath.

Parker looked back at the church doors. He could not bring himself to tell Mrs. Milligan that her husband was not at work today. The stress of losing her child appeared to already strain her ability to hold on. For the second time today he had caught Mr. Milligan in a lie. It seemed that everywhere he went to find answers, he came away with only more questions. When he found Kevin Milligan, he would get some answers.

8

Parker patrolled his beat early Sunday morning. Sundays were regular duty days for all five constables. Cameron called them "Drunk Days." While most of the citizens kept the Lord's Day holy, others celebrated their one day off from work each week with dancing and drinking. The constable's job was to ensure that the two groups' paths did not cross. But this Sunday morning started the third full day since the disaster, and as the fire had destroyed the buildings in his ward, Parker had no drunks and churchgoers to keep separate.

What would his duties be today? He helped victims during and after the fire, but what could he do for the people in his ward now? The immediate disaster was over. But thousands of people lost their homes and all possessions contained therein. Their current needs were food and shelter. For now, churches, public buildings, relatives, and friends took them in and fed them. Soon they would need other essentials including jobs and even simply clothes. Then they could begin to build or find new homes and start doing all the things needed to put their lives back together.

Late in the morning as Parker picked his way through some rubble at the intersection of Second and Front streets, a voice hailed him from behind. He turned around to find Howard Blakely, Esquire, approaching. The office from which Mr. Blakely practiced law had been on the block that the two men walked by now.

"Constable Parker, hello there," Mr. Blakely called.

"Hello, Mr. Blakely," Parker said.

Howard Blakely carried a large brown folder tied at the front. He caught up to Parker, "Constable Parker, I wonder if you might be able to help me."

"What can I do for you, Mr. Blakely?" Parker asked.

"Well, by way of explanation, the Relief Committee appointed three people from each ward to coordinate relief efforts by, or on behalf of, the ward — depending on whether their ward is donating or receiving relief. In turn, one person from each block in the Burnt District was appointed to identify everyone in their block who needs help. I am the person appointed for my block."

Mr. Blakely held up the folder and untied it. It was filled with handwritten, boilerplate certificates. "I need to find a person from each family or business on my block, and complete one of these Relief Certificates for them. Then I've got to sign and give them the certificate, which they'll use to prove that they're entitled to the relief that the mayor is arranging."

"I see," Parker said, "and I'll guess that you're having a hard time locating many of the block's former residents."

"Quite so," Mr. Blakely replied. "Would you help me locate some of these people?"

"Of course I will," Parker replied. "I'll be happy to help out. Do you have a list of people that you've found so far?"

"That list is very short, at the moment," Mr. Blakely admitted. "I found a few neighbors taking shelter at the courthouse and completed certificates for them. I was hoping to catch many of them here at work cleaning up their buildings. But I see that not many people are in the area right now."

"It's Sunday morning. Many of them may be at church," Parker reasoned. "Maybe you'll have better luck in the afternoon. Meanwhile, I can take some of your certificates, if you want, and keep an eye out for people while on my rounds."

"That's precisely what I'd hoped you'd say," Mr. Blakely replied. "Thank you so much, Constable Parker."

"There are several churches in the city sheltering fire victims," Parker pointed out as Mr. Blakely handed him a stack of certificates. "Maybe this morning you should try looking in a few of them."

"Splendid idea," Mr. Blakely agreed. "I very much appreciate your helping me."

"Don't mention it," Parker said. "I'm sure that under the circumstances it falls under my duties to help out."

Parker and Mr. Blakely walked together around the block for a while. They found Turner Frederickson picking through the rubble of what used to be his house. Parker looked on as Mr. Blakely filled out a Relief Certificate with Mr. Frederickson's name, address, ward, and the total number of people in his household. He had Mr. Frederickson sign on the line on the bottom left hand side of the certificate. Mr. Blakely signed the line on the bottom right hand side. He turned to Parker, "Your signature will be official for any certificates that you complete, Parker. I'll see to it."

The two men continued walking until they completed one circuit around the block. Once again at the corner of Second and Front streets, they parted company. "Well, Constable Parker, I'm off to try my luck in the churches. I'll start with the English Lutheran Church — I know that they're housing many fire victims."

"There are a couple of families from this block staying at the Third

Presbyterian Church," said Parker. "I'll go there."

"Very good," Mr. Blakely said. "Can you meet me at the courthouse at, say, five o'clock, so that I can list the people for whom you've completed certificates?"

"I'll be there," Parker said.

"Thank you again, Constable Parker," Mr. Blakely said. "You're being a tremendous help to me."

"You're welcome," Parker replied.

Parker felt better now that he had a tangible task through which he could directly help the people in his ward. Additionally, he also planned to use it as an opportunity to see if Kevin Milligan returned to his wife yet at the Third Presbyterian Church. Mr. Milligan lied twice about his whereabouts during and after the disaster. Why? Did his lies have something to do with his daughter's death? Parker hoped to find Milligan alone and compel him to explain himself.

Parker entered the Third Presbyterian Church and went down into the basement, past the rows of beds to the section where the Milligans and Gladys Dilworth stayed. He found no one near the bed on which Addie Milligan sat the previous day.

"They're not here," Gladys Dilworth's voice said from behind.

"Do you know where they are, Mrs. Dilworth? Parker asked.

"Up at St. Paul's," Mrs. Dilworth said. "They've gone to prepare for Grace's funeral. It's today at one o'clock."

"I see," Parker said. Then he remembered that he had business here with Mrs. Dilworth, also. He stood with her and completed a Relief Certificate, signing it at the bottom after she did.

"Keep this certificate," Parker instructed her, "and take it to the old courthouse to get provisions. It'll prove that you're a fire victim."

Mrs. Dilworth took the certificate with impatience that bordered on disgust, "If they want proof, they can come see my house burned to the ground!"

"Have you seen any of your other neighbors staying here, Mrs. Dilworth?" Parker asked.

"No, not that I've noticed," Mrs. Dilworth said. "We were some of the few residents left on the block. Most others were businesses."

"Thanks for your help, Mrs. Dilworth," Parker said. Gladys Dilworth did not answer, but nodded her head as she turned back toward her bed, reading the certificate to herself.

Parker was glad that he didn't have to spend any more time in the crowded basement. When he reached daylight up on the street, he realized that it was almost noon. Jenny would have lunch made for him already. Parker walked back toward home.

Upon entering Jenny's kitchen Parker found her ladling soup into a bowl. "Oh, hello, John," she said. "I was just getting some lunch in a hurry. I won't be able to sit with you for very long today. Grace Milligan's funeral is at one o'clock and Nora asked me to go with her."

"Why?" Parker asked.

"Well," Jenny replied, "she wants to go, but Tom won't go with her. Says he won't step foot in a Catholic church."

"I see," Parker said.

Jenny set two bowls on the table and then laid a spoon beside each. Then she sat down across from Parker and they both began to eat. "John," she said suddenly but quietly, "why don't you come to the funeral with me?"

"Me? Why?" Parker asked.

"I know you've been troubled by Grace's death," Jenny answered. "Maybe it would help you to go."

Parker considered for a moment. The only thing that would make him feel better was to know exactly how Grace died. He needed to know what Kevin Milligan was hiding, but he wouldn't find that out at the funeral. Just as he couldn't bring himself to tell Addie Milligan that her husband was not at work yesterday, he would never grill a man with questions at his own daughter's funeral. But Jenny was right: some comfort at least might be attained by seeing Grace laid respectfully to rest. It might ease his tortured vision of her lying in the ruins of the building on Try Street.

"Okay," Parker said finally. "Thanks, Jenny."

"Good," Jenny replied. "Nora will be here any minute, then we'll all walk up together."

The two finished their lunch just as Nora Fischer rapped on the back door, peered in to see Jenny beckoning, and then entered the kitchen. Jenny introduced her to Parker and told her that he was attending the funeral with them.

"I'm very sorry, ma'am," he said, "about your granddaughter."

"Thank you, Mr. Parker," Nora said. "I wish I could get my husband to go. But his heart is so hardened by prejudice that he won't attend his own granddaughter's funeral — prejudice and resentment."

"Resentment, ma'am?" Parker asked.

"He's mad that the Catholics and the Irish are in this country," Nora explained. "He's mad that one of them 'took' his daughter. He's mad that his daughter went off with him, and that she converted — *especially* that she converted. He's never forgiven her for giving up her religion for that man. He wouldn't even take them in after their home burned down.

"I tried to talk her out of marrying the man, more for our family's sake than mine — I've never taken to this *Nativism* and *Anti-popery* like my husband did — but she wouldn't hear of it. She was so blind in love that she'd have done anything for that man."

"I understand that she made some demands of him, too," Parker said. "She told me that she made him settle down and get a steady job in town before she married him."

"Well, truth be told, I'm the one who really pushed him to do that," Nora said. "I felt that he should at least give Addie something for the trouble he was about to cause her — meaning with her father, and all. I've never told anyone this, not even Addie, but I sat down with Kevin Milligan and told him I could prevent him from marrying Addie, if I wanted to. If he was going to take her from us, he was going to get a steady job here in the city so that he could provide for her and give her a proper home. He saw that I meant business."

"Is that so?" Jenny said.

"Oh yes," Nora said. "He and I had a very long talk that day. I found out everything there was to know about our Mr. Milligan. He was actually very charming. I could see how Addie was attracted to him."

"What exactly did you find out?" Parker asked.

"Well," Nora started, "he came over from county Kildare in Ireland in 'twenty-seven. He was recruited by a contractor for the canal, and worked for a couple of years on the Western Division. He worked on the sections along the Allegheny and Kiski Rivers, from Pittsburgh to Saltsburg. He was done with that by 'thirty-two — the year he met Addie. At that time he was taking carpenter jobs in the city at the time. He didn't know where he was going to go after those jobs were finished — until *I* told him he was staying right her if he wanted to marry my daughter."

Jenny looked up at her clock. "I think it's time we get going, Nora," she said

The trio walked down Jenny's front porch steps onto Sixth Street and strolled in no hurry toward Grant Street. They'd left Jenny's house early enough to take their time, and their destination was one that they all would have preferred to not have to reach. Turning right onto Grant Street, they soon reached Virgin Alley, a small lane that bisected the block between Fifth and Sixth streets. Across this alley, the east wall of St. Paul's Cathedral faced them. Three large Gothic windows filled the cathedral's rear wall, the center window being the largest and reaching up almost to the gabled roof. They crossed the alley and walked on the sidewalk along the cathedral, looking at the tall Gothic windows along its length. The cathedral occupied the entire block between Virgin Alley and Fifth Street. Evenly spaced buttresses rose along the long side of the cathedral, thrusting upward toward the ornamented spires that lined its roof. Progressing to the front of the cathedral that faced Fifth Street, they approached the large wooden doors at the base of the west tower. Flying buttresses supported the massive tower at each of its four corners. The tower reached higher than the cathedral's main roof but was still not completely finished, even though the cathedral itself was eleven years old.

Just as they were about to reach the front doors Nora stopped. Her face grew ashen and she raised her hand up to her breast. She looked as if she'd momentarily lost her breath. It appeared to Parker that it had suddenly dawned on Mrs. Fischer why they were here. At last she said, "The last time I entered this church was to attend Grace's baptism." She stood frozen for a moment, staring at the large paneled doors. Jenny wrapped an arm around Nora's shoulders, then Parker opened the door and they entered the church.

The trio passed through the vestibule and entered the immense body of the cathedral. They stepped into the wide center aisle, walking between tall columns that supported the galleries above. The ceiling was very high — even higher, Parker thought, than that of the Third Presbyterian Church. As they walked up between the rows of wooden pews Parker noted statues of saints standing in small alcoves throughout the church, including two flanking the steps to the sanctuary. An inclined table with rows of short candles sat in front of the saint on the right. A woman in a veil lit one of the candles, then walked back along a side aisle and knelt in a pew.

Up in the sanctuary Father Deane readied items on the top of the altar for the mass. Parker knew him, as he did most of the city's clergy, from his duties as constable. Two boys in black robes with white surplices assisted the priest. Soon they disappeared into the vestry.

The small number of people sitting in the first several pews made the church seem even bigger. Addie and Kevin Milligan sat in the first pew. Immediately behind them several men filled the second pew. Scattered mourners only partially filled the next three pews. The sounds of muffled praying could be heard as several of the women knelt with rosaries between their folded hands. Periodically one or more mourners erupted in a bout of keening. At the head of the center aisle near the steps to the sanctuary, a small coffin was laid atop a stand, draped in brown cloth.

Parker and Jenny stopped as Nora Fischer put her hand on a pew just before they reached the body of mourners. Nora appeared to be about to enter the pew when she looked at her daughter kneeling up front. She stood still for a moment, then walked slowly up to and entered the first pew. Addie looked up as Nora approached. Mother and daughter gazed at one another for just a moment. Hesitated. Then they embraced, crying.

Parker and Jenny entered the pew behind the group where Nora had first stopped, as Father Deane started the service. He sang the mass in Latin. Near the service's close he walked down to the coffin, flanked by the two altar boys. One boy held a small gold bucket from which Father Deane withdrew some holy water and sprinkled over the coffin. The other boy held a small vessel suspended on a chain. Smoking incense poured from the holes in the vessel's conical top. Father Deane took the vessel and, holding it high, walked around the coffin swinging the vessel and reciting prayers.

The entire service lasted almost an hour. When it ended the men in the second pew rose and walked to the front. They shouldered the coffin and followed the priest out of the church. Starting with Nora, Addie, and Kevin Milligan, the mourners in each pew filed out and joined the procession.

Outside Father Deane led the funeral procession to the parish cemetery on Boyd's Hill. The pallbearers rotated every few blocks to relieve their burden. At the gravesite Father Deane said another short service. When he concluded and it was time to leave Grace Milligan for the last time, a final round of keening rose from the mourners. Jenny broke into quiet tears and Parker put his arm around her.

Some of the mourners left the cemetery but most lingered to convey one last condolence to Mr. and Mrs. Milligan. Jenny and Parker joined the group. Parker could not help but study Kevin Milligan's face and actions, looking for signs of what might be within. The man was in deep pain — that was certain. Parker wondered if he didn't observe something more. Kevin Milligan looked no one in the eye, even as he accepted their words of comfort. His eyes stayed downcast, or occasionally wandered off into the distance over the crest of Boyd's Hill toward the Monongahela River.

Parker and Jenny reached them and found Nora holding her daughter's arm, physically supporting her. Jenny hugged Addie Milligan. "I'm very sorry for your loss," Parker offered to Kevin Milligan.

"Thank you, Constable," Kevin Milligan said. His eyes almost reached up to meet Parker's but not quite. He made no indication that he knew of Parker's discussion with his wife at the Third Presbyterian Church. Parker looked over at Addie Milligan. She did not act as if she recognized him or remembered their previous day's conversation. Parker felt certain she did neither. She kept the same vacant look that she had yesterday, except when her mother spoke to her. Only then did she appear to connect to the outside world.

Parker walked Jenny back to the house before going back to his rounds. At the front porch she stopped him before he walked away. "John, are you all right?" she asked. "You seemed very concerned when Nora was speaking, earlier today."

"I don't know," Parker replied.

"It's not just about ghosts, is it, John. It's about real people now, isn't it?" Jenny said. They weren't really questions as much as they were statements.

"Yes, you're right. It is about people — people who weren't where they said they were, people who died without any complete explanation. Maybe not just Grace. Maybe more."

"Who?" Jenny asked.

Parker didn't want to say just yet. "I may not be around tomorrow, ma'am," he said at last. "I need to find out exactly what *is* wrong. I need to go find some answers." He started walking across the street.

"But you're not even on duty tomorrow, John," Jenny said.

Already halfway across the street, Parker turned back toward Jenny and spread his arms out for emphasis, smiling in amusement for the first time that day. "I know," he called. "It's the only time I'm allowed to go do my job!"

9

Monday morning John Parker allowed himself to sleep past sunrise. A precious night of unbroken sleep made him loath to get up. From his experience, he knew that he had about one week or so before he had to start worrying about the nightmare recurring. After that, it could come at any time — maybe in a few days or not for several weeks. But this morning he slept until the sun illuminated the thin curtains of his window.

As today was Parker's only day off, he needed to travel to Freeport to find whatever answers that town might hold. He dressed, and then carried his overcoat downstairs. Jenny was nowhere to be seen, but a covered plate of food sat on the kitchen table. Parker ate and then put on his overcoat as he went out through the front door. The air was much cooler than it had been in the past several days, making this a more normal April morning. As he walked down the front steps, he unpinned the constable badge from his overcoat and dropped it into his coat pocket.

The easiest way to get to Freeport was by canal. With the aqueduct over the Allegheny River still under construction, Parker had to cross over to Allegheny City to catch a canal boat. He walked to the downtown area from the Wright House, turning toward the Allegheny River onto St. Clair Street. Parker pulled some change out of his pocket as he approached the tollhouse in front of the St. Clair Street Bridge. He handed the toll collector two cents, then entered the portal to the covered span. The wide entrance and many windows lining both sides provided enough light to see along the sidewalk inside the bridge. Up ahead, he saw the silhouette of an odd-shaped figure moving slowly along on foot. As Parker caught up to the person near the end of the bridge, he found a man struggling under the weight of large bolts of fabric. The man looked as though he was about to lose his grip on the bulky rolls.

"Can I help you with those?" Parker asked him.

The man, apparently hearing Parker's footsteps on the wooden sidewalk, was not startled but rather let out a grateful, "Oh yes, please." Parker took two bolts of black fabric off of the man, who kept two bolts of cream-colored linen.

"Thank you very much, friend," the man said. "I come to Pittsburgh every year at this time to buy my spring stock. But I've never had to walk so far to get on a canal boat to go home."

"Well, they tore the old aqueduct down last September and worked all winter building the new one," Parker said. "It should be finished in just a few weeks."

The two men exited the north portal of the bridge into Allegheny City. Walking a block farther, they turned left onto Lacock Street and approached the canal basin. Several boats sat in this long man-made pond, waiting for passengers to board or workers to load them with freight.

"That'll be my packet over there," the man said pointing to the canal boat closest to the basin's entrance to the canal. The two men carried the rolls of fabric past the second boat in line, the *Juniata*, to the lead boat, the *Cornplanter*. It was a long, low boat that reminded Parker of a barge, but was actually a passenger packet. The cabin covered most of the deck, leaving walking room along the sides and larger spaces in the front and back. Several chairs sat on the deck near the bow for passengers to sit on during the trip. At the stern the helmsman leaned on the long handle of the tiller that turned a single, wide rudder in the water. Most of the boat was painted white with green trim. Under the name *Cornplanter* stenciled in green on the white stern of the boat, "David Leech, Prop., " was painted in smaller green letters in rolling cursive.

The two men stepped aboard the *Cornplanter* and carried the fabric rolls down a small set of steps into the passenger cabin. The low ceiling made it impossible for them to stand completely upright as they looked for a place to set down their loads. The cramped quarters were full of male passengers, most sitting around two long tables in the middle of the cabin. Long planks lined the cabin walls in ascending rows. On the other end of the quarters a red curtain divided the cabin into two compartments. The sounds of women's voices and the rustling of their movements came from the other side of the curtain as they, too, prepared for their trip.

"Well, there's no room down here for my fabric," the man said. "We'll have to put them up with the baggage." They walked back up onto deck and handed the bolts of fabric to the two boatmen stacking baggage onto the roof of the cabin. The man then turned to Parker and held out his hand. "I am much obliged to you, friend," he said.

"You're welcome," Parker replied, "now if you'll excuse me I've got to go buy my ticket before we take off."

"I paid my passage previously," the man said. "Thank you again for your help."

Helping the man carry and settle his goods had slowed Parker's timing, and he now needed to hurry to purchase his ticket. He disembarked and walked to the ticket agent, who operated from a small building next to the basin surrounded by the larger buildings of the commission houses. Above the front door a sign proclaimed "Pennsylvania Main Line Canal — Schedules and Tickets." Upon entering he saw that there was only one person in line in front of him.

"Destination?" the ticket agent asked the gentleman.

"Leechburg," the man answered.

"That'll be seventeen and one-half cents," the ticket agent said. "The *Cornplanter* leaves in five minutes. It's eleven hours to Leechburg. You'll be there by six o'clock this evening."

"Destination?" the ticket agent asked Parker.

"Freeport," he replied.

"That'll be fifteen cents," the ticket agent said. "The *Cornplanter* leaves in five minutes. It's eight hours to Freeport. You'll be there by three o'clock."

"Will there be any boats returning to Pittsburgh tonight?" Parker asked.

The ticket agent looked up at a chart on his wall. "There should be a boat leaving Freeport at eleven o'clock," he said. "Would you like that ticket now?"

"Yes," Parker replied. He paid the agent and took his tickets.

Parker boarded the *Cornplanter* and handed his ticket to the captain.

"Welcome aboard the *Cornplanter*," the captain said. "I'm Joseph Redpath, her Captain."

"John Parker," Parker said while handing the captain his ticket.

"Freeport, I see," Captain Redpath said while looking at the ticket. "Well, we'll have you there before the day's out. Enjoy your trip, Mr. Parker." The captain wore a Prussian blue, long coat trimmed in thin red but with no other ornamentation. His hat was the same color, also trimmed in red with a short bill at the front. Around his shoulder and waist he slung a thin gold cord from which hung a brass horn.

Parker walked toward the ships' bow. The chilly morning air kept most of the passengers down inside the cabin for now. Parker stood on deck in front of the cabin and watched the crew prepare to embark. One man led three mules harnessed in tandem along the shore to the front of the boat. The man took the end of the long rope that trailed from the harness and fastened it to a catch on the side of the boat's bow. Then he took hold of the long reins that trailed from the lead mule and stood waiting for the captain's order.

On the cabin roof two boatmen finished stacking the luggage and swung a tarpaulin over the top of the pile. They tied the ends of the tarpaulin down, then climbed down and stood on the side of the deck nearest the towpath.

They, too, appeared to be finished with all of their tasks and waited for the boat to start. The helmsman now stood straight up with his eyes fixed on the captain as both hands grasping the tiller.

Captain Redpath stood in front of the cabin at the corner opposite the boatmen. He raised the horn to his lips and blew a strong, steady call. The driver flicked the reins and called to the mule team, who raised their heads and stepped forward. The towrope snapped taught. With a second snap of the reins the mules pulled the boat along. The helmsman guided the *Cornplanter* along the basin's shore through the channel that led into the canal. The boat glided noiselessly through the muddy canal water. With their boat under way, the two boatmen began talking and laughing in an almost celebratory conversation.

Parker walked to the very front of the boat. He looked down into the brown canal water and watched it lap gently onto the bow. This, he thought, was a truly peaceful way to travel. Suddenly, the captain yelled, "Bridge!" and Parker immediately ducked his head. The crew ducked without looking and went about their business. They passed under the bridge that crossed the canal at Federal Street.

The *Cornplanter* moved smoothly along the canal through Allegheny City. After it passed several blocks Captain Redpath's horn let out another steady blast. Looking ahead Parker saw that they approached a lock. The locktender emerged from an adjacent building and walked along on top of the lock's stone wall. He stood near the open wooden gate and waited for the canal boat to enter.

On board the *Cornplanter*, one boatman walked to the towrope and grasped it where it was fastened to the boat. The other boatman held a second rope and stood on the edge of the deck, watching the lock wall draw nearer. As the boat entered the lock gates, the captain yelled a command and the first boatman unfastened the towrope and threw his end up onto the towpath. The boat drifted into the lock chamber and slowed to a near stop. The boat bumped against wooden planks lining the stone walls of the lock chamber as the helmsman steered the boat from the middle of the entrance over to the side of the lock. Once inside the lock chamber, the second boatman tossed his line up to the locktender, who quickly tied it off around a snubbing post embedded into the wall. The boatman then climbed up on top of the wall himself and grabbed the line, pulling the canal boat to a stop.

The locktender walked atop the wall to the gates through which the boat had just passed. Grasping a long beam that protruded horizontally from the top of the gate, he pushed the thick wooden chamber doors tightly closed. Then he walked to the gates at the upper end of the lock. At this end, he gave several turns to an iron wheel. Parker suddenly felt himself being lifted, and saw that the water level was rising inside the lock.

During the water's rise, the boatman on the lock wall pulled his rope taught to keep the canal boat steady. Parker watched as his head rose above the level of the lock wall. The water's ascent stopped when it reached the same level as the water in the canal upstream. The driver then brought his team along the towpath again to the front of the boat and tossed the towrope to the boatman, who reattached it to the catch. The other boatman untied his line from the snubbing post and carried it back on board. With a command from Captain Redpath the driver set the team moving again, and the *Cornplanter* glided out of the lock chamber.

From their new height Parker could see up ahead the section of the canal that left the main line at a right angle, branching toward the Allegheny River and the nearly completed aqueduct. He watched the crews continue to fix timbers and planks into place in the aqueduct's trunk. Soon regular traffic would resume across the aqueduct and Pittsburghers would no longer have to cross the river to use the canal.

Parker looked across the river at the city of Pittsburgh. He seldom saw it from this perspective. The first thing that struck him was how the city, crowded with buildings and teaming streets, was hemmed in by nature. The Allegheny and Monongahela rivers bounded the triangle on two sides. Inland, three successive hills seemed to halt the city's spread further into the hinterland. The farthest of the three hills from Parker's position was Boyd's Hill, with its steep face along the Monongahela River. Moving left, Grant's Hill encroached farther into the city's center. Closest to Parker, Quarry Hill started farther away from the city center. A wide strip of level ground between Quarry Hill and the Allegheny River lay directly across the river from Parker's current position on the canal. These flats contained Pittsburgh's Fifth Ward.

As the canal boat moved farther along, the busy city's smoke and noise contrasted with its bordering woodlands. Very quickly the world became a different place. The hills lining both sides of the Allegheny River valley were quiet and forested with deciduous trees whose branches were just now awakening with green buds. Three weeks from now, thought Parker, this trip would be through a valley covered in green. But today the hills showed mostly brown, with only enough green to spur the longing for full-blown springtime.

Moving out of Allegheny City, the canal curved northward along the west side of the Allegheny River away from Pittsburgh. As the city disappeared around the bend, Parker looked one last time at the busy town couched in the quiet hillsides. Parker thought of all of the concerns and toils in the daily lives of the people living there. All of the aspirations and activities that made up their entire world now seemed somehow contained within a specific location. As a member of that community Parker shared in all of the city's dreams and labor, but he'd never seen any boundary to them. Now they seemed infants in the wide, ancient wilderness that surrounded them.

"Sure does look different from here, doesn't it?" Captain Redpath said, suddenly standing beside Parker. For an instant, Parker felt irritation at having his thoughts invaded. But turning and seeing the captain gaze at the city, Parker immediately realized that Captain Redpath had viewed this same scene and thought these same thoughts hundreds of times before.

"Most of the things you think and worry about don't seem so large when you look at them from a distance and compare them with the world around you," Captain Redpath noted.

"Most," Parker agreed, "but not *all*."

"You look like someone who's got a worry that would follow him anywhere," Captain Redpath observed.

"How long have you worked on the canal?" Parker deflected the conversation away from himself.

"Me? Well, let's see now," Captain Redpath said, "I started as a boatman ... must've been in 'thirty-two, up in Friendship. I did every job there is to do on a canal boat — all on Leech's Line. Ten years ago Mr. Leech made me the captain of the *Spartan* — now that was a freighter, mind you. I've captained several of his boats since then. This is my second year runnin' the *Cornplanter*. Passenger packets are a bit more work, y'know — keepin' on schedule, mindin' the passengers, and all that. Floatin' freight was a bit more peaceful. But, believe me, all those trips with havin' no one to talk to will give a man his fill of solitude."

"Leech — that's a name you see a lot when you ride a canal boat around here," Parker noted.

"Yes, sir," Captain Parker exclaimed, "Mr. Leech runs one of the biggest lines of packets on the Western Division. He built the Big Dam and the canal lock in Friendship, where I'm from. Let's see now, besides his boatyard, he runs a sawmill, a gristmill, and a wool factory there.

"There wasn't much to Friendship before Mr. Leech and the canal. He practically built our town up all by himself. So much so that folks there renamed the town after him," Captain Redpath said.

"That's quite a story," Parker said.

"Not really," Captain Redpath replied. "Lots of towns along the canal weren't much more than frontier outposts before the state built the canal through them. The canal brought people and commerce right to their doorsteps that would never have gone there otherwise. They …"

Suddenly a woman walking toward them, pointing her parasol at Captain Redpath, interrupted their conversation. "Captain Redpath. Captain *Redpath!*" the woman called as she approached. "Sir, I must protest the extremely cramped quarters of this vessel. Why, there is no room below for my daughter and I to sit, let alone stow our belongings. I'm forced to carry my carpetbag upon my person while the other ladies crowding our compartment push and stomp on my poor daughter's feet! You have taken too many passengers on board and some *must* be discharged. The situation is completely unacceptable."

The captain looked surprised by neither her complaint nor her request. He spoke in a demonstrably pleasant and calm voice. "Ma'am, we have the proper number of passengers aboard today. At the beginning of every trip there is some commotion while folks get their things settled in. Once everyone's situated, I'm sure you and your daughter will have a comfortable trip."

"Hardly," she retorted. She was a stout woman with a colorful dress and plumed hat. "We've just come up from New Orleans on the steamer *America* and quarters on board that beautiful ship were appropriately spacious. I see that the remainder of my trip to Philadelphia will not be as …" she looked around the canal boat, "adequate."

"We are quite a bit smaller than a steamboat, ma'am," Captain Parker said.

"Yes, quite," she replied. She looked over at the Allegheny River running parallel to the canal. "Why on earth did you dig this muddy little ditch alongside a perfectly good river that's already here, anyway?" she asked.

Captain Redpath looked out over the river. "No steamboat could go up the Allegheny today, ma'am. Too shallow. You'd need a good springtime freshet to get it deep enough for steamboats. Now, over on the Monongahela River they've built a dam to keep the water deep enough for steamboats year-round. Maybe they'll build one on the Allegheny. Still, there's no river that runs from Pittsburgh to Philadelphia. Only the canal does that."

The woman was not impressed, "Well, I'll tell you something *else* that runs to Philadelphia and that is the *railroad*. And when the railroads finally reach Pittsburgh they will put your silly little boats out of business!" She wheeled and marched back to the cabin with her parasol under her arm like a baton.

"Yes, ma'am," Captain Redpath said to her back. He looked again out over the Allegheny River valley. Parker saw a look of wistful sadness on the captain's face. "Ever ride in a rail car, Mr. Parker?" he asked.

"No, never," Parker replied.

"I rode one from Columbia to Philly — the last leg of the Main Line," the captain said. "They're fast, very fast. They make a lot of noise and they rush around just like the people back there in Pittsburgh, tryin' to get their work done. Canal boats are quiet and they can't be rushed. You might as well sit on a deck chair and look around and see what God has made in all His glory. If railroads do put the canal out of business, well, something will be lost."

Parker looked out over the river and its beautiful valley and nodded in understanding. The morning sun burned the chill out of the air and a few other passengers began to emerge from the cabin. Some relaxed on chairs placed on the deck and cabin roof, turning the trip into a relaxing sight-seeing tour for any who cared to enjoy it in that manner.

Captain Redpath excused himself and attended his duties. The canal boat continued its journey, passing through the community of Millvale. Across the river, homes lined the hillside in the town of Lawrenceville. Farther along they passed through the town of Sharpsburg. Captain Redpath's horn rang out from atop the cabin as they approached another lock. Parker climbed on top of the cabin roof and stood near the captain. From this higher vantage point Parker could see farther upstream than at the first lock. Less than one minute after Captain Redpath blew his horn, a similar horn sounded on the other side of the lock.

A canal boat traveling south approached. The locktender did not move immediately to allow the *Cornplanter* in, but rather stood on the wall and watched the two boats approach. By its lower, windowless cabin Parker saw that the other boat was a freight packet. Three men from the freighter stepped off onto the towpath and approached the lock.

"Why isn't he letting us in?" Parker asked Captain Redpath.

"He's waitin' to see who's first," the captain replied.

"Aren't we first?" Parker asked. "We did get here before them."

"That doesn't matter much out here," the captain said. "When they get off their boat, they're sayin', 'We're goin' first, see, an' if ya don't like it, we'll beat the tar outta ya.' Canallers are a rough lot, Mr. Parker, and that's a fact. Those fellas probably figure that we won't fight for passage, having a boatload of passengers, and all. They're wrong."

The two boatmen on board the *Cornplanter* had observed events and joined the driver on the towpath. Captain Redpath stepped down off of the roof and called in to the cabin. Shortly, the cook emerged and they, too, disembarked. The five crewmembers of the *Cornplanter* stepped up onto the lock wall without hesitation. The three men from the other boat stopped suddenly and held a brief conference. They then turned and walked back to their boat.

Captain Redpath nodded to the locktender, who now moved along the lock wall and lowered the water level in the chamber so the *Cornplanter* could enter. He opened the gates and the boat passed through the lock as it had through the first one. As the *Cornplanter* passed within inches of the freighter after exiting, none of the other boat's crew could be seen. Before long Captain Redpath again stood on the cabin roof.

"Your men are pretty handy in a pinch," Parker complimented him.

"I told you Mr. Parker — canallers are a tough lot. My men hardly need an excuse to fight. I need them like that. This canal winds at times through miles of wilderness. Sometimes, especially when we're tied up to a lock, we're sitting ducks. Gangs wait 'til after dark near a lock and listen for a canal boat's horn. When the boat ties to the lock, they attack and rob everyone on board. But a good crew can stop them. Yes, sir, I need my men to be tough."

Once through the lock, the boat resumed its northeasterly course. Leaving the environs of Pittsburgh and its surrounding communities, all evidence of the existence of humankind temporarily disappeared except for the watery path itself upon which the boat traveled.

During the morning Parker strolled to different parts of the deck to view the scenery. The wooded hills lining the Allegheny Valley never left them. Sometimes they rose close to the river, leaving only a narrow strip of ground through which the canal could pass. In other stretches the hills retreated, making a wide valley floor on one or both sides of the river. Small communities sometimes resided in these dales, and the canal boat stopped to pick up or drop off passengers. A break in the hills usually heralded a creek cutting its small swath to the river. The canal either crossed the creek via an aqueduct or used it as a feeder to maintain its own water level. Human settlement also appeared here, with gristmills and sawmills built on the streams.

Sometime before noon they approached Harmarville Station. At the small basin there a man led three new mules out of a barn and replaced the mules on the towpath with the fresh team. One of the boatmen relieved the driver, who also needed a rest from walking behind the mules.

By now they were several hours into the trip. Parker, having stood the entire trip so far, looked for a place to sit down. He saw that several chairs on the forward deck were vacant, and walked down the stairs off the cabin roof to sit and rest. He sat for only a few minutes before a man walked from around the side of the cabin and sat in the chair next to him.

"Hello, friend," a familiar voice said. Parker saw that it was the man whom he'd helped carry fabric bolts across the bridge that morning. The man extended his hand to Parker, "We parted without my introducing myself. I didn't mean to be impolite, I was just intent on getting to the boat on time. My name is Jacob Shoop."

"John Parker," Parker said while shaking his hand. "I got in a hurry too, by the time we reached the station. No harm done, I think. Where are you traveling to, Mr. Shoop?"

"Freeport," Jacob Shoop replied, "that's where I have my home and my business."

"Oh?" said Parker, now interested in more than small talk. "What kind of business do you run?"

"I'm a tailor. I own a men's clothing store in town," Jacob replied, "going on fifteen years now." Jacob Shoop looked to Parker to be just under forty years old. He wore a beard and a suit that looked like it was made of the same black fabric Parker had carried to the boat.

"Have you lived there all of your life?" Parker asked.

"No," Jacob said, "I moved to the area with my parents from the eastern part of the state, Royersford, back in 'fifteen. I opened my shop in 'thirty — the same year I got married."

"You must do good work to be in business so long," Parker noted.

"I do a fair amount of business," Jacob replied. "The town is my home. The people there are my neighbors — so we all know each other and work together. Plus I get business from the rivermen stopping in town on their way downstream to Pittsburgh. Every now and again a circus or camp meeting comes to town and brings some business with it. And of course I get customers from this highway we're on right now — the canal sure is a handy thing to have going through your town."

"Were you here when they were building it — the canal, I mean?" Parker asked.

Jacob Shoop nodded his head affirmatively, "We lived in the vicinity. They dug the ditch at Freeport in 'twenty-seven and 'twenty-eight. The next year the *Benjamin Franklin* started regular trips from Freeport to Pittsburgh."

"Was there much of a town there when they were digging it? I mean, did a lot of people live there?" Parker asked. "I've heard that some towns along the canal didn't really get started until after it opened up."

"It was a small village then," Jacob said. "I know the rivermen were stopping there for years even before we moved here, as a stop-off before the last leg on the trip to Pittsburgh. There was a tavern, of course, which was another reason they stopped. There was a blacksmith shop, I remember. The saltwater veins were discovered in the area in the 'twenties and that brought more folks into the area who sunk wells and sold salt. I guess there were a couple dozen homes in town in 'twenty-seven when they started digging the canal ditch. And of course the pioneer families' homesteads in the surrounding hills were there long before that."

"I see," Parker said.

"Do you have an interest in our town's history, Mr. Parker?" Jacob asked.

Parker paused, unsure exactly how to answer, "I heard a story once, about a little girl who died in town around that time — drowned, I'm told," Parker said.

Jacob suddenly looked away as he answered, "I remember the story, although I'm not the expert on the incident. The rivers can be our life's blood but they can also take their toll, Mr. Parker. My own mother drowned in the Kiskiminetas River, just above town, the year after we moved here."

"I'm sorry," Parker offered.

"That was a long time ago, Mr. Parker," Jacob said. "Now, will you be stopping in Freeport on your journey?"

"That's my destination," Parker said.

"So it is," said Jacob, now looking more thoughtfully at Parker. "Well, if you're really interested, I could introduce you to some folks who were around back then and know a bit more about that girl than I do."

"Yes, I am interested," Parker replied.

Jacob Shoop nodded again, with his eyes now fixed on Parker. Then he looked away at the valley corridor winding in front of them. After a while he started a new conversation. "That was some fire you folks had," he said.

"Yes it was," Parker said, "bigger than I ever imagined a fire could be."

"I spent an extra day in the city just to look around," Jacob said. "It sure covered a lot of ground."

"Covered a lot of ground, destroyed a lot of property, destroyed a lot of homes," Parker added.

"I heard that there were surprisingly few people killed for such a huge fire," Jacob said. Parker suddenly got the feeling that now he was the one being questioned.

"No, not many," he said, "only one person confirmed killed by the fire. Others are missing. Some, well, we're just not sure yet exactly what happened to them."

"I see," Jacob said.

For a long while the two men discussed details of the fire and the current state of the Burnt District. Jacob Shoop impressed Parker with his knowledge of many of the businesses that were lost and of businesses in the city in general. After about an hour the canal boat stopped for a short time in Springdale, a small village of only a few houses, a tavern, and a schoolhouse. "We're less than two hours out," Jacob said, as the boat left the basin.

They traveled now through territory that Jacob Shoop knew well. He told Parker the names of villages or landmarks they passed, along with stories of events or people of note connected to them. Later they approached the town of Tarentum. As they crossed over the small aqueduct spanning Bull Creek, Jacob pointed to the gristmills and other works along the stream. He noted that they were started by some of the earliest immigrants into the area. The boat navigated a lock as it passed through the town. Here the hills gave way enough for many streets to be laid out on the flats along the river, putting several blocks between the canal and the river during this stretch.

As they passed out of the north end of Tarentum the hills again closed in on them, leaving so little room that it seemed they might push the canal boat right into the river. The hills facing the canal were higher and steeper than they had been at any point in the trip so far. Jacob announced that this was the last leg of the trip to Freeport.

After about one half-hour or so the line of hillside to their left dropped abruptly to a valley on the northwest side of the river. Up head, running through another valley cutting in from the north, a wide, slow stream emptied into the Allegheny where the river made a sharp easterly curve. An aqueduct crossed the stream, and beyond that the buildings of a town clung to the hillside along the river. At the far side of the town a long island lined the shore. Past the island, the Allegheny curved again to the north, out of sight. "There's our town, Mr. Parker," Jacob said, "It'll only be a few minutes now."

On their left they passed a small clearing in the trees. There appeared no natural reason for the clearing — the area looked as wild as the woods surrounding it. Small trees and underbrush covered it. Looking closer, Parker saw what appeared to be the ruins of small houses — shacks, by the look of it. They had mostly fallen down and were covered by moss and other vegetation.

"Mulligan," Jacob said without warning.

"Excuse me?" Parker said.

"That's Mulligan. It was a camp that the Irish laborers lived in while they dug this section of the canal," Jacob explained. "You expressed a lot of interest in the subject earlier in out trip."

"Yes I did," Parker said. "Why only the Irish? Where did the other workers stay?"

"There were no others," Jacob said. "The men who dug the canal were almost all immigrants fresh from Ireland."

"I didn't know," Parker said.

"Sure," Jacob continued, "it was a monumental job that required a lot of laborers — more than this country had at the time. Contractors went across the ocean to Ireland to recruit workers and brought them back here — cheap labor from a place where they knew they could find men who would work for low wages."

"They must've worked on this section a long time, to have to build a camp like that," Parker noted.

"They spent a long time at Freeport. Besides the ditch they built a lock and two aqueducts here — the one up ahead across Buffalo Creek and a bigger one on the other side of town that crosses the river. There was another workers' camp, too, along the river on the upstream side of town. They called that one the Garry Owen."

The two men stood now at the bow of the boat. The canal made a sharp bend to the right to match the Allegheny River's eastward curve. The aqueduct across Buffalo Creek approached about two hundred yards away when Parker spotted something floating in the water just ahead of them. As they continued nearer he saw that it was a large animal floating on its side. Its head was submerged under the dirty water but from its thin legs Parker could see that it was a deer. The boat bumped the body, which bobbed and rocked as it was pushed to the side. The underside of its bloated torso was a sickly white and in places its flesh peeled from its body. As Parker stared at it, a deep sadness came over him. He closed his eyes and the pale image of Grace Milligan appeared before him. She never really left him, he realized, but rather had become a permanent fixture in his mind that he had to moved to a back corner so that he could carry on.

"Heavens, what a stench!" Jacob Shoop exclaimed. "That carcass will drift in the canal for weeks until it hangs up in some town's basin. It'll rot there until they finally pay someone pull it out and bury it."

The canal boat glided across the aqueduct into town. Buffalo Creek flowed so wide and slow beneath them that it might have passed for a river itself. With its high steep hills lining both sides, the creek looked like a miniature version of the Allegheny River Valley through which they'd traveled all day. As they entered the canal basin the captain's horn sounded, then he announced with a booming call, "Freeport Station." Parker helped Jacob Shoop receive his bolts of fabric as the boatmen unloaded them from the cabin roof. Captain Redpath met them at the short, bowed gangplank.

"There you go now, Mr. Parker, I told you that I'd get you here before the day was over," he said.

"You did, Captain Redpath," Parker said.

"Did you leave that worry of yours behind anywhere along the trip?" Captain Redpath asked.

"No, I'm afraid she's still with me," Parker slipped without realizing it.

"Well, God bless you then, and good luck to you," Captain Redpath said.

Parker looked out at the driver and the mules along the towpath, then back over the length of the deck and cabin of the *Cornplanter*. He thought of the peaceful trip and Captain Redpath's love of his life on the canal. He recalled the woman's prediction that the coming railroads would end that life. "Good luck to you too, Captain Redpath," he said. Then he and Jacob Shoop stepped ashore.

10

John Parker followed Jacob Shoop along the towpath of the canal. Freeport was bigger than he'd expected. Much of the town sat on a spur rising high from the confluence of the Allegheny River and Buffalo Creek. Although bordered on two sides by water much like Pittsburgh, any resemblance to his home city ended there. Freeport's narrow flats ran only one city block back from the river, then, wound around its own "point," to where the hillside faced Buffalo Creek. If the people had allowed the hills to stop their progress inland, it would be a tiny village indeed. But houses and streets occupied a series of slopes and small flats for about halfway up the spur. Above the uppermost houses a long, steep slope rose unoccupied to the hilltop. The canal flowed along the foot of the first slope, forming a dividing line between the riverside buildings and the rest of the town on the hillside.

The two men walked past the east end of the long canal basin where a lock formed a gate to the Main Line. They passed a short branch of the canal that bypassed the lock around to the doorstep of a factory. The sign in the factory's front read "Hope Woolen Mill." As he walked by, Parker watched workers unload large sacks from a freighter onto the mill's dock. He and Jacob continued past the lock, turning right onto a cross street toward the river. At the end of the street they turned left and stopped at the corner house, which faced the riverbank.

"This is my home and my store," Jacob announced. It was a large, two-story house with chimneys at both ends and two doors standing side by side in the center. Over the left-hand door a sign read *Clothing Store, Jacob Shoop, Tailor.* Jacob opened the shop door and walked in. Parker followed. Inside, racks of men's suits lined the left-hand side of the room. Most of the suits were of the same color and material as the bolts Parker carried. Others were work clothes. On the racks farthest to the back, the suits had slips of paper pinned to their shoulders with names written on them. On the right-hand side of the room long, glass-top cases were covered with neatly stacked folded shirts. Hats and other men's apparel accessories filled the cases. In the center aisle, a boy who looked to Parker to be about fourteen or fifteen swept the floor near the rear of the shop.

"Hello, Papa," the boy smiled as he greeted Jacob.

"Hello, Simon," Jacob smiled back. "Hard at work, I see."

"Yes, Papa," Simon beamed at the acknowledgement.

"Simon, this is Mr. Parker," Jacob said. "Take the bolts that he's carrying up to the sewing room." He continued toward the rear of the store and started up a set of stairs. Simon came over to Parker, took one bolt, under whose weight he sank for just a second, then motioned to take the second.

"I can carry one up," Parker said, then followed the boy upstairs. A large room at the top of the stairs contained long tables covered with lengths and cuts of fabric. Large rollers dispensing the fabric sat in carriages mounted atop each table. Near one table an elderly man in a vest and rolled up shirtsleeves sized a suit coat that was draped over a canvass mannequin. The man looked up from his work only long enough to greet Jacob. Jacob greeted him in return, then set his bolts of fabric onto one of the long tables while nodding to Simon and Parker to set theirs in the same place.

"Thank you again, Mr. Parker," Jacob said. "Now, I haven't eaten since breakfast on the boat, and I didn't see you at the table then, so I'll wager that you're even more hungry than I am. Let's go down and get a bite to eat. Then I think we can go talk to somebody who might be able to help you."

The two men walked back downstairs. They exited the store's front door, then turned and went in the right-hand door.

Jacob Shoop's home was sparsely but solidly furnished, and shortly Parker saw why. Upon the call of one child of, "Papa's home!" a charge of small bodies rushed and surrounded Jacob. Larger children crowded and hugged his waist while a toddler wordlessly hugged his leg. Then after the universal question of, "What did you bring us, Papa?" the mob stepped back only one-half step while Jacob produced treats from the pockets.

The crowd dispersed with laughs and giggles as their mother entered the room and shooed them away. "Well, I see that you stayed an extra day after all," she said as she hugged Jacob.

"I told you I would," Jacob said. "A horrible sight — where the fire was. It's an entire section of the city, bigger than our whole town. Everything inside is destroyed." Then he turned to Parker, "Hannah, this is John Parker, who has been most helpful to me on my trip home."

"Hello, Mr. Parker," Hannah Shoop said.

Parker nodded his head, "Pleased to meet you, Mrs. Shoop."

"Hannah," Jacob said, "it's been a long trip and our guest is hungry. Why don't we show him some hospitality and give him a bite to eat?"

"Oh, so it's *our guest* who's hungry, is it?" Hannah said, looking at Jacob from under raised eyebrows. "And I suppose you'll be eating with him?"

"Of course," Jacob smiled, "it would only be the polite thing to do."

"Of course," Hannah said, shaking her head. "Get yourselves cleaned up,

THE BURNT DISTRICT

then take Mr. Parker into the dining room." She turned and went to the rear of the house into the kitchen. Jacob led Parker to a small room just before the kitchen that contained a washbasin. The two men washed their faces and hands and went into the dining room. Near the entrance to the dining room sat a bassinet, over which a beaming Jacob Shoop leaned. "And how is our baby Catherine today?" he asked.

"She's sleeping at last," Hannah replied from the kitchen, "and I'll thank you not to wake her."

Jacob and Parker entered the dining room and sat down at a table with ten chairs around it. After a few minutes Hannah came in with two plates of food: beef and potatoes. "Here's what were having for supper in about an hour if some folks could've waited," she said with mock irritation.

"Peace, my love," Jacob said. "Where did the beef come from?"

"Tom Clawson brought it this morning for payment for his suit," Hannah replied. "He said that he still owes you five dollars cash to settle his balance."

"That, he does," Jacob said.

"Well, he said he plans to get it to you before the end of the month," Hannah added.

Parker sat a bit bemused by this line of conversation. Jacob, seeing his expression, explained. "Not everyone has cash around here, Mr. Parker, and payments 'in kind' still put food on the table, as you can see."

"I do see. And it is very good food, indeed, ma'am," he said to Hannah.

"What brings you to our town, Mr. Parker?" Hannah asked.

Jacob answered her in a matter-of-fact tone while continuing to eat his meal, "Mr. Parker is a constable from the City of Pittsburgh. A little girl has been killed there at the same time as their big fire. He doesn't know how she died. He doesn't believe the fire killed her. He believes that she was murdered. He doesn't know how or by whom. He thinks that somehow learning about a girl who drowned here in Freeport seventeen years ago might help him find out what happened in his own city."

Parker stared at Jacob Shoop. If he had not had a mouthful of food, his jaw might've dropped to the tabletop. Hannah now addressed her husband, "Who drowned here seventeen years ago?"

"Mary Woodburn. Her parents were Michael and Maria. They moved farther west about three years after she died — Colorado Territory, I think," Jacob replied.

"And what does he think that has to do with a girl being killed in a fire in Pittsburgh last week?" she asked, now becoming incredulous.

"He doesn't know. He's only heard a story. There's some connection, though, and he's come to find out what it is."

"Does he know someone here? Whom does he plan to ask about this?" she asked.

"He knows no one. He got on a canal boat and came up here. He doesn't have much of a plan after that — he's never been here before."

"Jacob Shoop, are you making this up?" she demanded.

Jacob looked at Parker, "Am I making it up, Mr. Parker?"

Parker considered for a moment. "No," he said finally.

Hannah shook here head, "You men are either daft or much too smart for my understanding. And I'm sure it's the former." She turned and walked back into the kitchen.

Jacob smiled at Parker, "Now don't look at me that way, Mr. Parker. I'm not from Pittsburgh, but I've been to enough market days at the Diamond to recognize a city constable's coat when I see one. You don't say much, and I believe that's from your own nature rather than trying to be deceptive, but you tell a lot by what you don't say. You tell even more by what you do. There's no reason in heaven or earth for a Pittsburgh constable to care about a girl who drowned in Freeport seventeen years ago, let alone get in a canal boat and come here, unless it has something to do with what's going on in his own city right now. You did tell me that for some victims in the fire, you just don't know what happened to them. And when the canal boat captain asked you if you left your worry behind, you said that 'she's' still with you. You see, Mr. Parker, I can't help doing more with my brain during an eight-hour trip than just sit and admire the scenery."

"I can tell," Parker said. "Now, I'm betting that you already have a plan for who we'll talk to about the Woodburn child and how we'll approach them."

"Who *I'll* talk to, Mr. Parker," Jacob said. "We're going to deliver a suit to George Weaver in a little while. His family's been in this valley for decades. He lives a mile or so back the Buffalo now, but in 'twenty-eight his family lived on Water Street, here in town. I don't know that much about the incident, but he will. It'll be best to let me do the talking."

After they finished eating, Jacob informed Hannah that they were delivering Mr. Weaver's suit. She followed them to the front door.

"Thank you again for supper, ma'am," Parker said.

"You're welcome, Mr. Parker," she replied. She spoke to him a little louder than before, as one who believes that the person to whom they're speaking is not deaf, but rather just a little slow. "Good luck on your mission."

Jacob kissed his wife good-bye, "We'll be a while, Hannah. I probably won't be home until after nightfall."

"Of course you won't," Hannah said to him. "Why should I expect you to be home, after all?"

"Peace, my love," Jacob called as they walked out the front door. Parker waited outside while Jacob went back into his store to get Mr. Weaver's suit. Across the street Freeport's own packed-dirt wharf bustled with activity. Keelboats, flatboats, and rafts of various types were pulled up onto its shore as workers loaded or unloaded freight. Out on the river, a group of men drove a huge raft of logs downstream. "Does it remind you of home, Mr. Parker?" Jacob asked as he came outside carrying the suit.

"All you need are a few steamboats," Parker replied.

"We get them when the river's high enough," Jacob said. The two men walked along Water Street in the direction of the large island that Parker had seen from the canal boat. A sawmill operated on the very tip of the island and just beyond it a small wooden bridge connected the island to the rest of the town. Beyond the bridge, residences lined the shoreline that faced the town. Before the two men reached the island, however, Jacob turned left onto a street that led up into the town.

After they crossed a canal bridge the street sloped upward. They turned right onto the next street as the slope leveled off. Freeport's streets were graded, but not paved. Townspeople passed them on foot, riding horses, and driving wagons and carriages. Everyone they passed greeted Jacob. They looked at Parker briefly but did not stare impolitely. "Strangers are common in our town," Jacob said without being asked, "they're a big portion of our commerce."

On the next block Jacob reached the building that was apparently their first destination and walked to the rear. Parker saw that the back section was a small stable.

"We'll ride out to the Weaver's," Jacob announced. He saddled two horses. "Do you ride, Mr. Parker?" he asked.

"I did when I was a kid," Parker answered, "but I haven't ridden much since then."

"You'll ride Wilhelmina," Jacob said. "She won't give you any trouble."

"Do you rent this stable?" Parker asked.

"No, I own this building," Jacob replied, "and seven other properties in town, including one on the Island."

The two men mounted their horses and headed back out onto the street. Parker found that horseback riding became almost instantly familiar again and Wilhelmina was indeed a friendly mare for riding. He followed Jacob, riding in the direction they'd just come from. Then Jacob turned right as they rode through the middle of the town all the way across to the side lined by Buffalo Creek.

Just before reaching the creek they turned right onto a dirt road that took them out of town. The lane became little more than two ruts running parallel along the bottom of the hillside.

After about one mile the hillside gave way to a wide meadow. They reached an area where most of the land between the hill and creek was tilled. On the far side of the plowed square a farmhouse and a barn sat in the lengthening shadows of the early evening. The dirt road skirted the field and curved toward the house before continuing on its way. As they neared the house, Jacob reined his horse closer to Parker's.

"George's mother, Mae, lives with him," Jacob said. "She lived in the valley back when the pioneers were settling in these hills during the early 1790's. She was a tough frontier woman back then, but now she's very old and quite senile. She's still full of fight, though. Just watch your step around her and hope that she's asleep the whole time we're here."

A young boy ran out from the porch to see who approached and greet them. "Hello, Mr. Shoop," he said.

"Hello, David," Jacob answered. "Is your father home?"

"He's out at the corn crib, bringing in a bushel for Grandma," David answered.

"Will you tell him that I've brought his suit?" Jacob requested.

"Yessir!" the boy answered, then ran off.

Jacob and Parker continued toward the front porch, dismounted, and tied their horses to a hitching post. A large man with broad features and light brown hair carried a bushel basket full of corn in from the barn. He wore a work shirt and bib overalls that looked similar to the ones hanging in Jacob's store. David walked along beside, talking to him. The man stopped and put the basket down as two young men approached. The young men appeared to be in their late teens and early twenties. Both were surely the man's sons, Parker thought, because they had similar features to his. After a brief conversation the two young men continued toward the field as the man picked up the basket and walked toward Jacob and Parker.

"Hello, Jacob," the man said.

"Hello, George," Jacob greeted him. "I've brought your suit."

"Can you bring it up on the porch?" George Weaver asked. "I've got to carry this up to Mum."

"Of course," Jacob replied. As they walked, Jacob introduced Parker, "George, this is John Parker, up from Pittsburgh. He helped me a great deal on my trip home from there and I've invited him to stay at my home."

THE BURNT DISTRICT

Parker nodded, "Pleased to meet you, Mr. Weaver."

"Any friend of Jacob's is welcome at my farm, Mr. Parker," George Weaver said.

The three men stepped up onto the porch, which extended along the entire front of the house. At the far end an old woman sat hunched on a bench. She wore a plain dress and a shawl over her shoulders. At her booted feet sat a small wooden bucket. Jacob stopped at the top of the steps while George Weaver took the bushel of corn to his mother. "Here, Mum," George said in a loud voice, "here's the corn you wanted."

Mae Weaver just nodded to the spot on the floor where she wanted him to set the bushel. She didn't look up. George put the basket down where she had indicated. He lifted a lantern to make ready to light it, as the daylight had started to fade for the night. "Don't need that yet," she bellowed. George set the lantern back down and started to walk away.

"Who's that?" the old woman yelled, not looking up but cocking her ear toward Jacob and Parker.

"That's Jacob Shoop, Mum," George replied, still speaking loudly.

"I know that!" she yelled, now irritated. "Who's the other one?"

"He's a friend of Jacob's. His name's John Parker."

"I never heard his name before," Mae yelled.

"He's up from Pittsburgh, Mum."

"What does he want?" she demanded.

"He doesn't want anything, Mum, he's just here with Jacob," George said.

"He wants something!" Mae Weaver said.

George Weaver shook his head and walked over to Jacob, who handed him his new suit. George held it up and admired it. "It sure is a dandy!" he said. "Can I get you two something to drink?"

"Water would be just the thing," Jacob said.

"Have a seat, gentlemen," George said as he took his suit into the house. Jacob and Parker sat in chairs on the far side of the porch from Mae Weaver. The old woman did not appear to pay any attention to them, but Parker had already seen that that meant nothing. She took individual ears of corn from the basket and removed the kernels from the cob. She accomplished this by grasping the ear tightly with both hands and twisting one hand. This pulled the kernels off of the cob and they dropped into her bucket. Although her head continually bobbed involuntarily while she worked, her hands moved deftly and her grip was obviously strong. She made good progress on her task.

After a few minutes George emerged from the house carrying two tumblers of water. He handed them to Jacob and Parker, and then sat down on a small wooden chair that facing them. "That is a mighty fine suit, Jacob," George said. "How about some venison in the next couple of weeks, then some bushels of fresh corn and potatoes at harvest?"

"Agreed," Jacob said as the two men shook hands. "So, George, how are you doing these days?"

"Just fine, Jacob," George replied. "I have Matthew and Mark planting an apple orchard on the back acreage. Hopefully we'll have an apple crop in a few seasons. How are things with you?"

"Business is good," Jacob said. "I was in Pittsburgh this weekend buying my spring stock — just got back this afternoon."

"At service yesterday they were sayin' that there was a big fire there last week. They said it burned down the whole city," George said.

"Well, not the *whole* city," Jacob said, "but a very large chunk of it."

"Were you there when the fire happened, Mr. Parker?" George asked.

"Yes, sir," Parker replied, "it was a horrible calamity. Over one thousand homes and businesses were lost. Lots of people fought desperately against the fire, but the water supply failed and the wind worked against us all day. We are fortunate that only a very few people were killed."

"Mercy," George said. His interest in the subject quickly dissipated, and he began surveying the scene of his large field in the meadow. Then he looked back at Jacob. "So, Jacob, did you take the canal into Pittsburgh?"

"Yes, I did, George," Jacob said. "Up and back."

"Y'know, I was living in town when they built that canal," George said. "I watched them build it from nothing."

"I know you did," Jacob said in an agreeing tone. He showed no surprise that George Weaver had just turned the conversation to the very period in time that they had hoped to discuss. Rather, he seamed to relax and settle himself in, as one who is about to be told a story that he's heard many times before.

"Yessir," George continued, "I was there when the surveyors and engineers planted the stone markers in the ground to show the contractors where to dig the ditch. I watched the Irish dig the thing with their picks and shovels. I saw them lay the first stones for the lock." He started to chuckle to himself. "Y'know, Jacob, after they finished that lock, me and Bill Bohlen and Benjamin Drum had us a contest. We tried to see who could jump from the wall on one side clear over to the wall on the other side. Now that's sixteen feet across, mind you. Well, Bill and Ben both tried it and didn't make it. Got a little wet for their trouble, too. Hah! But me, I took a start and jumped clean over to the top of the other wall. Sixteen feet and not a drop of water on me! Hah! No one has ever done it since. No one!"

"That's quite a feat," Jacob said. "Those were some big doings around here — building that canal. Seems to me that the work went on for quite some time."

"Yes it did," George said. "They started diggin' around here in 'twenty-seven, and the work went on through the better part of 'twenty-eight. That canal's what put Freeport on the map. Lots of folks have moved here since then."

"Lots have moved here," Jacob agreed. "Of course my family lived just around the corner on the Kiskiminetas River near Rumbaugh's Ferry. I moved into town and set up my store in back in 'thirty. Some moved away when it got too crowded for them — moved farther west for another frontier. Let's see, I remember the Woodburns moved away just a few years after the canal opened. Went to Colorado Territory, I believe."

George's face became serious again, "Yes, I remember them. They lost a little girl here, too — drowned in Buffalo Creek. I was one of the ones who found her. It was a sad day, very sad."

"Had she been swimming?" Jacob asked.

"No, I doubt it. We found her after the fact. She had all of her clothes on. We found her in the morning, so we thought she must've drowned the night before."

"I wonder what she was doing over that way," Jacob mused.

"There was a camp meeting in town here that day," George answered. "It set up on the flats near the point below First Street. That was open field, then. I remember hearing about the camp meeting on its way here weeks before it arrived. Folks were talkin' about the Reverend Isaac Longwell. He was a powerful preacher, saving souls and increasing his following as he went through the countryside.

"They got into town on a Saturday, I recall, and set up their tent. By Sunday morning's gathering, folks had showed up in pretty good numbers. Reverend Longwell gave a stirring sermon in the morning. He inspired all who listened to him and put the Holy Spirit in our hearts. Then there were prayers and hymn singing. Folks kept coming to the field all day. We took a long break in the middle of the day. By late afternoon when Reverend Longwell started his second sermon, the flats were jammed with people. The whole town was out.

"Well, the next day they were to have two more services, but early in the morning two boys who'd been fishing in the Buffalo came runnin' up to the crowd, yelling for someone to come and help. I ran back with them with Nathan Painter and Josiah McCue and a few others. We found her on the bank near the new canal. She was dead — drowned."

"You didn't find her in the water, then?" Parker could not stop himself from asking.

"No, she was just on shore in some high grass, but soaked completely through. She must've drifted onto shore soon after she died — not badly swollen, as I've seen in other drownings."

"But you were sure she'd drowned?" Parker asked.

"Well, there was some debate about that — her being out of the water and all. Doc Alter was there and he said it looked to him like her neck could be broken."

"There was a physician there?" Parker asked.

"David Alter? Sure was. Well, these days I guess he's more a chemist than a physician by practice, I suppose," George said. "Her neck did seam out of joint, but I couldn't see how it could've been broken, because it looked to me like she must've been calling for help. Her mouth had set open — her eyes, too. Poor thing — the crowd was making too much noise for anyone to hear her."

Parker saw Jacob betray a barely perceptible wince and downcast his eyes for just a moment. He realized that this line of conversation must be painful to Jacob, his own mother having drowned. Parker had heard all he needed to know about the girl's appearance. It was a description that was by now very familiar to him. He moved the topic past the description of the girl's body, "With so many people there, you'd think that someone would've seen her — a witness, I mean."

"No one came forward to say they saw anything," George said. "Some folks tried to say there was foul play, but mostly such talk was dismissed as rumor mongering."

Suddenly Mae Weaver erupted into a angry yell, "It was the Irish that done it!"

"Now, Mum, no one ever said or did anything to prove the Irish did it!" George yelled back. He turned back to Parker and Jacob in an almost apologetic tone. "Some folks tried to say that the Irish working on the canal here at the time killed the little girl. I guess when bad things happen there's a need for some to find someone to blame. For their part, the Irish brought suspicion on themselves, I suppose. They lived in two shanty camps on either side of the town, and they didn't always get along with the townspeople. They had no respect for others' property. If they wanted food for their supper or wood for their fire, they'd likely as not walk onto someone's farm and take it. If they were caught, they'd show no remorse. Instead they acted like they were entitled to it.

"And whenever they got paid they'd fill the three taverns that were in town. They were a raucous lot. I remember in 'twenty-eight the men from both camps got together on Saint Patrick's Day and made a long parade. They played music and marched all through town, ending up at the tavern at the end of the day, of course. I guess all Irish parades lead to a tavern," George chuckled as he finished.

"The damned Irish done it!" May Weaver yelled again, becoming increasingly angry.

"Now, Mum, settle down!" George yelled.

"Don't you 'settle' me!" she bellowed back. "It was the Irish that killed that girl! 'Citizens by choice,' my arse. Devils! Blackguards!" As she shouted the last word she let fly a corncob at George's head. It was apparently not altogether unexpected, and he ducked. But so quick was her release, and with such deadly accuracy did she send the projectile, that it still caught him full in the back of the head.

"Ouch! Mum, now you cut that out this instant!" George demanded, sounding as if he were the parent.

"The Irish killed that girl!" she shouted again. "That's what he wants to know! Ask him! Ask him why he's here!"

George Weaver now looked at Parker and Jacob, "I'm very sorry about this. Mum, well, she sometimes has these spells."

"Ask the Irishman what he wants!" Mae Weaver bellowed, then sent a corncob straight at Parker, hitting him on the side of the head. "Irishman! Blackguard!"

Jacob stood up, "I think we'd better be going, now, George."

Mae Weaver began cursing in a steady stream. All three men retreated down the porch steps amid a withering hail of corncobs and oaths. They regrouped at Jacob's horses, which were tethered off the corner of the porch in the front yard.

"Jacob, thank you for bringing my suit out here. It's a fine suit, indeed," George said. "I'll bring some venison into your shop next week. Sorry again about Mum, and all. She just gets excited at times."

"That's all right, George," Jacob answered. "You take care, now. I'll see you next week. Good night."

"Good night, sir. It was nice meeting you," Parker said.

"Good night, Mr. Parker," George said

Jacob and Parker mounted their horses and rode out to the double-rutted road. Riding side by side, they headed back into town.

"Thank you for doing this," Parker said after they had traveled a while. "I know some of that talk must've been hard for you to listen to."

"I was just a boy when my mother drowned, Mr. Parker," Jacob said. "It was a long time ago. Any holes in my life have been more than filled by my wife and my children."

By now the daylight was completely gone. Jacob looked up at the stars in the night sky. It looked to Parker as if he were counting them. Then a smile spread across Jacob's face. Parker had seen that smile before. It was the same look on Jacob's face as he put it down into baby Catherine's bassinet and stared at the sleeping infant. It was the same smile that he had when he handed out treats to his mobbing children, and when his wife teased him with feigned irritation that was actually thinly-disguised, deep affection.

"Yes, I see," Parker replied.

The two men continued riding under a sky full of stars, and returned to Jacob Shoop's home.

11

John Parker stood with Jacob Shoop at the canal basin in front of Freeport's Hope Woolen Mill. By Jacob's pocket watch, the eleven o'clock packet should be arriving any minute. Parker peered into the darkness past the lock along the canal's dark ribbon in the moonlight.

"I think I see it coming," he said as several figures emerged from the darkness on the towpath.

Jacob looked, "Yes, that's it all right."

Earlier, upon returning from the Weaver Farm, the two men had spent the rest of the evening at Jacob's house. They ate yet another dinner, this time surrounded by Jacob's children, who begged Parker to tell stories about "the big fire in Pittsburgh." Though he talked more than he was used to, he didn't mind doing so in the comfortable setting of Jacob's home. He tried to describe the ferocity of the fire and the valiant effort of all the men and women who fought it. The children sat wide-eyed as he recounted his wild ride through the burning streets with the box of gunpowder, and the collapse of the Monongahela House and Bridge. He didn't mention the looters, but did tell of his escape from the wharf by swimming out to the steamboat. It was long past their bedtime when Hannah Shoop finally stopped their endless questions and pried them away to go to bed. She said "good night" to Parker in a normal voice — apparently after hearing him talk for an extended time, she decided that he was not dim after all. Jacob went along upstairs to see them all to bed, and then returned downstairs to accompany Parker to the canal basin.

Now, as the boat came to a stop along the shore, Jacob turned to Parker, "Well, Mr. Parker, did you find what you were looking for here?"

"I found some answers, yes," Parker replied.

"I think you heard everything that you needed to hear and have decided exactly who you believe your murderer is," Jacob said. "I think you had halfway decided who it is before you ever got here."

"Jacob, are you a mind reader or am I just really bad at holding my thoughts to myself?" Parker asked.

Jacob laughed, "Well, let me answer that by giving you some advice, Mr. Parker. Never take up the game of poker."

Parker laughed too, "Thanks, Jacob." The two men shook hands. "Thank you for everything."

"You're welcome," Jacob said, "and good luck to you, *Constable* Parker."

Parker nodded and turned around toward the canal boat parked along the side of the basin. He stepped aboard and handed the captain his ticket. Then he turned around to see Jacob disappearing into the night toward his house. He stared after the departing figure. He envisioned Jacob walking into his home, with his wife embracing him and telling him that the children are asleep. What a warm, comfortable scene awaited him, thought Parker. Suddenly the blare of the captain's horn and the forward lurch of the boat brought Parker back from his reverie. Looking again, there was now only a dark, empty street where Jacob Shoop had been.

The weariness of his long day suddenly descended upon Parker. He resolved to get some rest, and went below into the cabin. In the dimness of a single lantern he saw the walls of the cabin lined with men sleeping on bunks. Each bed consisted of a single wooden plank affixed lengthwise along the wall via hinges. Ropes hanging from the wall just above each plank suspended its outer side. Each plank hung just about one foot above the next, leaving just a few inches of clearance between the top of the sleeping occupant and the next bunk above. Bunks lined the wall from nearly top to bottom. Parker thought the occupants looked more like merchandise sitting on store shelves than men.

Slipping past long tables and personal baggage, Parker found an empty bunk and climbed up into it. Getting up to it was not as hard as trying to lie down on the plank's narrow surface. Finally he managed to situate himself on his side with his back leaning against the wall. Fear of falling forward prevented his perch from being very relaxing while awake, and so he hoped that he would fall asleep from sheer exhaustion in order to get some rest.

He reflected on the events of the past several days. Jacob Shoop had been correct again. Parker started to view Kevin Milligan with suspicion even before he left Pittsburgh. Kevin Milligan, who lied about his actions during the fire. Kevin Milligan, who lied about his whereabouts after the fire. Kevin Milligan, who worked on crews digging the Pennsylvania Main Line Canal from the Conemaugh River to Pittsburgh — a stretch that included the town of Freeport.

Parker dozed. Scenes of work crews crept into his vision. Laborers hefted picks high into the air and brought them down with mighty swings. He heard the thuds of picks slamming into the earth and the clangs of picks striking rock. He heard the *slooshing* sound of shovels sliding into gravelly dirt and the shovel load of dirt hitting the ground after the worker heaved it out of the ditch. The afternoon sun bore down on the men, soaking their clothes with sweat. The work went on endlessly and Parker became tired even in his sleep. A horn sounded in the distance and the men stopped working and laid down their tools. But the horn was not that of a work crew boss, but rather of a canal boat captain approaching a lock. The sudden bump and scrape of the boat along the lock's stone wall woke Parker. He had no idea how long he had been asleep, but did not want to return to the exhausting dream. He climbed down from his bunk and went up on deck.

Parker stepped out of the cabin and started up the stairs to the deck. The locktender hung his lantern from a pole above the lock wall, giving just enough light for all hands to perform their tasks. The captain stood near the front of the boat while the boatmen worked their ropes. Parker just started walking along the cabin toward the captain when suddenly several shadows detached themselves from the darkness beyond the lantern and spread out along the lock wall. One figure ran to where the locktender and boatmen secured the line to the snubbing post. The figure swung a long club around, hitting the locktender who fell backward to the ground with a short scream. The intruder then menaced the boatman with the club, driving him farther away from the boat. Three men jumped aboard the boat. One of them knocked a boatman to the deck with another long club. The other two intruders simply walked up to the captain, where one leveled a long rifle at his chest.

"Right. Now, here's the thing," the intruder with the rifle, apparently the leader, said to the captain, "my friend here is going below and gather up some handbags and wallets and such. You'll die right here if you move." He then nodded to one of his men, who started toward the cabin.

Parker ducked back along the cabin wall. He climbed down into the shadows of the stairwell and drew his nightstick. As the highwayman descended the stairs, Parker sprang up and slammed his nightstick into the man's lower jaw with a forehand strike. The force of the blow sent the robber backward and he landed in a sitting position on the steps. With a backhand swing Parker clubbed the intruder full in the forehead, knocking him senseless. Parker then crept low along the cabin wall toward the leader, whose long rifle still pointed at the captain. When he progressed as close to the leader as he could go undetected, Parker stood straight up without saying a word. The rifleman, surprised at a stranger suddenly appearing beside him, swung the rifle around toward Parker. In an instant Parker's nightstick came up and knocked the rifle barrel aloft as it discharged into the night sky. In the same motion Parker brought his nightstick around and jammed it straight up into the rifleman's stomach, just below his ribs. The brigand might have slowly fell forward on his face if the captain at that time had not joined the fray, delivering a blow that knocked the leader backward onto the deck.

The third thief on board bounded over the prostrate leader with his club held high and swung it down on Parker. In a flash Parker blocked the blow holding his nightstick above his head with both hands. He drove the attacker's club sideways, then whirled around and drove his nightstick into the man's ribs with a backhand swing. The blow sent the intruder staggering backward. Parker instantly stepped forward and delivered a swift and crushing forehand blow to his head, sending the man reeling against the lock wall, where he collapsed onto the deck.

The boatman on the lock, seeing the captain no longer in danger, lunged at the highwayman who'd been holding him at club's length. The robber quickly left the boatman holding only the long club, as he disappeared into the darkness. The fourth highwayman recovered from Parker's assault enough to stagger up from the cabin stairwell and jump across the lock into the night. The mule driver, who had already taken the team up to the far end of the lock, returned upon hearing the rifle's report.

"What happened?" the driver called from above.

"A band of highwaymen got the drop on us," the captain growled, "or at least they thought they did." He turned and looked at Parker, "We're indebted to you, sir." Even though the bandits had been thwarted, the captain remained grim faced. He looked at Parker thoughtfully, almost suspiciously.

The boatman on shore helped the locktender to his feet and they both stepped aboard. "What do you want to do with these two?" the captain asked the locktender.

"I've got plenty of rope to hold them until I can get the area constable here in the morning," the locktender replied. "By God I'll not let them roam free to attack me again!" He brought several lengths of rope aboard and the canallers secured the two thieves. They dragged the men ashore and locked them in a shed beside the locktender's house.

The crew resumed locking through. Several male passengers came up on deck to see what all the noise and commotion was about. The captain assured them that all was well and bade them return below to resume their night's sleep.

After all had settled down and the boat exited the lock, Parker, no longer sleepy, remained on deck. He walked toward the front, where a few chairs sat, and chose one at the very bow of the boat. He sat staring into the darkness for only a minute when he suddenly felt the presence of another person nearby. The captain stood beside him. He pulled up a chair beside Parker.

"I'm Captain Thomas Bingham," he said.

"John Parker."

"That was quick work you made of those brigands, Mr. Parker — quick work indeed," Captain Bingham said in a quiet and serious tone.

"I just did what was needed," Parker said.

"Yes, what was needed," the captain repeated, staring at Parker.

"Is there something wrong, Captain Bingham?" Parker asked him.

"I've seen men use clubs before, Mr. Parker," he started, "but the way you wield that nightstick — I've never seen anything like it before. You move quicker than the eye can follow." His words were not just a statement, but also a question: *Mr. Parker, why is it that you carry a nightstick and just how is it that you are so proficient with it?* Parker finally understood the captain's reserve. He had trained himself to use his weapon skillfully years ago when he first became a constable. His display tonight might have impressed onlookers in the city, but knowing who he was, they would not have thought any more about it. This captain, however, needed to know exactly who was on his ship.

"I'm a constable from Pittsburgh," Parker said.

"I see," Captain Bingham replied, relaxing. "That explains much. I meant no harm, Constable, but I can never stop looking out for the safety of my passengers and crew."

"No harm done," Parker said.

"I suspect, Constable Parker, that the citizens in your district are quite safe from brigands and bandits."

"There aren't many citizens in my district right now," Parker said.

Captain Bingham looked at him quizzically for a second. "Ah yes, *the fire*," he said at last. "I have not been to the city since it happened. Today will be my first view of it. Well, I'd best get back to my duties, Constable. We're about two hours out of Pittsburgh. You have some time to salvage some sleep on the trip, if you like."

As Captain Bingham departed, Parker looked forward over bow of the boat. Sparkles of light reflected off of the water from the stars in the last hour of nighttime. In the darkness he closed his eyes and listened to the water gently lapping at the bow. It made an easy, comforting sound that had the potential to lull him to sleep. Each time he dozed, however, the sound of the picks and shovels started again, and he started digging and hefting dirt out of a deep ditch. He'd wake himself to end the toil, feeling exhausted from the very sleep that he needed to give him rest. Then he'd stare at the sparkling surface of the water and the process started all over again.

The sky over the hills on the opposite shore began to lighten. The bright blue pushed the darkness across the river and over the western hills, and a cloudless morning filled the Allegheny Valley. Parker marveled at how the trees seemed greener than they had just one day before.

Soon the forests gave way to the communities just upstream of Pittsburgh. As the river and canal curved westward, Bayardstown came into view on the opposite shore. The city was awake and hard at work. The Fort Pitt Foundry belched smoke, as did the Fifth Ward's other factories — glassworks, tanneries, paper mills, soap, tobacco, and breweries. The din of their operation traveled across the valley and ended Parker's peaceful excursion. As the canal boat entered Allegheny City he looked across the river at Pittsburgh in full view, already bustling at full speed at daybreak. He felt his own pulse seemed to speed up to match its pace, like an oarsman quickening his paddle when entering a set of rapids. The life of the city flowed in him once again. John Parker was home.

12

It was past seven-thirty by the time Parker walked up the steps inside the Watchhouse. The attempted robbery at the lock delayed the canal boat's arrival in Pittsburgh, making him over one half-hour late reporting for duty. No one sat in the meeting area on the constables' floor as he entered, but High Constable Butler's door stood ajar, meaning that he was still there. Parker gave two small raps on the door, then stepped inside.

High Constable Butler looked up from his desk. Upon seeing Parker, he blinked his eyes slowly with raised eyebrows, indicating that he did not expect to have to ask the question.

"I was traveling on the canal," Parker explained, "The boat coming back got — delayed."

"The canal? Where did you go?" Butler asked.

"Freeport," Parker said.

High Constable Butler's countenance dropped as if he'd just lost an argument. "So you went after all," he said. "Did you get your answers?"

"Actually, I did," Parker replied.

"Tell me."

"A little girl was killed there in 'twenty-eight. It sounds very similar to Grace Milligan — most figured that she drowned, others suspected otherwise."

"So a child drowns in a river town," Butler said. "Do you realize how common that is?"

"She drowned in a creek," Parker said.

"That creek is wide and deep at its mouth — almost a river itself," Butler pointed out. "I've been there. Remember, I'm an ex-riverman. Still, it's unfortunately too common an occurrence for us to use to start an investigation. Besides, the two deaths are seventeen years apart. There's nothing to connect them."

"Kevin Milligan," Parker said.

"What?"

"Grace Milligan's father. He lied to me about his whereabouts during the fire. He said he was at the factory. He wasn't. Kevin Milligan also worked on the canal when it was being dug. He worked on the Western Division, which meant he could've been in Freeport in 'twenty-eight."

117

"*Could've* been," Butler repeated. "That doesn't mean he *was*. We have lots of people living in this city who worked on the canal, John. You can go over to Bayardstown and talk to *hundreds* of Irishmen who dug the canal. That doesn't mean that they were at Freeport. Have you asked him if he was there? And even if he was, that doesn't mean that he killed someone."

"It would mean that he is a connection," Parker said, "and 'no,' I haven't asked him. But as soon as I find him, I will. He seems to be hard to get hold of these days."

"John, I think you've made something out of nothing. And now you're stretching it beyond all reason. I want you on your beat today. I want you to take care of the people who are really here and really need you. Do you understand me, John?"

"Yes, sir, I do," Parker said. "Were there any updates this morning?"

"They found Samuel Kingston's body yesterday," Butler said. "His sons found him while clearing the rubble from his house. Everyone's certain that it's him — witnesses saw him go back into his house on Thursday and never come out. They'll bury him today."

"Anything else?" Parker asked.

"No." Butler replied. "There's no word yet on the Councils hiring help to knock down walls. You still have to watch out for them and warn others to do the same."

Parker gave a short nod of understanding, then exited the office. Leaving the Watchhouse, he walked once again into the Burnt District. All morning he stayed on his beat, as Butler had ordered. Recovery activity seemed more widespread than before, as workers and residents toiled in more sections of the Burnt District. Many burned-out buildings remained untouched, however. Most of these had been abandoned buildings before the fire.

At noon Parker went home to eat lunch. Jenny worked at her stove as he walked in the kitchen.

"Well, he's here today," Jenny announced to no one. "I did not know whether or not to make lunch for you today, after your being missing for an entire day, and all."

"I had to travel yesterday, ma'am," Parker explained. "I told you on Sunday that I wouldn't be around. And you weren't at home to tell 'good bye' to when I left."

"Yes but you didn't say you were taking a trip for the entire day. You must have planned it for some time. You could've told me your whole plan at any time in the last couple of days," she said.

"I guess I wasn't completely sure I was going until Sunday," Parker said.

Jenny set a plate for herself and Parker, then sat down to eat. "So where did you go?"

"Freeport."

"What's in Freeport?"

"An unnervingly perceptive businessman with a large and wonderful family. And a farmer who remembered a little girl who died long ago."

"Died how?"

"Most believed that she drowned. Some felt the circumstances were, well, suspicious."

"I see," Jenny said. "Did this trip have anything to do with Grace Milligan?"

"It had everything to do with Grace Milligan."

"This girl from Freeport and Grace — they both seemed to die from accidents but you're not quite certain that they *were* accidents?"

"Yes."

"Just like Ruthie Bowden?"

Parker looked up from eating. "Yes," he said quietly. He and Jenny had become very close in the last five years. There were many nights during that time that she sat up with him after his nightmares, talking to him and keeping him company. Mostly they avoided the topic of death during those conversations. One night, however, he told her the whole story of Ruthie.

Jenny shook her head, "John, what am I going to do with you? Y'know, for a man who says that he doesn't believe in ghosts, you sure have enough of them following you around."

Parker bowed his head slightly with downcast eyes.

"Oh, John!" Jenny said suddenly and grasped his hand, "I didn't mean …"

"I know," Parker said. "I know you didn't."

Just then they heard a rap at Jenny's front door. She left to answer it while Parker finished his lunch. He heard Jenny speaking in a loud, welcoming voice inviting someone inside. The voices came closer to the kitchen, and soon Jenny stood in front of Parker with a family of a man, a woman, and one boy.

"John, I want you to meet the McKees: Harold, Muriel, and this is Harry Junior."

Parker stood up, "Pleased to meet you." He shook hands with Harold and nodded to Muriel and Harry.

"The McKees will be staying with us for a while. They lost their home in the fire. Reverend Stuhl announced at service on Sunday the names of several parishioner families who needed temporary homes. I volunteered the extra room upstairs."

"I just wish you'd let me pay you," Harold McKee said. "The fire took my job, too. But I should be able to get back on my feet, with all the rebuilding going on."

"There'll be no talk of paying me," Jenny said. Then she put one hand on Parker's shoulder a smiled a demonstrably over-sweet smile, "That's what I have *Mr. Parker* here for!" Parker gave a broad smile that matched hers. Jenny chuckled, and Mr. and Mrs. McKee let out small, nervous laughs. It struck Parker that the McKees had little to laugh about in the last several days, and they seemed uncomfortable doing so. But soon everyone noticed that little Harry's eyes could not tear away from Parker's finished plate of food.

"Oh, you all must be hungry!" Jenny said. "And just in time for lunch. Please sit down. We can get you settled in after we eat."

"Please excuse me," Parker said. "I've finished and have to get back to my rounds."

Parker put his coat on and exited through the front door. He crossed the street and headed toward the Burnt District. At a side street he heard a loud commotion and turned down the street to investigate. Crowd noises came from a tiny alley around the corner. As he came nearer, he recognized the sound of children yelling. As he turned the corner, a group of a dozen or so boys stood in a rough circle around two boys fighting in the middle. The spectators yelled to egg the combatants on. By the time Parker reached the mob, one boy attained the upper hand and sat on the other's chest, pummeling him. One of the spectators spotted Parker and yelled the alarm. Immediately the crowd scattered, except for the two boys fighting on the ground.

The boy on top had lost any sense of what was going on around him, so intent was he on defeating his foe. Parker hesitated for a second before pulling him off of the other boy. Something about him seemed familiar. He was dressed like most of the boys dressed: boots, knickers held up by suspenders, and a work shirt. He wore a cap, as many of the boys did, but rather than lying flat, his cap was puffed up, as if over-stuffed with … long hair. Parker reached down and pulled the child up to a standing position.

"Hello, Gretchen!" Parker said to the young girl as he held her up by the collar. "What are you doing way over here?" The girl was startled for a moment, but still full of fight.

"Teaching him not to call me names!" she said, and lunged for the boy on the ground. Parker held her fast. The boy scampered away on his knees, then stood up and bolted.

"Whoa!" Parker said. "I've got you now. What was it about this time?"

Gretchen Anderson pursed her lips taught in a scowl. Parker had seen that scowl before, and this was not the first time he pulled her off of a boy who had made the mistake of teasing her. She lived in the Second Ward, and Parker had known her since she was a small child. Absolutely a tomboy, he'd never seen her in a dress. Soon after she got old enough to attend public school the fights started. Boys who made the mistake of teasing "the girl who wore boys' clothes" soon realized their mistake. The teasing at the Second Ward's public school had stopped some time ago, as the boys wanted very much to avoid the humiliation of getting beaten up by a girl.

"I have to go to school over here since ours burned down," she said. "*He's* been calling me names since I started."

"What was he calling you?" Parker asked.

"Well, he called me different things. But today, the teacher was talking about a man from literature, Bay Wolf."

"Beowulf."

"Yeah, Bay Wolf. Anyway, Bay Wolf killed this monster named Grendel — yanked his arm right off." As she said this she made the motion of a violent pull with both hands. "Then he had to kill the monster's mom, who was a witch. And ever since the teacher told us that story, little Mr. Rufus Moore has been calling me 'Grendel.' I told him to stop it, or I'd make him sorry. He thought that was funny."

"I don't believe he thinks it's funny now," Parker said.

"Nope!" Gretchen agreed, as she punched a fist into the air in front of her. From what little Parker could see through the perpetual dirt on her face, Gretchen Anderson was a pretty child. He had never actually seen her hair, but from the dirty wisps that sneaked from under her cap, he guessed that it was blonde. And there must be a lot of it, judging by the way her cap bulged. They walked out of the alley as they spoke.

"Where are you going now?" Parker asked her.

"We're staying with my aunt and uncle on High Street, over past the courthouse."

"Do you think you can make it there without getting into any more fights?"

"As long as boys leave me alone, I can!"

Parker laughed, "Please try. Get going, now."

"Good-bye, Constable John," she called as she walked away toward the courthouse.

Parker watched her for a moment, then turned and headed again to his beat. When he started, he fully intended to go back to the Second Ward. But his feet took him through it almost directly to the Third Presbyterian Church. He found himself standing outside the church's front door. He hesitated for a moment, then went inside.

Downstairs, the basement was crowded and close as before. Parker walked directly to the area where he found Addie Milligan the last time that he was there. He saw her sitting alone on the edge of her bed. Kevin Milligan was not there. As Parker approached, Gladys Dilworth saw him coming and moved in front of him to block his progress.

"What do you want?" Mrs. Dilworth demanded.

"I wanted to talk to Kevin Milligan."

"He ain't here. He's gone."

"Well, then, I need to ask Mrs. Milligan where he is."

"I told you he's gone. He brought Addie back Sunday after the funeral. Then he went out and never came back. No one's seen him since. He left poor Addie there in her grief all by herself. She's barely holding on as it is, and now this. He's a worthless scoundrel, if you ask me!"

Parker looked past her toward Addie Milligan. "Now you leave her alone," Mrs. Dilworth said. "She'll be no use to you and you'll only send her into a fit. I've told you everything you need to know." He looked at Addie again. She sat unmoving with her back to him. Her head was bowed. He realized that Gladys Dilworth was right. "All right," he said and turned and walked out of the basement.

Outside, Parker started back toward his beat. Kevin Milligan's complete disappearance did not surprise him. Now the search was on. But where? Then he thought about his meeting this morning with High Constable Abraham Butler. Suddenly, something Butler said came to him. *You can go over to Bayardstown and talk to* hundreds *of Irishmen who dug the canal.* Parker stopped in his tracks for a moment. Yes, yes indeed he could.

13

At the Sunday noontime meal little Harry McKee wolfed down all of the food on his plate. He had gained color and maybe even a pound or two in the six days since his family moved into the extra room at the Wright House. Jenny insisted that he fill his plate again, but he declined with a polite, "No thank you, ma'am. I'm full up."

Previously, breakfast and lunch included Jenny, James Higby, and Parker, or any two of the three, eating at the kitchen table. But since the McKees arrived, the larger group ate all meals in the dining room. After meals, Muriel McKee always insisted on helping to clear the table. She was very grateful to Jenny, and helped out in every way that a woman might dare in another woman's house.

Harold Senior found work as a carpenter rebuilding businesses in the Burnt District. When he was at the Wright House, however, he never allowed Jenny to carry a bucket of water from the well outside. On Friday when he tried to give her some of his wages for the week, Jenny told him to save his money to build his family a new house.

It was Sunday, April 20 — a week and a half after the fire that destroyed the McKees' home along with one-third of the city. Parker sat preoccupied through the meal. Jenny and James were so used to this condition that they might not have noticed it on any day, but today the McKees helped them fill the meal with conversation, which doubly covered Parker's silence. He excused himself and walked through the kitchen toward the back door.

"Are you going back on duty without your coat, John?" Jenny asked him as he passed her at the stove.

Parker put his index finger to his lips, "Shhhh. I'm going under cover," he whispered loudly with mock gravity. "Secret duty."

"Oh, go on," Jenny shooed him out the door.

Parker had replied as if joking, but going incognito was exactly what he intended. He needed to find Kevin Milligan and, following High Constable Abraham Butler's unintended advice, he would start searching in Bayardstown, where a large community of Irish immigrants lived. If Milligan sought refuge among his countrymen, they might not give him over to the police. So Parker could not go in uniform, or even ask Constable Cameron, who patrolled the Fifth Ward, for assistance. His coat and nightstick remained in his room upstairs as he exited the kitchen and left through the back yard.

Parker walked the streets that took him along the Allegheny River in the upstream direction, taking the same route he did the morning he went to see Sam Reppert at the canal aqueduct the week before. But this time, when he reached the canal, he crossed over it on Liberty Street's bridge and entered Bayardstown.

When Parker was a young boy this area along the Allegheny River bordering the city was known as the Northern Liberties. After it became a borough its official name changed to Bayardstown, after its founder. Even then, like most towns adjacent to the city, upon leaving Pittsburgh and entering Bayardstown one could see no difference between the two. The bustle of ironworks, glassworks, factories and breweries were equal in both areas. The only difference that Parker knew of in their composition was Bayardstown's slaughterhouses and tanneries. The city had kicked the slaughterhouses out of its limits many years before, and they moved out to the Northern Liberties. When Pittsburgh annexed the area in 1837 and made it the Fifth Ward, the city gained back the abattoirs it had once expelled.

He continued down Liberty Street for several blocks, all of which mixed factories with the residences of the people who worked in them. Having passed almost halfway through the area, Parker stopped at an intersection. Looking to his right down a cross street toward the rise of Quarry Hill, he saw people out on the streets at the next block. He walked down this street toward them. At an intersection just before the hill started its ascent, small groups of people loitered on the sidewalks and in the middle of the street.

Stopping for a moment, Parker noticed that they weren't loitering at all. Rather, they started assembling into one substantial crowd at the intersection. Pairs of men carried wide wooden planks through the crowd into its center. The men laid the planks down beside each other until they formed a large square in the middle of the intersection. Parker walked into the fringe of the crowd, which by now made a rough circle around the wooden floor. Two men up front produced a fiddle and a fife, and soon lively music filled the air. Suddenly a man and a woman broke through the crowd, hopped up onto the wooden floor, and began dancing. Side by side, the couple danced a jig with their hands on their hips, lifting their knees high up into their waists. They smiled broadly at each other as they danced. Very quickly as they fell into the rhythm of the music their movements became looser and freer, and they added slight improvisations to their step.

The people in the ring around the dance floor clapped in time with the music. Some sang the words to the songs, others whooped at the dancers and

THE BURNT DISTRICT

cheered them on. More couples joined the dancers on the floor. The entire crowd, whether dancing or clapping, moved with the music. Laughter erupted constantly and filled the spaces between the music, singing, and calling. The assembled individuals transformed into one body of merriment. Even Parker felt the pull to be swept up in it.

Suddenly a jug was thrust into his chest. The strong odor of whiskey stung his nose. Parker had never drunk whiskey before, but knew its smell well from the drunks he'd hauled to the Mayor's Court over the years. He raised the jug to his lips and took a small swig. Not expecting the burn that hit the back of his throat, Parker gagged and nearly doubled over coughing. The man who'd handed him the jug reared his head back, laughing.

"I can see that you're no Son of St. Patrick," he yelled between guffaws. "If you want to wet your whistle at this party, maybe you'd best join the boys at the table and have some of their German brew. It doesn't have the bite of whiskey, mind you, but it'll set you alight once you've had a few!"

As he laughed, the man pointed behind them where several men had set up a table and placed on it a wooden barrel with a spout. Revelers from the ring walked to the barrel, filled their mugs with beer, and returned to the crowd. But a group of men lingered at the barrel, conversing as they enjoyed the music at a distance. Parker judged that in that group he was more likely to engage someone in a conversation. He joined them.

A man stood at the tap, dispensing beer for everyone. He handed Parker a filled mug.

"Thank you," Parker said.

"Hello," greeted another man standing next to the barrel. "Can't say that I've seen you in our neighborhood before." He extended his hand. "Daniel Fitzgerald."

"John Parker," Parker said as he shook Daniel Fitzgerald's hand. "I'm just visiting. I didn't know about this party. I was just walking and wandered into it. I hope I'm not intruding."

"Intruding?" laughed Mr. Fitzgerald. "This is an Irish cross-roads dance, my friend. There's no *intruding*. There's only dancing and music and laughing. And," he held his mug up in front of his face, "libations. Copious libations!" He lifted the mug to his lips and took a long drink. Parker took a drink from his own mug. The beer felt cellar cool, unlike than the burn of whiskey, as it washed down his throat.

Daniel Fitzgerald looked to Parker to be about sixty years old. Portly, as one who's led a successful life, he was dressed more formally than most of the men at the gathering. The others wore simple clothes and work outfits. The ladies' dresses were plain. But Mr. Fitzgerald wore a fine suit with a vest. His pocket watch chain curved up into his vest pocket. His stovepipe hat shined of newness, unlike the dingy dullness of the cloth caps worn by most men in the crowd. His speech hinted at just the slightest Irish accent, while the others around spoke with a thick Irish brogue.

"You'll find us to be a welcoming lot, Mr. Parker. It's America and its freedom that allows us to be so."

"Have you been in the United States long?" Parker asked.

"Been here long?" Daniel Fitzgerald laughed. "My friend, my family has been in America for over one hundred years. My grandfather, also Daniel, was one of the Wild Geese who flew from Ireland and William's reign to France. It was he who later made the journey across the ocean to these shores and a promise of a new life. My father, Robert Fitzgerald, served under General George Stanwix in the French and Indian War. He later joined the Pennsylvania Line, one of the most celebrated rifle regiments in the War for Independence."

The names he spoke aloud gained the attention of a few of the men standing near the table. They moved closer to join the conversation.

"I didn't realize ..." Parker started.

"That the Irish have been here so long?" Daniel Fitzgerald finished Parker's sentence. "Many Irish have been here for generations, my friend. We are indistinguishable from any other descendents of colonists.

"My friends here who arrived more recently, now, they're another story." Daniel Fitzgerald swept an open hand along the small crowd of men now gathered around him, as one who is introducing someone else. "The 'first generationers' who've come since the 'twenties and thereabouts, they're who you're thinking of. My grandfather's generation came as a result of warfare and oppression, but these lads before you have come simply seeking jobs and opportunity. Isn't that right, boys?"

"I had to leave," one man spoke up. "There was nothing for me back home. Everywhere you went there was more people than there was work. A 'population explosion' they called it then."

"When we got here there was work, all right," chimed in another, "the worst and hardest jobs available, but jobs just the same. We've broken our backs digging canals and gone blind mining coal. We've taken the lowest jobs in the mills and on the steamer lines. Lots of people look down their noses at us because of it, but I'll tell you, this country is being built up by Irishmen who put their backs into it!"

A round of agreements and lifted mugs followed the last statement.

"A friend of mine worked on the Pennsylvania Canal," Parker said. "He told me that it was very hard work."

"Hard?" one of the crowd said. "Why, you've never done harder work in all your born days! Diggin' and haulin' dirt and stones out of the ditch, cuttin' down trees and diggin' out their roots, hauling stones for the culverts. We started at daybreak every day and worked 'till nighttime when it was too dark to see. We worked in all weather. And we got paid a pittance for it — fifty cents a day from the contractors for the hardest work any man could bear."

"And they'd try to pay us even less, if they could get away with it," another man said as his comrades shook their heads affirmatively.

"Contractors posted bills over in Ireland promising everything to men who would go to America to work on the canal," said another. "Then after we got here, they gave us nothing. They made work crews travel all across the state to dig the damned ditch, and left us to build our own shanties in work camps if we wanted shelter over our heads to sleep in wherever we was workin'. They didn't allow us to build anything more than shacks. Most of the time we were out in the middle of the wilderness. Heaven help the man who got sick and needed some doctorin'. And food — they provided only the barest provisions, or nothing at all."

"We had to fend for ourselves," the first man said. "We caught what we could eat from the land. If there was a farm about, then, well, we had to take what we needed — whether it be livestock or fruits or wood for our fire."

"The contractors left us no choice but to steal like that," the second man said. "The locals hated us, but what were we to do? We were desperate — lots of times we were starvin'."

"A contractor paid my passage across the ocean," said one man. "When I arrived I was indentured to him. It took me two years of work to pay off my debt."

"And mine as well," said another man, "but I worked off that dead horse and I'm a free man today."

Another round of affirmations arose from the crowd, then all drank in unison as if a toast had been offered. Parker noticed out of the corner of his eye an old, small man at the fringe of the group. The little man eyed Parker suspiciously, then spoke in quiet tones to the man next to him. The second man looked at Parker, and his expression changed from friendliness to wariness.

"What's your friend's name?" Daniel Fitzgerald asked Parker.

"What?" Parker said.

"Your friend," Daniel said, "the one that worked on the canal. What is his name?"

"Oh, yes," Parker said, "Milligan. Kevin Milligan. Do you know him?"

"That's not a name with which I'm familiar," Daniel said. "Any of you boys know a Kevin Milligan?"

The men shook their heads negatively. As the conversation continued, the little man worked his way through the group, whispering to each man in turn. Sometimes he put his mug up beside his mouth as he talked, make the conversation private, and each listener stooped to hear his words. Parker noticed that the little man's other hand stayed at his side. It was small and deformed, with gnarled fingers that never moved. Parker tried to see what the little man was up to while listening to Daniel Fitzgerald.

"He's not from our neighborhood, then," Daniel said. "Where does he live?"

"He lives over in my ward, the Second Ward," Parker answered. As soon as the words left his mouth, he realized he'd just slipped mightily. Daniel Fitzgerald was unaware of Parker's mistake.

"Oh, you're from the Second Ward? That's where the great fire was. You're homeless then, I suppose," Daniel said.

"Um, yes," Parker stammered, "at the moment." *How could I have blundered like that?* he wondered.

"Your mug's empty," Daniel Fitzgerald observed. "It won't do to have an empty mug at a party like this. Please help yourself." He opened his hand toward the barrel. "Go on, then, don't be shy."

Parker parted through the group, which had become smaller in the last few minutes, and walked over to the barrel. As he opened the spigot and filled his mug, it occurred to him that another mug of beer was not what he needed right now. One mug had been enough to cause him to slip up. Since no one seemed to know Kevin Milligan, or at least they were not going to let on that they knew him, he need not stay any longer. He would find a way to exit the party.

"Well I shouldn't …" Parker turned back toward the group of men. They were gone. He turned and looked at the crowd around the dancers. Everyone on his side of the ring had their backs to him. He did not see the little man with the gnarled hand, nor any of the men who, one minute ago, stood in the small group by the barrel. He did not even see Daniel Fitzgerald's shiny silk hat. The music and singing and clapping and calling still went on, but now it felt quite separated from him. No one came to the barrel to get a beer. Parker stood for a moment alone, watching the crowd. Then he set his mug on the table and walked quietly down the street the way he came.

Parker crossed the canal bridge out of Bayardstown. He stopped at home to retrieve his overcoat and nightstick, then proceeded to the Burnt District. Although no one worked in the area today, he could see that the rebuilding

THE BURNT DISTRICT

of a few structures had commenced.

Eventually he found himself again at the burned-out house in the alley off of Try Street where they had found Grace Milligan. Over the past two weeks Parker kept returning to this spot, even though there seemed nothing left here for him to find. While much clearing and some construction had occurred in the Burnt District in the past two weeks, many structures remained untouched. This was one of them. He stared into the foundation. Rain had washed the ashes off of the burned timbers and a pool of murky water sat at the bottom.

The sun left the afternoon sky and the wind rose steadily, whipping the bottom of Parker's overcoat around. Behind him, a bank of heavy gray clouds approached. Ahead, lighter clouds lay in different colored and textured layers. Breaks in the sky above illuminated one layer, making it look like a vast plain in a white and gray landscape, with the sun shining on white hills in the distance. Every shade between bright white and dark gray appeared as a layer in this landscape, giving it a depth that made Parker feel he could walk across it like some mist-covered plain before a mountain range. Here and there above this plain, single dark gray clouds hung suspended, as if heralding the coming storm. Steadily, the mass of dark clouds advanced from behind him and pushed the landscape away. Rain began to fall in large, soaking drops.

Just then Henry Watts, supervisor from the Dallas Iron Mill to whom Parker had spoken to previously, rode by driving a team pulling a wagon. "Constable! You're just the man I'm lookin' for," he called. Parker turned toward him.

"Are you still lookin' for Kevin Milligan?" Mr. Watts asked.

"Yes, I am," Parker replied.

"I just saw him a few minutes ago — at least it looked a lot like him. I was just coming down Watson's Road. I saw a guy cross and go into the canal tunnel. I says to myself 'That looked just like Kevin Milligan!'"

"He went into the tunnel?" Parker asked.

"Yeah, I watched him. Looked like he was carryin' a little sack or something."

"Thanks very much, Mr. Watts," Parker said as he hurried off toward the tunnel. He walked quickly to the canal ditch, then trotted along the towpath. This section of the canal traveled between Boyd's and Grant's hills, then into the tunnel through Grant's Hill. The rain started falling harder as Parker crossed Watson's Road and entered the tunnel's arched portal.

Groundwater seeped through the tunnel's round, brick-lined wall and dripped into the canal below. Light poles rose intermittently along the wall.

Cross arms extended from the tops of the poles and held gaslight fixtures over the towpath. Because of the tunnel's disuse, the Watch stopped lighting these lamps long before the fire put the Gas Works out of service. Parker slowed, proceeding more warily through the darkening tunnel.

Up ahead, just before the darkness completely concealed everything, Parker could make out a figure that looked like a man. The figure moved strangely, as if it was no longer moving away but turning slowly. It was a slow, smooth swaying motion. Parker peered into the darkness as hard as he could. The man was ... swinging!

Parker bolted forward, calling out as he ran. Kevin Milligan hung by his neck on a rope tied to the arm of a gaslight pole. His feet were only a few inches from the ground. Milligan continued to turn as Parker reached him. Parker grabbed him full around the thighs and tried to lift him high enough to take his weight off of his neck. He felt a hard object against his shoulder at Milligan's belt. Moving furiously, with one arm trying to support the body, he moved his other hand up under Milligan's coat and found, as he had hoped, that it was a long knife in a sheath. Parker continued to yell Milligan's name as he worked. He took the knife out, reached up, and sawed at the rope behind Milligan's head. It was difficult to reach, and he had to relax his hold on Milligan's body to cut the rope. At last it broke free and both men tumbled onto the ground.

Parker rolled Milligan onto his back and yelled his name repeatedly. Slowly, Milligan's eyes opened. He moved his lips but no sound came out. Then he closed his eyes again as he wheezed, desperately fighting to breathe.

"Milligan! Kevin!" Parker yelled again. "Milligan, look at me!" Milligan's eyes opened again. "Milligan, did you kill Grace? Did you kill your daughter?"

Kevin Milligan's eyes widened just a bit. Then his face twisted as if he would cry. His lips moved again. This time, with great effort, he was able to utter a sound. "Anfaler," he said.

"What?" yelled Parker. "What did you say?" He put his face closer to Milligan's.

"Anfaler," Milligan said again, and a sickening gasp of air came out with the word. His eyes closed again and his features sank. His whole body shuddered. He went taught for just a second, then gasped again as he went limp. His wheezing stopped and he moved no more.

Parker yelled his name one more time, but received no response. He looked toward the tunnel's entrance in the distance, now dim from the rain outside. He started to yell for help, but quickly stopped. There would be few people out in the storm, he realized. He looked back at Milligan — it was too late for help, anyway. Kevin Milligan was dead. Parker sat back and cradled his face in his hands between his knees. There was no sound inside the tunnel except the drip, drip of water from the ceiling into the ditch. He stared into the darkness of the tunnel. *What am I going to do now?* he thought, *What on earth am I going to do now?*

14

It was well past dark when Parker finished reporting to High Constable Abraham Butler. By the time he had left the canal tunnel earlier that day, the only help he needed was a dray to haul out Kevin Milligan's body. They took Milligan to Coroner Eichbaum. Bodies were taken to the coroner for one of two reasons: either no known next-of-kin existed, or the death was brought about by unnatural causes. Suicide by hanging constituted an unnatural cause.

Why had he done it? Butler believed that Milligan simply succumbed to the trauma of loosing his daughter, house, and job all at the same time. And he pointed out that if Parker's suspicions about Milligan's involvement in his daughter's death were correct, then the guilt of such a monstrous act could drive him to suicide.

Parker wasn't sure. The latter theory certainly made sense, but it didn't feel exactly on target. When he asked the dying Kevin Milligan if he killed his daughter, the look on the man's face did not register a confession of guilt. It was more like ... heartbreak. There seemed responsibility in that look, but for murder? No. It wasn't there. And what did *Anfaler* mean?

It had been a very bad day. Kevin Milligan's death was a hard blow. Was he back to the beginning now, with no leads or ideas? Parker wandered through the dark streets. No gaslights yet. He walked in front of the Wright House, passing by it without the slightest intention of entering. He heard the watchmen calling out the time. Eleven o'clock. He walked along Liberty Street with no direction in mind but found himself crossing the same canal bridge that he had earlier that day. Bayardstown. The Fifth Ward.

As he walked through the area Parker heard singing. It grew louder as he moved toward the block that he had visited that afternoon. A lone male voice bellowed out the song. The singer knew the words well enough but massacred the tune. At certain parts for no apparent reason he sang even more loudly. Parker recognized the song. It was one that the fiddle and the fife had played and the crowd sang this afternoon. He moved toward it. It seemed to come from the next block over, near the intersection where the crossroads dance had taken place.

At the next corner Parker saw silhouetted in the darkness a small shack, just a bit bigger than an outhouse. It was a watchbox — one of the little holding shacks that the Watch put offenders in for the night before taking them before the Mayor's Court. Ten watchboxes sat on street corners scattered about the city; there had been two in Parker's beat. A watchman was allowed to stay in a watchbox during his shift if the weather was particularly inclement. For the most part, however, their occupants were drunks being held until they visited the mayor in the morning. There was a drunk in the box tonight.

As Parker approached the box, a voice hailed him from behind.

"Who goes there?" the voice demanded. Parker turned a saw a man holding a lantern in one hand and a long club in the other. It was William Fenlon, one of two watchmen whose beat covered parts of the Fifth Ward.

"It's John Parker, William," Parker answered.

"Oh, it's you, then, Parker?" Fenlon said. "I haven't seen you in this part of town for a while. One of your midnight walks, eh?"

"Yes, I suppose," Parker said. "I see you've got one in the box."

"Oh yes, that's just Paddy — one of my regulars. Too much celebrating today. Paddy's harmless. It's just that, once he starts drinking he never stops until someone stops him or he falls down. He's kind of a character around here. Everybody knows him. He doesn't work steady — just odd jobs and running errands."

"I see," said Parker.

Suddenly a wicked cackle erupted from the box and a face thrust outward from the small square window in the door. There was no glass in the window, just two small iron bars to keep occupants from causing mischief. One hand grasped the right bar. The other hand just set on the wood, its fingers gnarled and immobile.

"Well, if it isn't little Johnnie Parker," the face cackled derisively. Parker stared. It was the little man from the dance this afternoon. "He's *back*, isn't he, Johnnie? He's back and what are you going to do now? Can't run home to Mommy this time, can you, little Johnnie!"

"What are you ...?" Parker started.

But Fenlon cut him off, "Shut your mouth, Paddy!"

"Aw, shut yerself, ya bleedin' *lamplighter*!" Paddy yelled back.

Immediately Fenlon's club swung upward. "You watch your mouth with me, you decrepit little Mick!" Fenlon's club smacked flush up against the door, hitting Paddy's face and knocking him backward into the box.

"No!" Parker raised a hand to try to stop him. Too late.

Fenlon held his lantern up to the window. Paddy lay against the back wall in a heap. "Aw, damn!" Fenlon cursed himself. He opened the door and handed Parker the lantern. Fenlon went into the box and held Paddy's face in his hands. "Stupid little Mick. Look what you've gone and made me do." Then to Parker he said, "He's breathing. He's all right — just out cold. He'll sleep it off now, finally. I couldn't get him to stop that damned singing, you know."

Fenlon withdrew from the box and locked the door. "What was he going on about with you?"

"I don't know," Parker answered. "But I need to talk to him. Are you going to take him in?"

"I'll take him up at first light," Fenlon answered. "A cold bucket of water ought to be just the thing to rouse him for the walk up."

"Okay," Parker said. "I'll see him then."

Parker went home. He walked up the stairs and into his room without lighting a lamp or making a noise. After undressing he climbed into bed and lay with his eyes open. The little man's words rang in his ears: *Can't run home to Mommy this time, can you, little Johnnie!* What did that mean? Paddy's face seamed familiar. It caught Parker's notice the moment the little man stepped into the fringe of the group around the beer barrel. *He's back, isn't he, Johnnie!*

Parker lay in bed retracing the events of the day. He allowed himself to doze, but tried to keep from falling into a deep sleep. Weariness itself led him to convince himself that he could accomplish this. Enough time had passed since his last nightmare to require vigilance against the next one, inevitable as it may be. He woke suddenly, aware that he had indeed fallen into a deep slumber. Looking around parker realized that it was morning — he had slept the night through. No nightmare. Parker rose from bed with the feeling of one who had escaped a close brush with danger.

Awake before sun-up, Parker dressed and left before anyone else in the house was up and moving. He went straight toward Bayardstown, with the sun rising in front of him as he approached that district. By the time he got to the watchbox, full daylight shone on the city's denizens, most of whom had started their workday hours ago. Parker peered into the watchbox. It was empty.

Parker scanned the streets for William Fenlon. The watchman was not about — only civilians walking on the sidewalks and driving teams on the streets of a usual busy Pittsburgh morning. Parker sighed, depleted, then looked at his pocket watch. 6:30 a.m. He needed to head for the Watchhouse for Report.

Walking out of Bayardstown, Parker stopped in the middle of the canal bridge at Liberty Street and looked over at the new aqueduct. The construction workers were already busy on the nearly-finished trunk. The little man's words tugged at him, *Can't run home to Mommy this time, can you, little Johnnie.* And his face — was it really familiar? Did it come from his memory or just his need to find a connection? Instead of continuing along the street, Parker turned onto the towpath and headed toward the aqueduct. He stared at the workers as he approached, moving almost as a person being called along in a trance.

As Parker reached the aqueduct, Sam Reppert spied him from atop the flume and came over to greet him. "Hello, John. I had a feeling you'd be back soon."

"Hello, Sam," Parker said. "It looks like you're nearly finished here."

"Yes we are, as a matter of fact," Sam said proudly, looking back at the aqueduct. "We're scheduled to fill the trough with water in about two weeks. We'll test it out for leaks and general sturdiness, then it'll open for business."

"This is a great accomplishment for you, Sam. Congratulations," Parker said.

"Thanks, John," Sam said. "By the way, I told Beth that you stopped by. She insists that you come over for dinner."

"I will. Just tell me the day."

"Great! I'll talk to her about it tonight," Sam said. Then he changed the subject. "Any progress on your ... investigation?"

"I thought there was. Now I'm not so sure."

"Are you still thinking that someone murdered those girls?"

"I'm still thinking that, yes."

"I'm sorry, John. I've thought about it, and it doesn't add up. A guy going around murdering little girls like that would have to be touched, or something. Don't you think? If that's so, don't you think we'd find more girls around here killed like that? Wouldn't he do it more frequently — just because he couldn't control himself? I just can't see how he would be able to wait so many years in between murders. It doesn't make sense."

Parker thought for a moment. He studied the work crews bustling about the shore and aqueduct. "It makes sense if we stop assuming something," he said at last.

"Assuming what?"

"Sam, tell me something: The men that you have working here — who are they?"

"Which ones?"

"All of them. Generally, I mean. There are some faces that I know I've seen around, and even one or two names that I know. But most of these men — they just don't look familiar to me at all."

"Well," Sam started, "most of the supervisors and people directing the

THE BURNT DISTRICT

project are Mr. Roebling's men. He brought them with him from Saxonburg. Then we have some skilled tradesmen — carpenters and blacksmiths and such. Those are probably the people who you recognize or even know. They live here in the city.

"Then the laborers, well, they could be from anywhere. A few may be long-time city residents, but most are men who just follow the work from town to town. They're almost like drifters, but they'll stay in one place as long as there's work. I get them at every construction job I've ever done."

"Do you ever get the same men from one construction job to the next?"

"I suppose there are a few that I've seen before. But crews are just as likely to go to another town after a job is done. They may end up here years later, just following the work. Heck, I might have men here that haven't been in Pittsburgh since you and I sat on the bank as boys and watched them rebuild the Monongahela Bridge!" As soon as Sam uttered the last word he froze. He finally met Parker's gaze of even determination with his own gaze of understanding.

"Sam, do you have a list of names of the men working here?"

"My paymaster does. I can get it from him."

"That dinner at your house — maybe we could do that really soon. How about tomorrow night?"

"Yes. Tomorrow night — I'll have the pay list there."

"Good. I'll see you then. I've got to get to Report, now."

Both men turned again and watched the work crews. Just before Parker turned to leave, a large man stepped up from the embankment carrying a massive timber by himself that any other *two* men would've struggled with. It was the same man Parker noticed the last time he stood at this spot. As the man's huge boots stepped up onto the aqueduct's flume Parker felt a flash of memory. He closed his eyes. His own words to Abraham Butler sounded in his head: *just a colossal pair of boots.* He saw those boots again in his mind now as he had the day of the fire, when his face was pressed into the dirt on the wharf. The boots turned and walked away and as they got farther away, for the first time since that day, Parker was able to remember seeing their owner — the large man with blue overalls and a tan cap. Parker opened his eyes. That man was walking away from him right now, carrying a timber along the trunk of the aqueduct. The realization flooded his mind, and he felt like he'd just been released from some kind of magic that had cast a curtain in front of his eyes.

Parker marched forward onto the flume. "Hey! You!" he called.

"Whoa, John! Where are you going?" Sam Reppert stood suddenly in front of him.

"Sam, the day of the fire," Parker said quickly, "did your crews work a full day?"

"No, most of them left in the early afternoon to fight the fire or get to their families. Why?"

Parker pointed toward the large man. "That man, there. He was one on the looters. He was looting on the wharf the day of the fire!"

"John, calm down. What are you doing? You can't go up there," Sam said.

"He was a looter! He attacked me and knocked me out cold!" Then Parker yelled to the man again, "You! Right there. You come here!" The large man with the blue overalls and tan cap set his timber down on the deck of the flume. As he turned to look at Parker he stood up at full height, rising like a grizzly bear defending a position. He stared a Parker with narrowed eyes. Then, recognizing either the constable's coat or the constable himself, he suddenly turned and bolted. Parker ran after him.

The large man ran through the crews of workers to the Allegheny City end of the flume. He was adept at traversing the intermittent planks of the unfinished structure, and easily outdistanced Parker who tripped several times on timbers strewn about the worksite. The man did not wait to reach the end of the aqueduct, but rather jumped off the side onto the embankment below. Parker looked over the edge at the spot where the man had jumped and watched him run up into the city.

Parker ran to the end of the flume, then onto the city street. He turned down the street in the direction the man last headed, but could see only unhurried citizens traveling on the streets and sidewalks. Parker stood in the middle of an intersection and turned a full circle, looking desperately around on all sides. Nothing. He stood panting for a moment, trying to decide which direction might be best to try. Finally he realized that it was useless. This was not his city. He would not know where to look. Parker turned and walked slowly back to the river.

15

"You want me to carry this all the way to Lawrenceville?" Parker asked Jenny Wright, who pushed a warm pie into his arms.

"Well, it's not as if you're *walking* up the hill," Jenny said, "you're taking the hack, aren't you?"

"Yes, but …"

"John Parker, you are not walking into someone's house for dinner *empty-handed*! I baked this today just so you could take something with you."

"What about James and the McKees? They would probably like a pie after dinner tonight!"

"I made two. Now take it and go!" Jenny pushed him out the door.

Parker stood on the front porch, holding his pie. He shook his head. No one could defeat him so completely as Jenny did whenever she felt strongly about something. He had no defense against her. He looked back at the front door, then turned and walked down the porch steps to the street.

He walked down Sixth Street toward the Allegheny River, crossed Liberty Street, and then stopped on the corner of Penn Street. He pulled out his pocket watch, then looked down Penn Street expectantly. After about five minutes a long, enclosed carriage approached, pulled by a team of two horses. The bright letters painted on the side proclaimed it the *M. Nasser Line*. As Parker boarded he found the hackney almost full, with about eight people on board. He sat across from an old woman dressed in finery appropriate for attending a grand social function. She looked at the pie on Parker's lap, then up at him and smiled a polite but amused smile. Embarrassed, he gave a quick half smile in reply, then turned and looked out at the streets through which they passed.

Penn Street paralleled Liberty for a few blocks as the hackney first traveled through the Fifth Ward. At one point Parker spied a familiar watchbox at an intersection one block away — the one that held Paddy two nights before. Parker found it empty the following morning when he went back to question the old man. It wasn't until after his shift was over that he finally caught up with watchman William Fenlon in front of the courthouse as the Watch reported for duty. Fenlon confessed that he had felt so badly about clubbing Paddy that he let the little man go free in the morning, rather than take him to face the Mayor's Court for his drunken disorderly conduct.

He gave Parker some tips on where to look for Paddy — locations of favorite taverns and friends' residences. But right now Parker had another appointment.

He was on his way to his long-time friend Sam Reppert's house for dinner. He and Sam grew up together in Pittsburgh, but now Sam lived about a mile outside of the city limits in the borough of Lawrenceville. Sam moved to Lawrenceville six years ago when he married the former Elizabeth Fisk. Elizabeth's father owned several large plots of land in the area and gave one plot, with house included, to the couple as a wedding present.

After passing through the interjacent town of Croghansville, Penn Street started a smooth grade up to Lawrenceville. As Penn Street angled to the right up the hill the hackney passed the Allegheny Arsenal on the left. The grounds of the Arsenal occupied several blocks from that point down to the Allegheny River. The hack passed the magazines on the northeast corner of the Arsenal complex. Parker got off at the next block.

He crossed to the north side of Penn Street and walked about one half of a block to Sam's residence. It was a two-story brick house with a large wooden porch on the front that Sam added after they moved in. It sat in the middle of a large yard that looked to be almost a full acre. Parker stepped up onto the porch past its ornate railings and posts and knocked on the door. A woman in her mid-twenties opened the door.

"Hello, Beth," Parker said.

"Hello, John!" Beth Reppert smiled a warm and welcoming smile. "Come in."

"Thank you," Parker said. Then he added awkwardly, "I brought a pie … Jenny made it."

"Bless her heart," Beth smiled, taking the pie. As Parker took off his coat she pointed to the coat stand beside the door. Beth Reppert wore her dark brown hair pulled to a single, thick braid in the back. As they walked out of the foyer her brown eyes and slender face changed from gladness to concern. "How have you been, John?" she asked as she slipped an arm through his. "I worry about you." Parker was very fond of Beth Reppert, but she always treated him with the same sympathetic tone as she had immediately after Angelina died.

"I'm fine, Beth. Really. And you?"

"We're doing very well, John." As they walked through the house they approach the stairs to the second floor. "Sam and the boys are upstairs — building a model, of course. What else do they do? We daren't have any more children because the extra bedroom has been tuned into a model shop! Go on up, John. Dinner will be ready in a few minutes."

THE BURNT DISTRICT

"Thanks, Beth," Parker said, and ascended the stairs.

At the top of the steps Parker followed the voices to the room at the end of the hall. Stepping into the doorway he saw Sam at a table working on a model of a bridge, assisted by a boy about five years old. Another boy, three years old, sat on the floor and played with small scraps of wood. Shelves covered nearly all of the walls of the room. On all surfaces sat wooden models of bridges and buildings, steamboats and canal boats, and some structures that Parker could not readily identify. Wood parts and small tools sat on the table next to Sam and his son.

"Do you think you could make a carriage for me?" Parker announced his presence. "I could use one so that I don't have to walk everywhere I go. Of course, then, I *would* need a horse."

"Well, there he is!" Sam Reppert said, laughing. "A carriage, you say? We can do that!" The two boys looked up at Parker. "Sam Junior, Matthew, you remember your Uncle John, don't you?" Sam Jr. nodded affirmatively, although his face registered that he didn't fully remember his "Uncle" John. It did not occur to little Matthew to even pretend to know who Parker was. Parker smiled. He did indeed remember these two boys. He attended both of their christenings and, though not a frequent visitor to the Reppert house, enjoyed seeing how they grew from visit to visit. Parker had learned one lesson from Jacob Shoop, though. He produced two candy sticks that he purchased earlier that day from James Higby's shop.

"Hello, Sammie. Hi, Matthew," he said as he handed the boys the candy.

"Well, what do you say to Uncle John for that candy?" Sam said.

"Thank you," Sam Junior said. Matthew was too busy with a mouthful of candy stick. He said something that sounded close enough to a thank you for his dad.

"We can go downstairs now," Sam said. "I think supper is ready."

Beth Reppert cooked a spring gobbler with pickled beets and other vegetables on the side.

"Canned from last fall," she said. "I made a pie for dessert, but we'll have Jenny's instead. It smells delicious." Everything *was* delicious and Parker enjoyed his meal with the Reppert family. Sam Junior sat straight and used perfect manners throughout the meal. Little Matthew, however, had little use for manners or even utensils for that matter. By mid-meal his lips, cheeks, chin, and fingers were covered with the red of pickled beet juice. Every topic of conversation somehow led Beth to mention some woman who was "available."

After the meal was over, Sam and Parker retired to the parlor. Sam brought in the pay register he'd obtained from his paymaster. They sat at a small table with the register. "Now, exactly what are we looking for?" he asked.

"I think we're looking for one of the itinerants that you told me about," Parker said.

"Well," Sam replied as he leafed through the pages, "then we can eliminate Roebling's men from the start. And the tradesmen, too — they're locals, most of whom I know by name."

"One more thing," Parker said, "I think we're looking for an Irishman. That might help us narrow down a list of names."

"Why an Irishman?" Sam asked.

"The work crews on the canal — they were Irishmen imported to do the labor."

"And ..."

"*And*, I went to Freeport to find out about the girl that died there."

"You did? You really *are* serious. What did you find out?"

"It was just like the little man said back when we were kids at the river. A little girl was killed there. Sam, when the man there that I talked to described the girl as they found her, it sounded just like Ruthie Bowden, and Grace Milliken. Now, they decided that she must've drowned. But some townspeople at the time felt that that wasn't the case. They were sure that the Irish laborers in town at the time were responsible."

"Which people felt that way?" Sam asked.

"Well, one that I met in person," Parker said, as he rubbed the back of his head where a corncob had struck him. "But she indicated that there were others that felt the same way at the time."

"I hate to say it, John, but that's really not that much to go on. You still know very little about what happened," Sam said.

"You're right. But I have to go on what little I *do* know, because there's so much that I *don't* know it would take me a lifetime to wade through it," Parker said.

Sam Reppert raised his eyebrows and shook his head affirmatively, conceding to Parker's sentiment, as he continued leafing through the register to the section listing the general laborers.

"What about our looter?" Parker asked. "What's his name?"

"Well, he would be a good suspect in that this is the first one of my jobs I've ever seen him on. When we first started work on the aqueduct, I thought that he looked vaguely familiar. But I looked on pay lists from previous jobs, and he wasn't on any of them. That could mean that he's just come to town recently. But I don't think his name fits with what you're looking for. It's Frederick Rhinehart."

"That doesn't sound very Irish to me — German, I guess," Parker said. "Have you ever spoken to the man?"

"I haven't. But I'll tell you something: there are a lot of people on that job that are mad as hell at you, John. Rhinehart hasn't been to the site since you chased him. He was a workhorse. They tell me that it takes two or three men to make up for the work he did."

"Believe me, I wish he'd show up again a lot more than they do," Parker said.

"Well, then, you'd have *one* of your criminals. Let's see if we might have another here." Sam came to the sheet he wanted and put his finger on the page on the top name. His finger slowly trailed down the page as he read the names silently to himself. Parker pointed at a name.

"What about that one: Aaron McGuire?"

"No. I know him. He has a family and has lived in the area for years."

"Michael Moran?"

"Same. Hey, here's one I don't know: Sean Foley."

"Let's put a mark beside any possibilities."

"Here's another that I don't know: Darren Kelly. And this one: Brendan O'Neill." The two men went down the entire pay list. When they finished, they had five names. "That's not a lot," Sam said.

"But it's more than we had before we began," Parker noted. "Tomorrow I can start to question these men."

"John, why don't you let me talk to my paymaster first? He'll know these boys. Maybe we can eliminate some names without spooking anyone. You've already chased one man away."

"Okay. Can you talk to him tomorrow, first thing?"

"First thing. I promise."

"I'll be around as early in the day as I can get over there," Parker said.

Sam nodded affirmatively. For a moment, neither man spoke. The silence seemed to rise to an introduction of the topic they did not want to discuss. "Y'know, John, this all has gotten me thinking about Ruthie Bowden again and that whole springtime at the bridge."

"I know, Sam. I'm sorry."

"No, it's all right. It was a terrible thing, but a lot of other things happened that spring. You and I became best friends. I got to watch them build the bridge. I think that's had a big influence on my life."

"I hadn't noticed."

"What?" Sam asked. Then realizing that Parker was teasing him, said, "Oh, yeah. I guess I have made building things my life, professional and personal, haven't I?"

"And you've done an outstanding job, Sam." Parker replied, cocking his head toward the kitchen where Beth and the two boys were. "No joke."

"Thanks," Sam said. "Hey, do remember the circus that came into town that spring? It arrived just a few days before the day Ruthie died. I remember because the circus' last night in town was the night before I found her."

"I remember," Parker said. "That was some circus. I liked all of the animals it had. They had a troop of bears. And there were lions all the way from Africa. I remember the lions most of all. I never thought I'd see one in my whole life, but there they were, right in front of me."

"I liked the show horses," Sam said. "They were all white with sparkling saddles and big plumes on their heads. The way they pranced around — they were just beautiful."

"And the acrobats," Parker remembered, "I remember watching them fly through the air."

"It was the biggest circus in years, before or since," Sam noted. "I remember their last night here was their big finale. All of the acts performed and then they had a big parade. They'd been billing the thing all week and the place was packed with people inside the tent and out. The whole town was out."

Parker nodded in agreement. But as he did, Sam's last statement struck him. He'd heard it somewhere before. He tried to think of where.

"Is something wrong, John?" Sam asked.

"What you just said, '*The whole town was out.*' That sounds familiar." Then the answer came to him. "George Weaver!"

"Who?"

"George Weaver. He's the man from Freeport who told me about the girl who died there. He spoke those exact words when describing the camp meeting held the night Mary Woodburn was killed."

"Okay, but what does it mean?

"On the day and evening of the fire, everyone in the city was out either fighting or fleeing the fire," Parker speculated. "So, could not the same statement be made for all three murders?"

"So, are you saying our murderer likes crowds? Maybe he uses them to cover his attack," Sam said.

"Could be," Parker considered. "Sam, didn't you say before that anybody who would do this kind of thing would have to be 'touched'?"

"Yeah," Sam replied, "I think he would have to be crazy somehow."

"Well, maybe a big commotion, like a crowd or some big excitement, sets him off. Maybe it kind of causes him to snap — go mad a bit — and do something wild."

"Could be," Sam agreed, "but madness is not a subject with which I'm familiar."

"Well, me neither," Parker said, "but it could be another connection."

Just then Beth Reppert came into the parlor with the Sam Junior and little Matthew. Matthew's face was cleaned of all pickled beet juice and both boys were dressed for bedtime. "I'm going to take the boys up to bed now," she announced.

"It's late," Parker suddenly realized. "I shouldn't keep you folks up any more. I should get going."

"Say 'good night' to your Uncle John," Beth ordered the boys.

"Good night," Sam Junior said.

"Good night, Sam," Parker said. He leaned down, putting his hands on his knees, and looked into little Matthew's face. "Good night, Matthew," he said. Matthew simply stared at Parker expectantly. "No more candy, Matthew. Sorry."

Little Matthew let out a long, drawn-out, "Okay," then, leaning his head down nearly on his shoulder in disappointment, turned and walked out of the room with his big brother.

"Don't leave without saying 'good-bye,'" Beth said. "I'll get the boys in bed and be down in a minute."

Parker and Sam got up from the table and walked to the front door. Parker lifted his coat off of the rack. "Thanks, Sam, for everything," he said.

"Don't mention it," Sam replied. "I'll start talking to those men as soon as I get the opportunity."

"All right. And I'll stop down at the work site at the end of the day," Parker said.

Beth came down the stairs. She walked over to Parker and hugged him. "Good-bye, John," she said. "I'm so glad you came over tonight."

"Thanks very much for dinner, Beth. It was delicious," Parker said. "And those are beautiful boys you have there. And they're getting so big!"

"Thank you, John," she said. Then the look of concern that had been there when he arrived returned to her face. "Are you sure that you're all right, John?"

"Yes, Beth, I'm *fine*," Parker said.

"Well, I worry about you," Beth said.

"You needn't," Parker said. "Good night, Beth."

Beth Reppert turned and walked back up the stairs to her sons. Sam followed Parker out onto the front porch.

"Can I give you a ride home, John," Sam asked. "It would only take a few minutes to get the horses hooked up to the carriage."

"Oh no, Sam, don't bother," Parker said. "The hack should still be running. It ought to be through any time now." After he spoke, Parker looked into the house, shaking his head.

"What's the matter?" Sam asked.

"Beth," Parker replied. "She still acts as if Angela just died last week."

Sam's face became serious and gentle, as someone about to say something difficult to a friend. He put a hand on Parker's shoulder. "That's because *you* still act that way, John."

Parker was not prepared for that answer, but he saw that it was delivered with much care. He shook his head in resigned agreement.

"I don't have an argument for that," he said. "Good night, Sam, and thanks again. I'll see you tomorrow."

"Good night, John," Sam Reppert said.

16

Parker stepped off of Sam Reppert's porch and walked out to Penn Street. He stood at a corner where the hackney would see him and stop. He thought for a while about what Sam had said. Sam was right, of course. Sam and Ann Reppert were both right. Abraham Butler was right. Even Jenny, with her unintentional comment, was right. Parker realized that five years ago a part of him went into mourning and never made any attempt to come back out again. He himself was trapped in the very place that he tried to warn Alice Wickersham not to go.

Suddenly Parker felt like walking. He wouldn't have gone straight home after the hack dropped him off anyway, he realized. It was time, again, for him to stay out walking until absolute exhaustion finally drove him home to sleep. Were his nightmares the cause or just another effect of his extended mourning? He did not know.

He walked past the Allegheny Arsenal grounds. Its buildings were solid hulks in the darkness. Past the arsenal he traveled silently down the street's grade through Croghansville and into the Fifth Ward. Most of the residences were dark. It was late Tuesday night, the middle of the workweek, and the workday started before dawn for most people in the city.

The taverns were still open though. Music, laughter, and shouting came from within any that Parker passed. He stopped suddenly across the street from one tavern, as the noises from it reminded him of the revelry in the crossroads dance. The moment he stopped, however, he heard a racket in the street behind him. It sounded as if something had been knocked over. He turned around quickly. In the darkness he could see nothing moving. Parker stared for a while, then turned back toward the tavern.

It was a German alehouse. As he watched, a well-dressed and somewhat portly man strode in front of it toward the entrance. As the man opened the door, the light from inside shown on him and Parker saw that it was Daniel Fitzgerald. Parker wondered if he might be of some help, considering that the search was now for someone other than Kevin Milligan. He walked across the street, looking over his shoulder as he went.

Opening the front door, Parker winced a bit from both the bright light and the tobacco smoke inside the alehouse. The tavern was surprisingly full for a Tuesday night. Parker saw Daniel Fitzgerald sitting at a table by himself, beaming at a newly poured stein of beer. Parker walked over to his table.

"May I join you?" he asked.

Daniel Fitzgerald looked up, "Well, if it isn't my friend, *the constable*. Come in uniform today, did you? Given up sneaking around? Or have you found your Mr. Callahan?"

"Milligan," Parker said. "And yes, I did find him."

"And did you put him behind bars? Did our undercover sleuth bring the criminal to justice?"

"He's dead," Parker said flatly.

"Whoa, now, aren't you the efficient one! Saved the city the cost of trying and jailing him, did you?"

"He committed suicide."

"Well, saved you the trouble, did he? An accommodating boy, that one."

"Look, Mr. Fitzgerald," Parker said with patience starting to wear just a bit, "I'm sorry that our last meeting was a deception, but I'm looking for a murderer."

Daniel Fitzgerald also became more serious as he leaned toward Parker. "And you didn't think that you could tell me that on Sunday? You thought you had to be sneaky?"

"I didn't know," Parker said. "I didn't know anyone. I wasn't thinking in terms of talking to an individual. I just wanted to know if anyone knew him — knew where he was. He could've been friends with all of you, for all I knew.

"And we Irish rogues all stick together, don't we, Constable?"

"I said I was sorry," Parker said. "Now I need your help. I'm looking for a man who murders children. He has killed three that I know of, and who knows how many that I don't know of. If I don't find him, he'll most likely kill more. Now, will you help me?"

Daniel Fitzgerald looked down into his mug of beer. "Y'know, Constable, folks more recently arrived from the *Old Sod* like their whiskey. But me? I've grown a fondness for this German brew. *Once removed*, I guess you could say I am." He took a long draught from his mug, then looked at Parker. "What is it that you want, Constable?"

"The last murder occurred Thursday the tenth around or after the time of the fire."

"I have not heard of this murder, by newspaper nor word of mouth," Daniel said.

"The murderer always makes the death look like an accident. A girl did die: Grace Milligan. Did you hear of that?"

"Yes, they have put the names of confirmed dead in the paper. No

THE BURNT DISTRICT

mention of foul play, though."

"I was one of the ones who found her. She was murdered. You just have to trust me."

"Go on."

"I have no material clues to suggest who the murderer is. Only common threads throughout the murders."

"And they are …?"

"Violent murders. He broke their necks and possibly strangled them first. All were young girls. All happened after a large gathering in the town where the murder took place."

"And now that you obviously no longer suspect the late Mr. Milligan, why do you think that I can help you?"

"I think the murderer is an Irishman."

Daniel Fitzgerald arched one eyebrow.

"Because one of the murders was done by someone on a work crew on the canal," Parker quickly continued. "As I understand it, they were all Irishmen newly brought over from Ireland."

"Many were, but not all. Constable, the canal was finished over a decade ago."

"I told you that there've been several murders over a period of years," Parker said. "To me that means that it is on-going. As long as this man is alive and free, the murders will continue. More children will die."

"And that, of course is where I come in, my being an Irishman and all that," Daniel Fitzgerald said.

"I don't think he is a permanent member of your community," Parker said. "He follows work all over the countryside. He just arrived back in the city within the last year. It's the first he's been here in many years. You would know who is a long-time resident, at least of the people who live in your neighborhood, and who is not. I have a list of names here …"

"Names? From where?" Daniel Fitzgerald asked.

"My friend is a superintendent building the new aqueduct. We picked several names from his paymaster's register," Parker said.

"You picked names from a list? How did you choose them?" Daniel Fitzgerald asked.

"We picked Irish names. I told you …"

"Did you know these men?"

"Not all of them …"

"You mean that you looked at a list of names and decided which ones were Irish? Hahaha!" Daniel Fitzgerald let out a loud belly laugh. He took another long drink from his mug.

149

"And let me guess: you picked all the O'Brien's, O'Reilly's, and O'Toole's!" After some more laughing, Daniel Fitzgerald became serious again. "Tell me, Constable, was James Smith on your register?"

"I don't recall."

"And what about George Taylor?"

"I don't know."

"And if they had been, would you have picked them for your 'list of Irishmen'?"

"I don't think so, I ..."

"James Smith and George Taylor were both signers of our Declaration of Independence. Both were born in Ireland. My point is, *boy-o*, that if you're only going to look for people with 'O's' in front of their names, you're going to miss a few Irishmen. You can't just look at a list of names and know who's Irish," Daniel Fitzgerald said. "Plus, over the centuries waves of Norsemen, Scots, and Englishmen moved to the Old Sod and added their names to the pot — not to mention Frenchmen, Germans ..."

"Germans?" Parker asked.

"Palatines," Daniel said.

"What?"

"Palatines," Daniel said, "German Protestants from the Palatinate. Seems that about one hundred and fifty or so years ago, Louis XIV of France's sister-in-law gave him her word that that little German territory was hers. Louis, always wanting to keep peace in the family, invaded the Palatinate and took it over for her. He made life a bit rough for the Protestants living there. Some years later the English took in some Palatine refugees and sent them over to the Old Sod to live. The Protestant Parliament in Ireland gave the Palatines a better lot than most Irishmen had at the time."

"So a man named *Frederick Rhinehart* could be an Irishman?" Parker asked.

"Frederick Rhinehart — you pick any name you like," Daniel said while lifting his mug again to drink.

Parker thought for a moment. So it *was* possible for Rhinehart to be on their list. If so, he might fit every connection Parker had made between the three murders. A*nd* Parker knew painfully first-hand that Rhinehart was on the Monongahela side of town at the time the fire raged.

"I think you've given me something to go on," Parker said.

"So go, then," Daniel Fitzgerald said.

"Can I buy you a beer — to thank you for your help?" Parker asked while pulling some coins out of his pocket.

"I can buy my own beer, Constable," Daniel replied. Parker rose from the table gave a resigned nod. Daniel Fitzgerald did not need or want his thanks. He exited through the tavern's front door.

The light and clamor of the alehouse made the night outside seem darker and quieter than before. Parker walked down the street toward home. After he'd gotten a few doors away, the noise from within the tavern came out into the street. Parker turned but saw no one, only the closing door. As he continued down the sidewalk, the feeling that someone was following him returned. Every now and then Parker heard a scrape or bump behind him, but when he turned around he saw nothing. He turned left into an alley, walking casually in the middle of the street. But after he turned the corner, he quickly darted up against the side of the building.

Parker stood motionless among some barrels and piles of trash, watching the sidewalk on the main street. After a moment, a small figure appeared from around the corner. Parker saw a man peer into the alley, then proceed cautiously into it.

When the figure walked past, Parker seized the man by his coat front and threw him up against the building.

"What do you want?" Parker demanded.

"I don't want nothin'. I wasn' doin' nothin'!" the man cried.

The man's voice was familiar. Parker saw his face, close now in the darkness, and smelled whiskey on his breath. Suddenly he recognized the little man in front of him.

"Paddy!" he shouted. "Why were you following me?"

"I wasn't!"

Parker pressed Paddy against the brick wall. "You know why I'm over here. You know my name. You know everything." The little man's eyes widened with fear as Parker's narrowed with realization and anger. "*You know everything*," he repeated. "You know who killed them, don't you? That's what you were talking about the other night!"

"I don't know nothin'!"

Rage surged inside of Parker — the outrage of the heinous murders and innocent victims, the frustration at his fruitless search. All welled up inside. Parker wanted to lash out, to drive the little man right through the brick wall behind him. Parker stepped back, lifted Paddy off of the ground, and coiled to slam him into the wall.

He stopped. He stared at the pitiful creature who cringed as he winced and braced for impact. Parker let Paddy go slowly, and the little man slid the whole way down to a sitting position between the barrels and trash piles. Paddy looked as if he were about to cry. Parker squatted down in front of him and said in a calm voice, "Paddy, you followed me. You've been following me so that you could tell me who murdered those girls, so go ahead and tell me."

Paddy's face twisted until it looked as though the little man really would weep. Then he said, "It was Rinie. It was Rinie that killed those girls."

"Who's Rinie?"

"Rinie is *Rinie*. He's ..."

"Frederick Rhinehart?"

"Yes," Paddy said at last. His face was pointed down and twisted in anguish.

"How do you know this, Paddy?"

"Me and the boys, we all came over together from County Limerick. That's where we read the bills posted up all over the place talkin' about steady work over in America on the canal for good pay. Most of us came over for the work. But Rinie, he was well-to-do compared to the rest of us. Some of the boys said he came over with us to get out of some trouble back home. They said he killed some girl, and folks was gonna hold him accountable.

"When we got off of the boat the contractor who signed us on was on the dock waitin' for us. He made us all one work crew, so we traveled everywhere in the same group. We was all at Toddstown together when the little girl was killed. We all felt that Rinie done it, but no one said a word. He was so big and mean, all the boys in the crew were afraid of him.

"After the canal was finished most of us followed work wherever there was work. A bunch of us ended up working on the Monongahela Bridge when they rebuilt it. That's where he killed that other little girl — the one your little friend found in the weeds. That's when I went and opened my big mouth."

"What do you mean?" Parker asked.

Paddy looked up, "All I said was, 'She looks like the wee lass they found up in Toddstown.' That's all it took. Rinie found me after work that night. 'Now, Paddy,' he says, 'I heard that you had your mouth workin' over at the bridge today.' Then he knocks me to the ground and pushes his big boot down on top of my curled hand while I was layin' there. 'You'd better watch that mouth,' he says, 'or it could bring ya to trouble.' Then he stomps on my hand and grinds it down into the street. He was so big, I couldn't do nothin' but cry in pain. Then he just glares at me and walks away." Paddy cradled his useless hand in his good one as he spoke. "And I've kept my mouth shut ever since. All these years, I've spoken to no one about it."

"Where is he now, Paddy?" Parker demanded.

"I don't know," Paddy whined. "I swear I don't know."

Parker believed the little man was telling the truth. He had one more question, however, "Paddy, *you* sought *me* out. You *wanted* to tell me. Why?"

Paddy raised his deformed hand. "I lost use of my hand that day. Lost it forever. I couldn't work at the job at the bridge no more. I couldn't hold down any kind of a real job no more. I've had to take grubby little jobs ever since: runnin' errands for nobodies, delivery boy, any kind of odd job," he really was crying now. Then he spoke again, "A woman don't want a man who can't work. I lost any kind of a normal life with a wife and a family. I became a drunk and a joke to anyone who knows me. That's no life for a man. No life at all. *He* took my life away from me. He may as well have killed me then, like he did that girl.

"And there's nothin' I can do to make him pay," Paddy continued while shifting from sadness to anger. "But *you* can. You can stick his hide in a dark jail cell to rot or even get him hanged. And if you don't, there's gonna be more girls dead. You know that."

"I know," Parker said. He felt very sorry for the wretch in front of him. The little man really did have nothing. "Paddy, is there anything I can do for you?"

Paddy's face looked confused in the darkness. It was as if no one in his entire life had ever offered him any help, and he could not fathom the question. Then he said in calm voice, "Sure, you can pull those coins back out and buy *me* a beer."

Parker emptied his pocket and handed it to the little man. "Here. I've got to go, Paddy, but you take this." He stood up, then reached down to help Paddy up.

"I'm not ready to get up yet," the little man said. "Besides, this might be as good a place as any to spend the night."

"All right, Paddy," Parker said. He turned and walked away.

"You get that bastard!" Paddy called after him.

Parker walked back out onto the main street. He got almost a block away when suddenly he heard a scream of terror and pain from behind. Running back the way he had just come, Parker heard barrels crashing in the alley. He reached the spot where he'd just left Paddy. It was difficult to see in the dark, but he could discern a dark heap among the trash. He knelt down and pulled the heap toward him. It was Paddy. His neck was cruelly twisted and his eyes stared unseeingly upward. "Paddy?" Parker tested to see if the little man was alive. He expected no response and got none.

Suddenly two massive hands grabbed Parker's head from behind and hauled him upward. The attacker lifted Parker so high that his feet left the ground. Parker grabbed the hands and tried to pry them off of his head. He could not budge them. Parker yelled for help as loud as he could as he writhed and kicked at his assailant, trying to break free. The attacker wrapped one thick arm around Parker's head, cramming it into the crook of the arm. Then he moved his other hand around to the side of Parker's head. *He's going to break my neck*, Parker realized, and called again for help.

A light appeared from behind them and threw their shadows onto the building. An immense shadow of a man held Parker's shadow in the air. "Who's in there? What's going on here?" Watchman William Fenlon's voice demanded.

Parker tried one last time to yell, "Fenl …"

The attacker roared with rage at the intrusion. He heaved Parker higher by the head and threw him into the air. Parker slammed face-first into the building and crashed down into the barrels and trash. He heard Fenlon cry out and then the smash of glass. The light went out and Parker knew no more.

17

"I think he's waking up," Parker heard a woman's voice say. He became aware of light around him, and people. He lay on his back in a comfortable, familiar place. It was his own bed. Just before opening his eyes Parker became aware of pain. Intense pain throbbed the entire way around his head. The pain spread down his neck and covered his shoulders. It shot the entire length of his back down to his waist. As he opened his eyes, he realized that the pain paralyzed nearly his entire upper body. He squinted as Jenny Wright and Muriel McKee came into focus.

"Try not to move, John," Jenny said.

"I *can't* move," Parker declared.

"Dr. Irwin said that most of the muscles in your back and neck are sprained," Jenny explained. "You've got a terrible bruise on your forehead and both of your eyes are black and blue. Dr. Irwin said only time and rest will heal you and you should not move."

"Ma'am, I swear I'm not moving," Parker said. "How did I get here?"

"Some watchmen brought you here in the middle of the night," Jenny explained.

"How they know where I lived?" Parker wondered.

"You were conscious in fits, and quite animated at times. You probably told them. One of them was seemed to be a very responsible fellow. He was in charge, by the look of it. What was his name …?"

"Lieutenant Rowe?"

"That's it. Lieutenant Rowe. He was quite a gentleman. Not at all like the others."

"Yes, that's Lieutenant Rowe."

"He sent one of his men for Dr. Irwin, who came right away."

Muriel McKee turned to little Harry, "Harry, go on up to the Watchhouse and give the High Constable the message that Constable Parker is awake. Run along, now."

Jenny explained to Parker, "High Constable Butler sent word asking us to tell him when you woke up. John, what happened? The watchmen said someone had been killed."

Parker waited until little Harry left the room. "I found him, ma'am, the man who murdered Grace Milligan — and Ruthie Bowden."

"How? Who?" Jenny asked.

"The old man who was killed last night knew about both murders. He knew who committed them. The murderer threatened him long ago, after killing Ruthie. There was at least one more — in Freeport. The old man was there, too. He told me everything." Parker paused. "Then he was killed for it."

Muriel McKee cupped her hand over her mouth. Jenny said, "You were almost killed, yourself, John."

"The men here last night — did they say anything about another watchman, William Fenlon?" Parker asked.

"One of them had a broken nose and an awful bruise on his face," Jenny replied. "Dr. Irwin attended to him, too, while they were here. He had to push the man's nose back in place. He said if the blow had been any more square, it would've been driven his nose up into his brain and killed him. It was dreadful."

Upon hearing that Fenlon was alive, Parker relaxed a bit. He felt very tired.

"You rest now, John," Jenny said. "I've made some soup downstairs. Can I bring you some?"

"Not now," Parker said, slumping back into his pillow. "Thanks, ma'am." Jenny Wright and Muriel McKee left the room. Parker drifted in and out of sleep. He was exhausted, but the pain made it difficult to sleep.

An hour later his door opened again. Jenny came in, "You have some visitors, John." High Constable Abraham Butler followed her in with Constable Cameron in tow. The Fifth Ward was Cameron's beat. Jenny stepped aside and allowed the men to pass by her to Parker's bedside. Then she left the room, closing the door behind her.

"There now, Constable Parker, I see that you are alive, if not well," High Constable Abraham Butler said.

"Yes, sir," Parker replied.

"One man is dead. Two officers of the law have been assaulted," Butler started. "Watchman Fenlon has already told us all that he knows, which is scant. We need you to tell us what happened last night."

Parker told Butler and Cameron everything, starting from the morning they found Grace Milligan. He did not speak of theories or hunches — he put everything in terms of facts. And as he put the whole story together, the facts fell into line. When he was finished, Butler questioned no part of it. Even Cameron made no remarks.

"Cameron," Butler turned to the other constable, "have you noticed a man of this description in your area?"

"Off hand, I'd have to say, 'no,' sir," Cameron replied, "but I'll start a search for him."

"He's been living in an apartment house or boarding house, probably," Butler said.

"Yes, sir," Cameron said.

"You go ahead and start now," Butler said to Cameron. "I'm going to stay here for a few more minutes."

"Yes, sir," Cameron said. Thus dismissed, he turned and walked out of the room.

After Cameron left, Parker said, "Rhinehart's probably gone, sir. He is a drifter."

"If he's smart, he left town," Butler said. "But we don't know that he *is* smart. You said that he follows the work. There's plenty of work in the city right now. And it is a big city. Maybe he thinks he can move to another section of town and work a different job."

Parker did not feel hopeful of this possibility.

"In any case," Butler said, "we must look for him. At least you know that Kevin Milligan had nothing to do with it."

"Yes," Parker said. He thought about the Milligans for a moment, then asked, "Has Eichman released his body to the family yet?"

"Eichman is finished with his work," Butler replied, "but from what I understand, Mrs. Milligan is in no mental state to arrange for burial. I believe that Eichman has spoken to their priest, and will keep the body until she's recovered enough to at least attend the services."

"If you find out when that happens, can you let me know?"

"Of course," Butler said, "I'll get word to you if I hear anything. You are to stay here and recover."

"Yes, sir," Parker said.

High Constable Abraham Butler turned to leave. "I don't want to see you at the Watchhouse any time soon. Is that clear?"

"Yes, sir."

18

One week after the attack by Frederick Rhinehart, Parker recovered to the extent that he could get up out of bed and walk around the house. Movement remained painful, but lying in bed became even more painful. On the whole, moving around seemed to improve his condition.

His injuries provided a positive side effect. Parker got more sleep in the past week than he had in a long time. One night the nightmare returned, but when his body started writhing in reaction, the pain of his movement woke him before the nightmare progressed very far.

The first time that he tried to shave was also the first time he looked in the mirror. Both eyes were black and blue, with a large bruise on his forehead above his left eye. Parker's face had hit a building. He looked like it. By now, however, the black around his eyes showed signs of fading.

Sam had stopped briefly the first evening of Parker's convalescence, after Parker failed to show up at the work site. Sam reported that his conversations with the listed workers had proved fruitless. He learned why.

Parker stood looking out his window, leaning on the sill, when someone knocked on his door. Jenny came in. "I saw High Constable Butler over by the courthouse earlier. He said Coroner Eichbaum turned Kevin Milligan's body over to the family two days ago. I stopped by St. Paul's on the way home. Father Deane told me they laid him out at Addie's sister's house the first night. They moved him to the church yesterday. They'll be showing him until noon, when the service will start."

"Thanks, ma'am," Parker said.

"Are you sure that you feel up to going?" Jenny asked.

"I want to go. Besides, I need to get outside. Moving seems to help me get better," Parker said. "Are you going?"

"No. Nora did not ask me to go with her this time. She'll be there, but only to be with Addie," Jenny said. Then she added, "Try to eat something before you go."

"Okay."

Dressing was still a bit painful, and took some time. He drew soup from the pot that Jenny seemed to keep perpetually cooking over the past week. By the time Parker finished eating and made it out the door it was nearly twelve noon.

Parker arrived at St. Paul's just a few minutes before the service started. Kevin Milligan's casket was still open. He was garbed in a brown burial habit. A crucifix lay between his hands. Parker lingered near the casket behind several mourners for a few moments, then moved to the back of the church. Father Deane appeared and spoke softly to Addie Milligan. He then moved to past the altar to the pulpit, as two men approached and closed the casket. As they gently lowered the lid, the sound of keening erupted from the mourners. Their lamenting rose in volume throughout he church, and did not subside until Father Deane started the service.

Parker had been only to a few Catholic masses in his life. He could not follow it, as Father Deane conducted the service in Latin. He alternately stood and knelt as the others did. When this was over, he followed the procession to the cemetery.

Father Deane again led the funeral procession to the parish cemetery on Boyd's Hill. This time it stopped at an open grave beside Grace Milligan's. He conducted a brief service there. As the coffin was lowered into the grave, another round of keening arose from the mourners. Two women held Addie Milligan upright and helped her walk as the crowd departed. One was Gladys Dilworth. The other was her mother.

As the mourners left the site Parker remained. He watched them go, then stared at the two new graves. He thought again of Grace lying in the burned-out building, and of Kevin dying in his arms. Although he now knew that Kevin Milligan did not kill his daughter, questions remained about how their deaths were connected. Why did he kill himself? Was it purely grief? Where was he during the fire and in the days afterward?

Suddenly Parker noticed another figure lingering in the area. Standing off to the rear among a trio of thick trees, a lone figure stood facing the Milligans' graves. Parker walked toward the figure, unhurried, as he could not have hurried if he wanted to. It was a woman. She wore a dark scarf over her head. Even so, as he got closer Parker felt that the woman looked familiar.

She reminded him of someone whom he had known years ago. Before he became a constable, John Parker worked at Bakewell's Glass Works. He aspired to be a supervisor, and his own supervisor was an able young man also rising in management at the works. Ben Fowler was not only a helpful and fair supervisor, he was someone Parker looked up to and emulated for his industry and energy. Ben Fowler was only two years older than Parker, and the two became good friends. He often invited Parker over for supper. In those days Parker was much more social, and always accepted. Fowler lived in Kensingon, down over the other side of Boyd's Hill from where they now stood, along the Monongahela. Ben's wife cooked wonderful meals, then the three sat and talked into the night. Parker enjoyed evenings in the Fowler household. But those happy times ended forever in a horrible accident one day at work. Ben Fowler was killed with two other workers as a furnace inexplicably exploded in the middle of a shift.

Ben Fowler's young wife was instantly a widow. Parker visited her periodically for a short time after her husband's death to make sure that she was okay. But their lives took different turns. Around that time Parker met and began courting Angelina Dougherty. His visits to the Fowler home became more infrequent, until they stopped altogether. He and Mrs. Fowler drifted apart, and had not seen each other for several years.

"Hello, Ann," Parker said as he reached her.

"Hello, John," Ann Fowler said.

Parker stared at her wordlessly for a moment. She studied his gaze, and a look of realization spread across her face. "You *know*," she said.

"I do now," Parker replied.

"How ...?"

"Kevin told me as he was dying, or at least he tried to. Your name was the last word he uttered. I didn't know what he was saying at the time. I never figured it out until just now when I saw you. Tell me, Ann, do you know why he did it — why he killed himself?"

"Oh, I know," Ann Fowler replied. "Kevin and I met about a year ago, and we started, well, we just started, and that's all I'll say. He'd meet me before or after his shift. He always told his wife that he was working overtime.

"On the day of the fire he showed up at my door. He said that the fire line made a wall the whole way from the cliff of Boyd's Hill to the river. He couldn't get past it to go to home, so he came to me. He didn't know what sections of the city were burning, but he knew that his daughter was in school way over at St. Paul's and thought that she at least would be safe. He stayed with me and brought water up from the river and splashed it on my roof, expecting the fire to reach my house. It burned out before it reached me. As soon as it subsided enough for him to get past, he left for home.

"He came back to me the day after and told me that his daughter was killed. He was completely distraught. He felt that her death had been his fault. He was inconsolable. I tried to tell him that under no circumstances could he have gotten to his daughter that day. He wouldn't listen. He came back after the funeral and sat in a corner. The guilt seemed to burn in him — to hollow him out from the inside. It destroyed his spirit until it became like the wasteland that surrounds my house. He had his own Burnt District right inside of him. He deteriorated before my very eyes. I could see him sinking further down, day-by-day, hour-by-hour. The day he got up and walked out of my house, I could see in his eyes that he was finished. I knew that I would never see him again."

Ann Fowler looked over at the graves, then back at Parker. "Don't judge him too harshly, John. He was a good man."

"I'm not judging him," Parker said, "even if I were inclined to."

"Why are *you* here, John?" Ann asked.

"I'm not sure," Parker said. "The night of the fire, Addie Milligan asked me to find her daughter. I found her dead. I was the only person with Kevin when he died. Somehow, since the fire, my life has been entwined with theirs. And it has all been tragic."

"Well, it's over now," Ann Fowler said.

"No," Parker said. He looked out over the city laid out below them. "It is not over."

19

On a Saturday morning in early May, John Parker ascended the Watchhouse stairs for the first time in over two weeks. He could not return sooner, as High Constable Abraham Butler had made it clear that he would not accept Parker back for duty until he was one hundred per cent recovered from the attack from Frederick Rhinehart. Reaching the meeting area, he saw all four of the other assistant constables seated, ready for Butler to come out of his office at any moment. All conversation stopped as they turned and watched him come into the room.

"Well, you're finally back," Albert Perry said. "You look pretty good for someone who was tossed up against a brick wall by a giant. How are you doing?"

"Healed for the most part," Parker said, as he sat down in the chair next to Perry, which was the closest. "I was forbidden to return until I was."

The other three were seated in a group. "You look a lot better than the last time I saw you, Parker," Cameron said.

"Thanks," Parker replied. "Any luck in the manhunt?"

"For a week we inquired in every public and private house that offers lodging," Cameron said. "If anyone knows him, they're not telling. Since then there's been nothing for it but to keep an eye out in case he shows up again." Ihmsen and Keller nodded affirmatively at his report, indicating that they had done the same in their wards.

"What about the workers at the aqueduct?" Parker asked.

Ihmsen spoke up, "A few knew his name, but none knew where he lived or really anything about him. It seems he wasn't very social." Just then High Constable Abraham Butler entered the room and stood in front of his men.

"Ah, Assistant Constable Parker," he said, "returned to work at last, I see. I was beginning to wonder if you were ever going to decide to come back. I would give you an update of the search for Frederick Rhinehart, but I'm sure the others have already done that."

"Yes, sir," Parker said. "Do you know if the Watch has also been looking for him?"

"I gave Lieutenant Rowe the full story, to which I'm sure Watchman Fenlon added in detail. But which of his men he directed to actively engage in searching, I do not know. It is possible that he did not ask watchmen in the

Burnt District to search, just as I did not tell Perry to. Besides, since they work at night, they simply do not conduct a search the way we do. But I will put the specific question to Lieutenant Rowe when I see him at the start of their shift tonight.

"Now, to our task for today. The official opening ceremonies for the new canal aqueduct are today …"

That's right, Parker thought, *Sam did tell me they would open it soon.*

"… there'll be a parade starting at noon. The companies will assemble in the public square over in Allegheny City, march across the aqueduct, down Penn Street, then end at the Fort Pitt ruins. They've erected a platform at our end of the aqueduct where the mayor and other officials will give their speeches after the parade. Since many of our city fathers often have much to say, the festivities could go on until anywhere from three to five o'clock. There'll be fireworks at eight o'clock."

"Fireworks?" Cameron said. "Who's shooting them?"

"The Pyrotechnical Association," Butler answered. A round of low laughter sprung from the group. Even Parker chucked. The Pyrotechnical Association had been providing Pittsburgh with fireworks for about the last eight years, but their record of proficiency proved spotty at best. Butler continued, "They're shooting them off from a barge just off the Point."

"Maybe they'll get it right this time," Ihmsen laughed. "Anyway, we're off duty by then."

"One more thing before you leave," Butler addressed the group. "On Monday the remains of Audrey Maglone were found in the rubble in the basement of her home. That accounts for the last missing person on our list."

There was no response from anyone after his last statement. No comments or quips were appropriate for that piece of information. The men simply got up and left to go on their rounds. Parker and Albert Perry walked into the Burnt District.

"Do you think that he's left town — your murderer, I mean?" Perry asked.

"It would seem to be the way that he works, but I don't know. The others have found out nothing about him, not even where he lived. Either he relates nothing about himself to the people with whom he works and lives, or they just won't tell."

"It would be easy for a man his size to keep people quiet," Parry noted.

"Yes," Parker agreed. "The only person who was willing to tell anything about him is now dead. It's certainly a lesson for anyone around who does know anything about him."

"*You* know something about him, now," Perry pointed out.

"Yes, I do, don't I?"

THE BURNT DISTRICT

Parker had heretofore only considered how much he *didn't* know about Rhinehart. It hadn't occurred to him that he might now know more than anyone else about the man.

"Maybe he'll stick around just to come after you," Perry said.

"That *would* be convenient — for him to come after me," Parker mused.

"Well, I'm off to my ward," Albert Perry said. "I'll see you later, Parker. Are you going to watch the parade?"

"Yes, I'll be there," Parker answered. "See you later, Albert." The men parted for their own areas. Parker walked through the Burnt District for the first time in over two weeks. For the most part, it remained desolate and dreary. Many pieces of walls still stood, only partially blocking their gutted contents from view. The streets were cleared of rubble. Here and there individual buildings had been cleared and their reconstruction was well under way. At noon Parker walked down Front Street, heading toward Penn Street where the parade would run. He passed Jonas Burbridge's commission house. Here workers laid runs of brick on the newly cleared stone foundation. The runs reached shoulder-high all around the foundation. Jonas walked around the corner, observing the work. Parker walked over to him.

"Hello, Jonas," Parker greeted him. "I see things are coming along pretty well for you."

"Oh, hello, John," Jonas said. "Yes, the rebuilding is going nicely. Right on schedule."

"I see you're building with brick this time."

"Oh yes. You'll see a lot more brick and stone, and a lot less wood, in the buildings that rise from these ashes."

"Y'know, Jonas," Parker said, "with all of the activity I saw here in the first two weeks after the fire, I guess I expected to see more buildings going up by now. But there's not. Why is that?"

"Money," Jonas replied. "In the immediate aftermath people came and cleared to see if they had anything left to salvage. They also cleared, of course, so they could rebuild. But some insurance companies went under, and could pay out only pennies on the dollar or nothing at all. So lots of people simply don't have the money right now to build. The banks are coming through with capital, though, which is where I got the money to build.

"Some of these other properties that haven't been touched are owned by landlords who may have no intention of rebuilding — the same for businesses that weren't doing that well before the fire. They'll be looking to sell. Those ruins might stand for months until someone buys the lots.

"But don't you worry, John, business will resume here better then ever. As a matter of fact, speaking of business, the aqueduct reopens today.

Opening the canal back up to the downtown will be a needed boost for businesses."

"That reminds me," Parker said, "I'm on my way over there now to watch the grand opening parade."

"That's right! The parade!" Jonas exclaimed. "I love to see the Pittsburgh Blues on parade. Can you wait one minute, John, then I'll go with you?"

"Of course," Parker replied.

Jonas walked around the corner, then reappeared a few minutes later. The two men walked to Penn Street, which paralleled the Allegheny River, then started along it toward the canal. Crowds lined the street. Parker could see that some schools had let their teachers bring the children over to watch the parade, and some shops let their clerks step outside to view it. As they got closer to the canal they could hear the bands playing in the distance. Then the aqueduct came into view, and they saw the lead band was just reaching the Pittsburgh side of the aqueduct. The rest of the parade followed, spanning the length of the new towpath.

The procession turned right when it reached Penn Street, and passed the spot where Parker and Jonas stopped to watch it. Companies of local uniformed militia made up the first sections of the parade. The Duquesne Greys' color guard led the way, followed by the company's band, and then the soldiers themselves. The officers sported smart dress uniforms with gray jackets, trimmed in black and gold, with black pants. Their black epaulets were also trimmed in gold and their large gold buttons flashed in the sunlight. The Greys' gold, star-shaped unit insignia adorned the front of their black, plumed parade caps. The enlisted men followed in step, wearing soft kepi caps and gray and black uniforms, slightly less ornate than the officers'.

The Washington Guards followed second in the procession. Their officers wore solid black jackets with gold-braided epaulets. A wide, infantry-blue stripe wrapped around their high collars. Their pants were the same infantry-blue as the collars, with a white stripe down them. Next came the Pittsburgh Blues. Their captain wore a patch on his shoulder that read "1812," identifying him as a veteran of that unit's service in that war. The Irish Greens were the last unit to pass. All companies marched with their bands in front, heralding their approach.

Behind the Irish Greens followed an open carriage carrying Mayor William Howard and several members of both the Select and Common Councils. Next began a procession of the volunteer fire companies, a standard feature of most parades held in the city. The Eagle Company led the way in their green and white parade uniforms. Black stovepipe hats replaced their conical fire-fighting helmets for the parade. Horses, not firemen, pulled their gleaming engine, leaving the men free to raise their fists in the air as they shouted "huzzahs" for their company. After another carriage of city officials passed the Allegheny Volunteer Fire Company came up next in their tan parade garb, followed by the Vigilant Company in their fire-red parade uniforms. Next came the Neptune Company in blue and finally the Niagara Company, also dressed in red.

Parker smiled to himself as he imagined the fisticuffs that broke out in the parade mustering area as the firefighters decided which company would go first. He noted that a carriage of public officials was placed in between the successive companies in the parade, no doubt to keep the men separated. Considering their order, though, he realized that they must have decided to go in order from oldest to newest company.

After the last of the parade passed, Parker and Jonas continued walking to the aqueduct. As the music from the military bands died in the distance the carriages of the city officials made their way back to the aqueduct for the official ceremonies. A canal boat covered in red, white, and blue bunting crossed from Allegheny City and entered Pittsburgh for the first time in many months amid cheers from the crowds lining both sides of the canal. After it passed, Parker saw that tables were set up on the grounds where the aqueduct's plume met the shore. There were two very long tables lined end-to-end with a podium between them. A group of men sat at the tables facing the crowd. The mayor sat at a central location next to the podium. He was flanked by members of the Select and Common Councils, the street commissioner, and other city commissioners and committee chairs. Seated next to the mayor was the man with the bushy goatee and penetrating eyes whom Parker now recognized as John Roebling. Sam Reppert and a few other engineers sat at the far end of one of the tables.

After the noise of the bands drifted off into the distance, Mayor Howard rose to speak. He paid tribute to "the meritorious designer and builder of the grand structure before us, who not only completed his great work on the date prescribed, but also did so not exceeding in expenditures the amount that he specified to us some nine months ago: sixty-two thousand dollars." Other city officials rose to speak in turn. They toasted Mr. Roebling. They toasted each other. They gave speeches on how the new aqueduct will help Pittsburgh fulfill its destiny of becoming one of the great cities of the United States. They toasted the Commonwealth of Pennsylvania, its legislature, and its governor, who had recently approved sending fifty thousand dollars to the city for disaster relief and also suspending state and county taxes for the next three years. They toasted in turn each of the fourteen states that sent disaster relief money. They toasted the Union itself. They toasted the citizens of

Wheeling, West Virginia; Economy, Pennsylvania; and Meadville, Pennsylvania for their large donations of food to the city. And finally, they toasted their fire companies and citizens who had helped fight the Great Fire of April 10.

Parker stayed for all of the speeches. He was particularly pleased when John Roebling named Sam Reppert among the invaluable construction superintendents who helped him complete the aqueduct. Although Parker did not expect to see Frederick Rhinehart standing out in the daylight with the entire city government assembled, he could not help scan the crowds along the streets and before the podium to see if he could spot the large man. When the toasts and speeches were over the people started leaving to go back to their work and homes. Parker lingered, watching the layers of the crowds peel away. Nothing. Finally Parker and Jonas Burbridge also left the completed ceremony and returned to the Burnt District.

Parker patrolled his beat for the remainder of his duty day. He approached the ruins of Bakewell's Glassworks for the first time since the fire. As often as he'd visited the building where they found Grace Milligan, he had avoided close inspection of his old place of employment merely one block away. He feared memories that might surface — memories of both good times and of tragedy. As he drew near, he saw that the rubble had been cleared from the sidewalks around the building. The debris inside its foundation had been cleared and separated much like that of the Dallas Iron Works a few weeks earlier. Rebuilding had not yet begun; no workers toiled at the site that afternoon.

Parker spotted a lone man picking through the piles of rubble. The man struck an odd sight, wearing not workers' clothes, but rather a business suit. A large wicker basket hung from the crook of his arm. He repeatedly picked up items from the rubble and held them toward the sun, inspecting them. Most pieces he chucked back onto the ground. Every once in a while he looked at one a little longer, then placed it in his basket. Parker wondered if the man was touched, and approached him slowly. As Parker came close to the man, he saw that the pieces he inspected were hunks of glass melted and cooled into misshapen little globs. Parker stood just inches behind him, looking over the man's shoulder at a hunk of glass he held up into the sunlight.

"Not this one," the man said, aware now that Parker was with him, and tossed the glass to the ground.

"What are you looking for?" Parker inquired.

"Colors," the man answered, picking up another piece of glass and holding it toward the sun.

"Which colors?" Parker asked

"All of them," the man answered as he threw that piece away. He turned around and, seeing Parker's constable coat and insignia, and asked, "Am I trespassing, Constable?"

"I don't think so," Parker answered. "Besides, I don't think you're after anything valuable."

"It would be valuable to me, if I found it," the man said. "I'm looking for a piece of glass that might help me see what I cannot see on my own. But it eludes me so far." He seemed to realize that Parker was eyeing him for transport to the Home for the Insane. "My name is David Alter, and I'm looking for pieces of glass suitable for conducting some experiments."

"David Alter?" Parker said. "Now why does that name sound familiar to me?"

"It would not be familiar to you unless you lived in Freeport," David Alter said.

"Freeport! That's it. I *was* there. George Weaver mentioned you when I visited him with Jacob Shoop — you're Doctor Alter."

"Yes I am, and they are two very good friends of mine," Dr. Alter said. "What were you doing in Freeport, Constable?"

Parker saw no need now in going into the whole story. A couple of weeks ago he would have had many questions for Doctor Alter. But now, all questions had been answered. All except one. "Searching for something, much like you are," he said.

"And did you find it?" Dr. Alter asked.

"I came very close," Parker said, "but it eludes me still. At this point I don't even have a plan for how to pursue it further. But I haven't given up."

"Well, Constable," Dr. Alter said while holding up yet another piece of glass toward the sun, "maybe if you look at it under a different light you might be able to see something that you could not see before. Perhaps an array of colors might draw out that which is hiding." He became involved in his search again and appeared to forget that Parker was even there.

Parker let the conversation end. He did not fully understand what Dr. Alter had just said, but thought he grasped the general sentiment. He would continue to look for ways to find Rhinehart. "Thanks, I'll keep that in mind."

"Good luck in your search," Dr. Alter said as he picked up another piece of glass.

"And good luck in yours," Parker said as he walked away.

Parker's first day of activity in over two weeks seemed a very long one, fatiguing him both physically and mentally. He walked home in the early evening, arriving at the Wright House after Jenny, James Higby, and the

McKees had already finished dinner. Parker ate alone. As the evening progressed, he felt so tired that he considered going straight up to bed. But he decided that he'd spent too much time over the last couple of weeks in bed, and instead joined Jenny and James in the parlor. The lamps flickered on Jenny's walls as she and James sat chatting and drinking tea.

"Hello, John," James greeted him

"Hello, James," Parker replied.

"Did you eat your supper?" Jenny asked.

"Yes, ma'am. Thank you."

"How was your first day back to work?" Jenny asked.

"I'm tired," Parker confessed.

"How are things looking over there?" James asked.

"I guess I expected more development as far as rebuilding. To be sure, there is a lot of progress there. Many businesses are rebuilding and some shops look like they're nearly ready to reopen. But there are still a lot of properties that haven't been touched yet. I talked with Jonas Burbridge. He seemed confident that things were moving along."

"He's right," James declared. "Every previously-available space in the city is now taken up by merchants who are temporarily relocated until their buildings are finished. And a tremendous number of properties in the Burnt District are being bought and sold even as we speak. The Recorder of Deeds office must be up to its elbows in transactions. Much of the activity going on now is behind the scenes. But mark my words: business in the city will be as vibrant or more so than it was before the fire."

"Yes," Parker said, "that's was Jonas' opinion. He and I watched the parade and the opening ceremonies for the new aqueduct today. He believed its reopening was another boost for the city."

"It certainly was," James agreed. "I let my clerk go to watch, but I stayed in the shop and did a pretty brisk business for the day before and after the parade."

"How was the parade, John?" Jenny asked.

"It was very grand," Parker replied. "All the local military companies and their bands were there. Seemed a lot of 'to do' for a bridge."

"John Parker, they have opened every bridge ever built in this city with a parade," Jenny declared. "Were there a lot of people there?"

"Yes," Parker noted, "the crowds were fairly big. Lots of people were at work, of course, but many still turned out to see it."

"Well, there'll be even more people out tonight for the fireworks," Jenny declared.

"Oh yes, the fireworks," Parker said. "I'd forgotten all about them."

THE BURNT DISTRICT

"Let's see if the Pyrotechnics Association can get it right this time," James quipped.

"Now you be nice!" Jenny chastised him. "Don't pick! They haven't had an opportunity to perform in quite some time. They'll do fine. And besides, with all that we've been through in the last month, this city needs a party right now. People love fireworks. Everyone I've talked to is really looking forward to them. The whole town will be out."

Parker jolted at her last statement. "What did you say?" he blurted out so forcefully that it startled both Jenny and James.

"I only said that the whole town will be out, John. What's the matter?"

Parker stared blankly at Jenny as conversations of the past several weeks raced through his mind. In his weariness Parker had given no thought to the fireworks and had no intention of going. Now, he had the sinking feeling of one who has made a terrible mistake.

"What time is it?" Parker demanded.

"Seven thirty-five," James replied quickly. "John, what's wrong?"

"Yes, John," Jenny said, now well past concern and moving into alarm at Parker's sudden behavior. "What in heaven's name is the matter?"

"I have to go," Parker said as he jumped out of his chair and ran out the room. He rushed to the front door, picking up his coat and nightstick on the way. He bolted out the door and off of the porch barely touching the steps.

Lengthening shadows darkened the city streets. If this were the Fourth of July, the fireworks would not start for another hour, waiting for the long summertime day to end. But in May, darkness had arrived earlier, and Parker had only a few precious minutes to get near the Point, where the crowds would assemble to watch the display. As he ran through the city streets most pedestrian traffic and conveyances traveled in the same direction that he did. By the time Parker arrived nearly breathless at the ruins of Fort Pitt, where the largest crowds gathered, it was completely dark.

Parker stopped behind a large mass of people lined along Penn Street on the Allegheny River side of the Point. He stood craning his neck and straining his eyes, trying to spot a man who, even in dim moonlight, would stand out in any crowd. Many people carried lanterns to light their way home from the event. Parker darted in and out of the outer layers of the throng, standing and pausing at different locations to see everything that he could.

Suddenly he spotted a familiar figure strolling along the back edge of the crowd, keeping his distance and watchful eyes on them. It was Watchman Kevin Fisk. Parker ran over to him.

"Fisk, have you seen a large man with overalls and a cap here tonight?" he panted.

"What large man? There are hundreds of men over here," Fisk answered shortly.

"Didn't Lieutenant Rowe tell you to look about for a large man who we're trying to find and bring in for murder?" Parker demanded.

"No one said anything to me," Fisk replied, affronted. "And you don't tell me my business!"

Parker tried to calm himself and speak reasonably. He put his hands out, palms down in a calming motion, "There is a man at large, probably wearing blue coveralls and a tan cap. If you saw him you would notice him, because he is big, very big — probably the largest man you'll ever encounter. I need to find him. *Now*."

Fisk considered quickly, "I've only seen one man like that tonight, but he was with his family, Parker," he said.

"Who was he with?" Parker demanded.

"He was with his daughter," Fisk said. "The poor girl had fallen asleep from exhaustion. 'To much excitement waiting for the fireworks,' he said to me as I passed them. He was cradling the child in his arms."

"Where were they?" Parker demanded. "Which way were they heading?"

"He was walking on Water Street, upstream along the Mon. They were almost into the Burnt District when I saw them," Fisk answered.

"That was him!" Parker was shouting now. "That was not a man and his daughter! That was a murderer taking his next victim!" Parker started away toward the Mon, then stopped. "C'mon, Fisk, you have to come and help me! Let's go!" Parker's palms were now turned up and toward his body.

"Now you wait one minute," Fisk said. "I'll not leave my post to go traipsing off with a raving sleepwalker!"

Parker threw his hands down in exasperation and ran. He did not have time to argue. He bolted across the wide thoroughfare of Liberty Street, then headed down a short alley that cut across the Point to Water Street along the Monongahela Wharf. Crowds of spectators lined the streets waiting for the fireworks to start. Groups clustered on the wharf also, interspersed among the stacks of freight. Steamboat crews gathered on their ships' decks, waiting for the show.

Parker ran along Water Street, staying on the side of the street that lined the wharf. Several blocks farther along, he passed the ruins of the Monongahela Bridge and those of the Monongahela House. He stayed on the street for the length of the wharf. Just before reaching the hull of what was Bakewell's Glass Works, the wharf stopped and Parker veered toward the river, staying on top of the small hillside between the shore and the block of destroyed buildings. His head throbbed from running and his side ached in a stabbing pain. Parker crossed the mouth of Suke's Run and the canal above the spot where they both emptied into the Monongahela River. When he passed the burned-down boatyard in Kensington he spotted them.

The moonlight showed Rhinehart making his way upriver along the shore just below the line where the grass and brush hillside met the rocky shoreline. Under his right arm he carried a young girl. She wore a light dress and her long, light-colored hair draped over her face and nearly touched the ground. She seemed limp, and did not move except when her body bounced as Rhinehart stepped.

Parker flew along in the grass until he was just above them. All pain disappeared. He dove from the bank with his arms outstretched and latched onto Rhinehart's neck as he landed on him.

The impact knocked all three bodies to the ground. Parker drew his club as he rose and squared himself. Rhinehart, disoriented for a second, focused on his attacker, then snarled and walked forward. In one swift, fluid motion Parker advanced and swung his club upward, striking the side of Rhinehart's forehead. The huge man's head jerked to the side from the crashing force of the blow, but recovered almost immediately. He seized Parker's club hand and raised it straight into the air. Then Rhinehart grabbed Parker's throat with his other hand and lifted him up until his feet were off of the ground.

Suddenly Parker heard the girl cough, then gasp for air. *She's alive*, he realized. The iron grip around Parker's throat cut off his air. His free hand flailed in the air. He now resolved to live long enough to occupy Rhinehart until the girl could recover and escape. For a moment the big man squeezed Parker's neck, then with one hand tossed him backward into the air.

Parker landed on his back in the river. Rhinehart leaped on top of him. He sat on Parker as again the huge hand seized his throat. But this time he didn't squeeze as hard as before. Instead he held Parker's head under the water, drowning him. Parker's nose was less than an inch from the water's surface, but he could not lift his head to breathe. The strap of his club still wrapped around his wrist and he tried to strike Rhinehart with the nightstick. He couldn't manage a real swing — having to bring his arm up from under the water. He tried to twist his body to wrest free of Rhinehart's grasp, but the huge man's grip and weight prevented even the smallest movement. Parker felt a slight thud, then a flash lit up the sky behind Rhinehart's head. Rhinehart looked up for just one second.

At Rhinehart's distraction, Parker tried again just to lift his head, but could not move it in any direction. He looked up at Rhinehart's blurry face through the shallow water. As the cold river flowed over his own face it suddenly hit Parker that he really was going to die. Another flash of light filled the night sky, and Parker wondered if his last conscious thought would be that the Pyrotechnical Association had finally got it right.

Suddenly Rhinehart's head snapped violently to the side. Another figure appeared from behind him. The second figure moved again and knocked Rhinehart completely off of Parker. Parker lifted his torso and rolled to get his head out of the water, then knelt on all fours choking and gasping for breath.

He looked over to see the girl with long, light, curly hair repeatedly beating Rhinehart on the head and shoulders with a rock. It was Gretchen Anderson. *My God*, thought Parker, *he picked Gretchen Anderson*. He might have laughed, had the situation not been so deadly. Gretchen held a large rock with two hands and screamed as she struck Rhinehart. She did not have the confident look of the girl beating the bully, rather a wild-eyed look of an animal fighting for its own life. Rhinehart did not fight back. He wore a dazed look of confusion, almost as if it had never occurred to him that one of his victims could or even would fight back. His expression registered a complete loss of any idea how to proceed.

A well-placed blow to the head brought Rhinehart out of his stupor. He swiped one arm around as he arose, knocking her backward onto the ground without effort. He wheeled toward her, his face twisted in a grin of hate. He would get her now, that expression said. No trace of humanity remained, just a mask of pure madness. He pounced on Gretchen Anderson and seized her neck with both hands.

John Parker staggered onto his feet, coughing and sputtering. His nightstick had proved to be ineffective against the giant. What, then? He picked up the stone that Gretchen had dropped as she fell. It was solid and unexpectedly heavy — a rounded rectangle, perfectly balanced. He saw that it was not a rock at all but rather a quarried stone, probably a large cobblestone from the wharf. He staggered over to Rhinehart and raised the stone up high as the huge man maneuvered the girl's head into the crook of his arm. Parker knew he must strike not to distract Rhinehart or simply hurt him so that they could escape. He needed to kill him. Now. The sky flashed again in an array of colors and stayed lit as multiple booms filled the air. Using the full weight of his body and swing of his arms to bring to bear all of the force he could create, Parker brought the stone down. It struck the back of Rhinehart's head with a sickening crunch. The huge man slumped down on top of Gretchen Anderson, then did not move.

With the release of her throat, Gretchen Anderson let out a half cough and then a long, sustained scream. She kicked at Rhinehart with disgust as she pulled herself out from under him. Then she sat up, crossed her arms in front of herself, and started sobbing. Parker went over to her. She shrieked at him in a long, guttural scream.

"It's all right," he said, almost having to yell. "It's over."

Gretchen stopped screaming but continued crying. Parker knelt beside her as she discharged some of the pain and terror of the attack. After several minutes he stood up and helped Gretchen to her feet. Frederick Rhinehart lay motionless on the ground next to them. Gretchen stared at him for a moment. "Why was he so mad at me?" she sobbed.

"He wasn't really mad at you, Gretchen," Parker answered.

"Who, then?" she asked.

"I honestly do not know," Parker said. "Maybe someone he knew. Maybe no real person at all."

"Why was he like that?" Gretchen wanted to know.

"I don't know," Parker said. "Some people have a rage inside of them, or a pain. Some try to keep it inside. But it always seems to fight its way out somehow, in some way."

Parker put his arm around the girl and walked her up off of the shoreline to the top of the riverbank. They stepped onto the street and headed toward the city. Parker noticed that Gretchen walked with her arms crossed tightly in front of her. Her head pointed down and her face was sullen. *She's closing up*, he thought. He couldn't let her get dragged into the despair and desolation that had consumed Frederick Rhinehart.

"I've never seen you wear a dress before," he tried.

"Mom made me wear it for the parade today," she replied with no change.

Parker thought for a moment. "You know, you saved my life," he offered suddenly.

Gretchen brightened as a look of realization came to her face, "Yes, I did. Didn't I?"

"I'd say that makes you a hero," Parker said.

"That's right. I *am* a hero!" Gretchen brightened. As she lifted her head again a look of wonder, then a smile, spread across her face. She raised a fist into the air and declared, "I'm not Grendel. I'm *Bay Wolf*!"

"Yes," Parker laughed. "You are Bay Wolf."

20

Parker went to the Watchhouse after walking Gretchen Anderson to her aunt's house. There he found the captain of the Watch in his office on the first floor, and reported the night's events to him. The captain sent word for two of his watchmen to fetch Rhinehart's body and take it to Coroner Eichbaum. Parker would have to give a full report to High Constable Abraham Butler in the morning.

Parker exited the Watchhouse and walked down Grant Street toward home. He turned down Sixth Street, but when he reached the Wright House he stopped before approaching the porch. He looked up at the window to his room. The blackness inside his room was much darker than the night sky. It was the same absolute darkness that surrounded him in his nightmares. He stood for a long while in the street, staring up at it. *Some people have a rage inside of them, or a pain. Some try to keep it inside. But it always seems to fight its way out somehow, in some way.*

John Parker turned and walked away, back down into the city. He retreated into the Burnt District: a place of emptiness and desolation that had been a part of his life for so long now that it was becoming familiar, approaching something of a refuge. He guessed that Frederick Rhinehart had been trapped inside the Burnt District his entire life. Parker wondered if the poor man had ever had the inclination to escape it or even the awareness of where he was. The big man's crushing boot sentenced Paddy to life there, too. Kevin Milligan could not endure his own Burnt District even for a few days. It destroyed him by letting him destroy himself. Now Parker wondered if he, too, would be trapped inside until the end, or would he gain the strength to drag himself out?

The gaslights remained dark throughout the city. Parker walked toward his beat and crossed Fourth Street where the silhouettes of broken walls and building shells now mixed with a few rising solid structures. Now among the acrid odor of stale ashes Parker could detect new smells. Passing through the streets he smelled new-hewn wood and the strong odor of fresh paint. He could even smell the fresh mortar between the new runs of bricks and blocks.

Parker stopped in front of a small shop. The two tall storefront glass panes flanking its door still had white X's painted on them from top to bottom from their transport from the factory. A long banner hung across the top of the store's façade. Even in the darkness Parker could read the high-case black letters against the banner's white background. "RE-OPENING SOON!" it proclaimed. Parker stared at the banner for a long time, considering. Finally he moved on.

Parker walked through the Burnt District the entire night. At dawn he found himself again at the ruins of the Monongahela Bridge. He stood on the abutment, staring out over the piers that stretched in a silent row across the river. Even in the first light of morning they looked like lonely hulks separated from each other.

Suddenly a commotion behind Parker startled him. He turned around to see Sam Reppert wrestling a tall, slim sack upright on the abutment. Sam looked up, "John, I thought that was you. What are you doing here?"

"I found the murderer, Sam. It was Rhinehart — the man from you crew. I caught him just as he was about to kill again."

"Oh my God, John, I don't believe it! How did you do it?"

Parker recounted the entire story starting from the day after Sam visited him. Sam stopped what he was doing and listened, enthralled.

"John, I don't know what to say!" Sam exclaimed when Parker finished.

"*I* know what to say," Parker said. "Thanks, Sam, for all your help."

"I really didn't help that much. Plus, I didn't even believe you at first."

"But you still helped, Sam." Parker said. "You still came through for me. By the way, what are *you* doing here?" Parker asked.

Sam's face instantly beamed with pride as he dropped the sack to the ground, revealing a transit on tall wooden legs. "I'm surveying!" he declared. "John Roebling just won the contract to replace the Monongahela Bridge." He extended his arm out to the side, as one who is about to give a bow, "And you are looking at the man whom Mr. Roebling again selected to be one of his top superintendents for the job!"

"That's great, Sam!" Parker said. "That's really fantastic news." Then he laughed. "Sam, this is the job that you've been dreaming about for thirteen years, isn't it?"

"Guilty!" Sam said as he set up the transit. "Take your last look at the tops of those piers, John. Soon they'll be supporting a beautiful new John Roebling suspension bridge!"

Parker looked out over the line of piers. The thought of them connected and made whole again by a new structure seemed to draw a feeling of lightness and life into his chest. "So they will," he said. "So they will."

Historical Notes

Since setting this story in a real time and place, anchored by an actual event, I feel obligated to separate fact from fiction in selected places.

All incidents depicting the Great Fire, as well as descriptions of the fire in dialogue, represent true conditions and incidents of the fire and the city's recovery, as found in sources named in the "Acknowledgments."

The makeup of Pittsburgh's police force and city government is represented as faithfully to their true makeup in 1845 as sources directed, with the exception of a Watchhouse as described in this story. The addition of new wards, new city charters, and disputes between the mayor and the councils, all changed the size makeup of the police force frequently from the 1830's through the 1850's. All names of individual city officials in this story, except Mayor William Howard, are fiction, though the offices they held were real. Official documents and letters read by city officials in this story are quoted from period newspapers.

Pittsburgh locations and street names are named in the story as they were in 1845. Therefore Mt. Washington is referred to by its original name, Coal Hill. The bluffs on which Duquesne University now stands were called Boyd's Hill. Penn Avenue was Penn Street. Diamond Alley no longer exists, being replaced by Forbes Avenue. The Diamond Market still exists as Market Square. Allegheny City was annexed by Pittsburgh in 1907 and became Pittsburgh's "Northside," currently being referred to in city signage and publications as "The North Shore."

Pittsburgh readers who may have raised an eyebrow when John Parker touched bottom in the Monongahela River should note that the system of locks and dams in place today, that keeps the three rivers at a uniform depth year-round, did not exist in 1845. The rivers' depth, and so navigation by larger craft such as steamboats, relied on the weather. At the time of this story only one dam existed, upstream on the Monongahela River. The island that Captain Sayre mentioned did previously exist and local residents did plant crops on it.

Most characters are fiction. Surnames for some characters were taken from lists of names of real people living in Pittsburgh at that time, to give the story more flavor of the real setting, but the real people themselves were not depicted. So local history experts may recognize some familiar surnames given to fictional characters.

One real person depicted in this story was Marina Betts. Ms. Betts was a frequent firefighting volunteer, said to be very aggressive at recruiting men to help put out blazes, although she may have been active in the decade before this story takes place.

John Roebling, of course, designed and built the second aqueduct for the Pennsylvania Canal in Pittsburgh and also the second Monongahela Bridge. His revolutionary wire-cable design for these two spans made them precursors of his masterpiece, the Brooklyn Bridge.

The Pyrotechnical Association was a real fireworks company that operated in Pittsburgh during the time of this story. However, allusions by characters to its level of proficiency are purely fictional.

Another real person depicted in this novel was Jacob Shoop, a tailor from my boyhood hometown of Freeport, Pennsylvania. I first met Jacob Shoop through his great-great grandson, John Shoop, who still runs the men's clothing store in Freeport in an unbroken family line from Jacob starting in 1830. John allowed me to edit Jacob's diary, *Weather Book 1848-1870*, for my Master's thesis at Indiana University of Pennsylvania. In his diary Jacob recorded events in his town and the conditions of the river and canal. Jacob's diary gives few insights into his personality, and so it was with great pleasure that I brought him to life in this story.

The two Irish work camps at Freeport — the Mulligan and the Garry Owen — did exist. And the workers did hold a St. Patrick's Day parade in the town. George Weaver's feat of jumping from one side of the canal lock at Freeport was based on the actual leap of one John Karns across that structure. All are reported in Robert Smith's 1883 *History of Armstrong County*.

Dr. David Alter was a real Freeport physician and inventor who conducted pioneer, and published, work on spectrum analysis. Leland Baldwin states that Dr. Alter picked the glass for his experiments from the ruins of Bakewell's Glassworks.